WHEN A LADY Dares

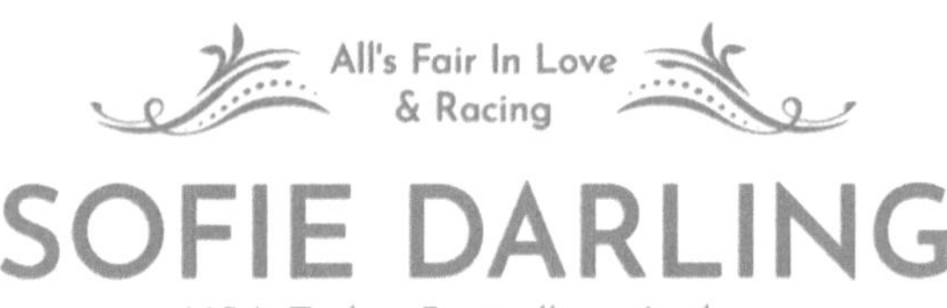

SOFIE DARLING

USA Today Bestselling Author

CHAPTER ONE

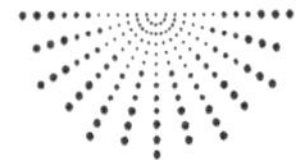

THE DRUNKEN PIEBALD INN, APRIL 1827

From her discreet corner, Saskia held herself quiet and small—and watched.

Taprooms made excellent venues for watching, and the taproom of a coaching inn at the edge of the Suffolk countryside was better than the average. A convivial atmosphere, it was, as the locals all knew each other. Here were villagers and farmers and the like, recounting their days with bluster, laughter, regret, and more than a few shakes of the head.

But so, too, were there travelers, which provided added interest to a coaching inn. Those passing through on their various ways south to London or east to the sea or north to Norfolk and beyond. They would require a hearty meal. Or perhaps they had a thirst that needed quenching, or bones that needed warming beside the fire, or simply souls longing for easy conversation with their fellow man—or all of the above with a bed for the night for good measure.

Then there was her.

Saskia required little. She needed neither drink nor conversation. She barely picked at the roast chicken and turnips she'd been served for her evening meal. Her wool travel pelisse sufficed for keeping her bones warm.

Not that she was an entity entirely unto herself.

The pencil in her right hand and the paper below it needed the people populating this taproom—their laughter, their tears, their whispered conversations, their jolly songs bellowed beside the fire, their enmity, their conviviality…that which imbued this room with *life*. That life which she observed and which flowed through her pencil and onto this half-filled page in the form of words. In her capacity as fifty-percent partner in a successful circulating library and publishing house, Saskia was a known purveyor of words. To most, that was all she was.

But she had a secret when it came to words.

She also wrote them and told stories with them.

Novels, in fact.

Novels, in further fact, that had attained an astonishing level of success these last two years. But no one, other than her closest sister, Viveca, knew that fact about her—that the popular romance novelist Miss Harriet LaPlume was none other than Lady Saskia Calthorp, sister of the Duke of Acaster *and* the Marchioness of Ormonde.

And that was just how she liked it. With her anonymity intact, she could sit in her little corner, be that lowly rural tavern or opulent London ballroom, and observe—and not be the observed.

Except, tonight, she wasn't sitting in this taproom as a novelist.

She was here in an altogether different capacity.

The enterprise that had her in this taproom tonight had been set in motion three years ago at a society musicale, of all places.

At the time, Sirens had been doing well as a circulating library and middling as a publisher. Her sister Viveca had been determined to see it reach higher pinnacles of success, and at that fateful musicale she'd happened across an idea. What if Sirens could publish the memoir of the most famous jockey in all England?

The famous jockey in question was none other than Liam Cassidy, who had been on the ascendency in the horse racing world for a few years and had been flattered by Viveca's offer. Still, he'd politely declined, citing the fact that not only wasn't he a writer, but he hadn't yet accomplished enough to warrant a memoir. In true Viveca fashion, she hadn't given up. She'd assured Cassidy he wouldn't be the one actually writing his memoir and had convinced him to commit to setting all his past and future accomplishments down on paper because, in three years' time, he would surely be more accomplished and even more famous.

Now, it was three years later.

And Cassidy was, indeed, more accomplished *and* more famous.

Aside from the king and maybe the Prime Minister and perhaps a few dukes and one couldn't forget a handful of scandal-prone lords, Liam Cassidy was the most famous man in England.

Viveca remained determined to have his memoir—and for Saskia to write it.

She'd tried to wriggle out of it, of course. "I may wear spectacles and look like one, but I'm *not* an amanuensis."

The words had precisely no effect on an undeterrable Viveca. "But you'll be so much more than that, sister. You won't simply be relating facts. You'll be telling a story, and you're already very accomplished at that."

Saskia crossed her arms over her chest. "No flattery, Viveca."

"And think of all the sales and new members this will bring Sirens."

"My books have done that for us." Saskia could be stubbornly undeterrable herself. "Their sales have exceeded every measure of success." She wasn't boasting, but merely stating fact.

Even as Viveca nodded with agreement, dissatisfaction yet glinted in her eyes. "And…"

"*And?*"

Viveca was about to say something Saskia wouldn't be able to refute.

She'd just known it.

"*And…*" A smile curled the corners of Viveca's mouth that Saskia didn't much like. "Now is the time to invest that popularity—and all those pounds and shillings—into something new, so we can diversify our interests."

"*Diversify our interests?*" Saskia scoffed. "Has Blaze been whispering in your ear?"

A light blush stole up Viveca's décolletage, pinking her cheeks, and Saskia immediately regretted the question.

But it was Viveca's answer that made her regret it even more. "Every night," she said, leaning forward conspiratorially. "And most mornings. And some afternoons, too. Oh, Saskia you wouldn't believe the things my husband whispers in my ear."

Saskia held up a hand, stopping the flow of Viveca's words. She would, in fact, believe them—but that didn't mean she wanted to hear them. So, she'd agreed to Viveca's idea for the memoir.

Which brought her to this place and moment in time—Suffolk in the spring of 1827.

As tomorrow would be her first interview with Liam Cassidy, she'd arrived a day early to collect her thoughts and gain a feel for his reputation off the racecourse and outside London society. He trained nearby at Somerton Manor, the racing estate of the Duke of Rakesley, his brother by law and for whom he rode exclusively.

Tomorrow.

Tomorrow wasn't a simple interview with Liam Cassidy.

That implied a beginning *and* an end.

Tomorrow was only the beginning.

Tomorrow signaled the first of many interviews, months of them, in the company of one of England's most famous men, as she followed him through the racing season—attending races… observing him in training…even perhaps speaking to his family.

Right.

She inhaled a slow breath and attempted to settle the little wobble that occurred in her stomach whenever she thought about the shape the next six months of her life would take. A shape around six feet tall, lean and rangy, possessed of sun-streaked auburn hair and green eyes that glinted with gold flecks.

With an irritated exhalation, she reached into her worn leather satchel for the notes she'd begun preparing for tomorrow's interview. Or, more accurately, she reached for the blank journal where she would enter those preparatory notes.

Her pencil poised above open white space, she adjusted her spectacles with her other hand and wracked her brain for her opening. Harriet LaPlume never had so much trouble filling a page. But then, when she wrote as Harriet LaPlume, she already knew her characters inside and out—their wants and motivations and goals, which, by the end, would unify into the hero and hero-ine's wants, motivations, and goals being only each other.

But this writing was different. Liam Cassidy was a flesh and blood man, and the simple truth was she didn't know a single solitary thing about him beyond the easily observable. She needed more information to be able to ask intelligent questions beyond *"Have you always enjoyed riding?"* and *"Is it true that every woman you meet falls madly in love with you?"*

She wasn't strictly certain about the validity of the second question. An assumption, that, as she'd never spoken a single word to Liam Cassidy. She'd made sure of it. She had no business falling madly in love with Liam Cassidy.

She gave her head a clearing shake. It would be better to get out of her own mind and into the mind of someone else. After all, as Somerton's lead jockey, Cassidy would spend much of his time in this area. So, really, there was one brain in particular she should pick.

Pencil and journal in hand, she stood and ventured from her discreet corner, weaving through the taproom, careful to avoid myriad impediments that appeared in her path—gesticulating arms flying wildly to illustrate a point…dogs lying in wait for their masters to have had their fill, be that food or drink…serving maids bustling around tables and chairs, one hand holding three mugs of ale and the other weighed down by a joint of mutton. At last, all obstacles narrowly avoided, Saskia reached the bar, where she waited several minutes while the barman added a few logs to the fire in the hearth across the room.

Upon his return, he asked with an expression somewhere between a smile and a frown, "What can I get you, milady?"

"What makes you think I'm a lady?" She'd dressed without the trappings of wealth. She wasn't even wearing a single piece of jewelry. So, though it wasn't the question she'd come to ask, she wanted to know.

The barman lifted his brow as if to say, *"Well, ain't ye?"* and that was answer enough.

She cleared her throat, slightly abashed, and plunked a guinea onto the bartop. "I believe that should cover my meals for tonight and tomorrow."

"Aye," he said with a nod, "milady."

"May I inquire about a patron who might frequent your establishment?"

The barman's expression had frozen in that state between a smile and a frown. "You can inquire."

"Liam Cassidy."

The man's face made up its mind and tipped into a smile, though Saskia sensed it had been a near thing. "He's a lad who enjoys a pint on the odd occasion."

Saskia opened her journal and held her pencil ready. "Is there anything else you could tell me about him?"

The barman turned to the serving maid who was presently grabbing an impressive four mugs of ale by their handles. "Now, Molly, didn't you have dealings with Cassidy when he was laid up?"

Dealings...

Well.

But Liam Cassidy's *dealings* with the comely, dark-eyed Molly were nothing she could ask about, so Saskia skipped to the next most relevant question. *"Laid up?"*

"Four...five years ago, it were," said Molly, expertly lifting the mugs brimming with a thin layer of foam, not a drop spilled. "Broken leg."

"Other parts of him were not broken." The barman winked at Molly.

"That would be kissin' and tellin', now wouldn't it?" The glint of fire in Molly's dark eyes looked ready to catch. "And me man, Jim, don't need to be hearin' those tales, now does he?"

The barman, chastened, said, "Fair play."

With a toss of her head, Molly and her ales rushed away.

Saskia might've needed to peel her eyebrows off the ceiling.

But what had she expected?

A man like Liam Cassidy wouldn't be short on dalliances.

"Anyhow," said the barman with a jut of his square, dimpled chin, "you can ask him for yourself."

And Saskia felt it—a charge whizzing through the air... elements transfiguring.

And she knew.

Liam Cassidy had arrived.

Slowly, as if not to disturb newly altered air, she turned. The atmosphere of the taproom *had* shifted. It wasn't her imagination. Every patron tossed a smile his way, and he threw smiles right back in that easy manner of his.

Criminy, but he was handsome.

Somehow, it struck her anew every time she saw him. When

she wasn't looking at him, his handsomeness fell into the category of memory, which could be unreliable. But when she was directly beholding him, she could take no such shelter from the truth.

With his sun-streaked auburn hair...his straight nose and sharp cheekbones...his lean, rangy form...his easy smile, he *was* that handsome. And that smile of his, which provoked smiles from others, could've been the smile of a politician. But it wasn't. His eyes held qualities which no politician possessed—*warmth... playfulness...sincerity.*

All wonderful qualities in a person, to be sure.

However, those wonderful qualities struck to the heart of a secret, slightly shameful truth she harbored.

In her capacity as a novelist, she'd written numerous heroes. Some dark and olive-complected...others light and pale. Some with eyes black as midnight...others blue as a crystalline sky...yet others gray as the sea on a cloudy day...some green as the moss beside a bubbling Highland stream. Some heroes had wide, muscular shoulders...others lean and rangy. She could write any man on the page and outfit him with any number of handsome features.

But 'twas a single man who inspired the depth of feeling she needed to access so she could write those other men—*Liam Cassidy.*

He was—*secretly...slightly shamefully*—her Platonic ideal of a hero.

No matter how the hero was described to the reader on the page—*short...tall...blond...dark*—in her mind's eye, he was always Liam Cassidy.

She'd made her peace with it.

And, really, where was the harm?

He wasn't truly in her orbit.

He was wealthy and famous; she was a bookseller-publisher-author.

When one thought about it, she'd come to a perfect arrangement of artist and muse.

Still, she thought as she pushed away from the bar and edged along the periphery of the taproom toward her discreet corner, it would be for the greater good if she legged it out of here.

Tomorrow was when she was to meet Liam Cassidy.

Not tonight.

She needed an uninterrupted, restorative sleep between now and then.

At her table, she grabbed her satchel and began shoving her writing materials inside, her heart a thundering stone in her chest, even as the possibility occurred to her that she was being overly dramatic. In all the years they'd been orbiting the same circles of society, he'd never noticed her once. What made her think tonight would be any different?

Luck, that was what. *Bad* luck.

She secured her satchel beneath her arm, then noticed a haze in the taproom—except the air was clear. It was her spectacles. In her haste, she must've smudged the glass. She set her bag down, pulled a soft cloth from its depths, and set to wiping the lenses.

Which was how she lost track of Liam Cassidy.

"Do I know you from somewhere?" came a masculine voice at her back.

Mid-wipe, she froze.

A low, resonant voice.

The very same voice all her heroes happened to possess.

"I sincerely doubt it," she tossed over her shoulder, the glimpse she caught of the speaker confirming what she already knew.

Liam Cassidy, seated at the table next to hers, addressing…*her*.

"Are you sure?" came his next question.

"I'm sure," she returned, her voice thankfully devoid of a wobble, the edge of her eye noting the cock of his head that hadn't been there before.

As if she'd piqued his interest.

Criminy.

And she felt them.

His eyes on her back, waiting.

She would have to turn and directly address him, even if it was a simple parting, *"Good evening."*

So, breath steeled in her lungs, she pivoted to find him sprawled on a bench, elbows propped on the table behind him, fully facing her. She opened her mouth to bid him that farewell—and he smiled.

His smile… She'd observed it from afar, but had never once been its recipient.

She'd described this smile in every book she'd written, but without one detail she only now noticed. In the instant before the smile curved his mouth, it lit within his eyes.

The farewell she'd meant to speak retreated in her mouth.

"It's just that"—his smile went knickers-meltingly lopsided—"I never forget a pretty face."

Her lungs forgot how to breathe.

It was a line—the practiced line of a handsome man accustomed to getting anywhere he wanted with any woman he wanted.

She knew this, for he hadn't seen her face until two seconds ago.

It is a line, she repeated to herself.

Yet that line's effect on her was…*enlivening.*

It was absolutely sobering, the enlivening effect that line was having on her.

"I'm Liam."

His confidence struck her.

But it wasn't simply his confidence in himself.

It was his confidence in *her*.

That in the face of his easy smile, indisputable handsomeness, and sparkling charm, she would, of course, give over.

She nodded.

Expectancy, along with a dollop of humor, entered his eyes. "And you are?"

"I'm…" A name made its way to her mouth, and when she spoke it, she found it wasn't her own. "Arabella."

"*Arabella,*" he said as if testing each syllable on his tongue. "Can't say I've ever met an Arabella."

Well, neither had Saskia.

The essence of his smile shifted, and he angled forward. They were entering a conspiracy together, this smile said. "I like firsts."

He was a sportsman.

He would like firsts.

Yet she sensed another meaning weaving between the spaces of his words.

A provocative, *stirring* meaning.

The appropriate response would've been a blush, except Arabella didn't seem the blushing sort—a trait she and Saskia shared.

She found herself faced with a palmful of choices. The most obvious would've been to reveal herself as Lady Saskia Calthorp, tell him she'd been having him on, that she would see him on the morrow for their interview, and leave.

Another choice would've been to let him keep believing she was Arabella tonight—and also leave. Tomorrow, she would tell him she'd been playing a jape on him.

Yet it was a third choice that pricked and pulled at her.

She could let him believe she was Arabella and…*stay.*

A tempting choice, this third one.

More than temptation, it was opportunity, for wasn't *Arabella* a character of her own creation? She was quite skilled at fashioning characters, which wasn't her blowing her own trumpet. Members of Sirens had said as much, unknowingly within earshot of Harriet LaPlume.

Really, when viewed from that perspective, *Arabella* would be research.

Except Saskia had only ever created characters on the page; never had she done so in real life. She'd never even acted out scenes from Shakespeare or Sophocles with Viveca, choosing instead to direct the performance while her sister played each role.

And though these ideas, choices, opportunities, and temptations came to her in the snap of a second, she knew it was already too late.

For the rest of this evening, she was Arabella.

And here was something Saskia already knew about the character of Arabella: she wouldn't be the heroine in one of Harriet LaPlume's novels.

No, Arabella was too worldly for virtuous heroine status.

Arabella would smile indiscriminately and flirt audaciously.

Lady Saskia Calthorp, on the other hand, would *never*.

So, here, within reach, for just one night, was experience of the empirical variety.

Experience she could use in her writing.

Experience that would serve to *deepen* her writing.

When viewed thus, wasn't it *necessary* experience?

CHAPTER TWO

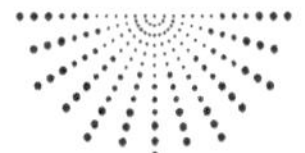

*L*iam had come to the Drunken Piebald prepared for his weekly pint and the usual banter that met him in such public places—did he have any tip-offs for next week's races at Newmarket? Would his three-year-old colt, Morningstar, be up to the task for the season? Was it true he'd met the king?

Nothing that couldn't have been easily answered with a straightforward *no, yes,* and *no.*

Yet it wasn't coincidental timing that he'd picked this night for his weekly pint.

Tomorrow, he would be starting his racing memoirs.

He snorted.

Actually, tomorrow he would be meeting the person who would be committing his career to paper.

He still didn't know what to think about it. Likely, he shouldn't have agreed. But one didn't say *no* to Lady Viveca Calthorp, as she was three years ago and who was now Mrs. Blaze Jagger. One didn't say *no* to Mrs. Blaze Jagger, either. Not easily, anyway. And three years ago, it had been easier to say *yes* in the moment and let the future sort itself out.

Well, the future was now—*tomorrow*—and it hadn't forgotten that long-ago *yes*.

But tonight, while he'd been in pursuit of the steadying usual, something new in the Drunken Piebald had snared his eye—or rather someone. The instant he'd entered the taproom, he'd noted her standing at the bar chatting with old Sam. Over the years, he'd honed that ability—to locate every pretty lass in a room within ten or so seconds. As she returned to her table, he'd seen that she was, indeed, pretty with her light strawberry-blonde hair and figure that curved in all the right places. Even the round spectacles perched upon her straight nose added, rather than detracted, to her appeal. So, as he'd greeted his way through the taproom, he'd kept her at the edge of his eye.

The truth was that though he noted every pretty lass in a room, he didn't usually seat himself at the table next to hers.

Which was what he did.

Arabella.

The fact was this *Arabella* possessed something both familiar and unique, and he wanted to understand why. So, he settled against the table at his back. "And what is it you're drinking tonight, Arabella?"

There.

She'd done it again—gathered her brow ever so incrementally and blinked at her own name.

Well, she blinked at the name *Arabella*, anyway.

All wasn't what it seemed with *Arabella*. He'd gathered that much from her first utterance of her name. For in the split-second hesitation before she'd uttered *Arabella*, it was as if she'd forgotten her own name. People didn't forget their own names, that was the thing.

Arabella was a false name.

Of course, people had their own reasons for concealing their identities. Five years ago, he and his twin sister, Gemma, had needed to do exactly that when they'd taken to the road to escape their father's reach. So, Liam wouldn't judge this pretty lass. And really, whatever *Arabella*'s reasons, why should that stop them from having a little fun tonight?

"What is it you're having?" She smiled, tremulously, as if she suddenly had too many teeth in her mouth.

He twisted around and called out, "Melton, all right if we have a dram or two of your whiskey?"

Without glancing up from his conversation, Melton waved him on.

When Liam turned, he was holding a bottle. "Whiskey."

Arabella's apprehensive smile returned, and he realized he was in the company of two women—the woman this woman was pretending to be and the woman she truly was.

And the woman she truly was had never taken a sip of whiskey in her life.

A surprising, bold smile found its way to her lips. "I adore whiskey."

His brow lifted. He could only admire her audacity. "Scottish?"

"Irish."

"Ah, well, then." He grabbed two small glasses with the hand not holding the whiskey bottle, then efficiently transferred himself from his bench to hers, straddling it as he faced her. "You're in luck, Arabella, as Irish whiskey is what we're drinking."

He poured a dram into each glass and held one out to her. She accepted it in a manner that suggested she couldn't fully believe events had come to this.

He held up his glass. "To new friends. *Sláinte.*" Then he tipped his whiskey back and drank it down in one smooth gulp.

Smile frozen on her lips, she took a quick sip of air, held her breath, and did exactly as he'd done, tipping the amber liquid back into her mouth—which was where all similarities between them ended.

She sputtered.

She coughed.

Her eyes watered.

And when her fit ended, and she was able to open her eyes again, he had a glass of water held out for her. Gratefully, she accepted and drank it down to the last drop in three large gulps.

When she'd somewhat composed herself—her eyes still glassy…her skin still prettily flushed—Liam suspected she might confess her deception, and he wanted to have a little more fun with her first. So, he poured more whiskey into their glasses and asked, "Now, how do you spend your days, Arabella?"

He hoped she hadn't detected the irony in that *Arabella*.

"I'm, *erm*, an actress."

"Is that so?" He respected her quick thinking, for in keeping with the lie, she was telling a truth. She was, indeed, an actress. A poor one, aye, but an actress, nonetheless.

She took a second tentative sip of whiskey. "And you?" She was wise not to dwell on Arabella's career as an actress, which would swiftly lead her down the murky path of more lies. "How do you spend your days?"

He shrugged. "I'm Liam Cassidy."

A single strawberry-blonde eyebrow lifted as if to say, *"That full of ourself, are we?"* and Liam felt like, at last, he was seeing the true woman below Arabella.

A woman who wasn't afraid to take the piss out of *Liam Cassidy*.

Perhaps, he allowed, he'd come across as a hair too confident.

Arrogant, even.

All right, breathtakingly arrogant.

Yet it wasn't a sharp retort that issued from her mouth, but a chirrup of laughter. "And spending your days as Liam Cassidy is a full-time occupation?"

This woman could give as good as she got, couldn't she? "I'm a jockey."

She nodded. "So, riding is a favorite activity of yours, then?"

A shocked chuckle burst from him.

Arabella's brow creased. Her head canted. "Have I said something amusing?"

His smile fell away. With her question, she hadn't been flirting in the least. She was serious, in fact. He cleared his throat. "Well, yes, riding is very much a favorite activity of mine."

"Then," she continued much too earnestly for both the conversation they were having *and* for the one happening below it, "you must do it often."

"Every chance I get."

"You must be exceedingly skilled at riding."

How? How could she possibly be an innocent?

Yet…she must be.

Still, because he couldn't resist, he said, "On more than one occasion, I've been told I'm the best."

Her head tipped to the other side, as if she'd suddenly heard the conversation they were having below their surface one.

He shifted forward, his voice gone like velvet. "I could show you if you like."

His ears picked up her delicate, little gasp.

His cock did, too.

"Could you?" she asked, breathless.

He nodded. "Aye."

How close they were now.

So, it was with great reluctance that he had to say, "But, not tonight."

For here was the thing: Arabella, or whatever her name was, was tipsy. And he wasn't about to tup a tipsy woman he'd just met in a tavern—or not *this* tipsy woman. For he had a golden rule when it came to women he was interested in tupping: if she looked the sort to regret it in the morning, he didn't tup her.

It was that simple.

And this woman looked very much that sort.

A pity, that.

~

Saskia froze.

Well, her brow didn't freeze.

It furrowed.

"Why not?"

She sounded no small bit petulant.

"It's getting late." Liam Cassidy stood. "You should be retiring to your room for the night, yes?" He extended his hand to help her to her feet.

Her first impression of his hand when she took it was how much larger it was than hers. Then came a cascade of impressions—*warm...calloused...strong.*

And there was something else about his hand.

She—*suddenly...voraciously*—wanted it on other parts of her.

"May I carry your satchel for you?" he asked, taking his hand back once she was on her feet.

"I hardly need help carrying my satchel."

It was only after she spoke the words that she realized they weren't in the least flirtatious.

In fact, they might've been snappish.

And, in a flash, she understood why.

He'd denied her what she wanted.

His hand...on other parts of her.

Was she...*drunken?*

Was this—*unreasonable...hot...excitable*—what that state felt like?

She summoned what was left of Arabella in her and said, "But then I would miss watching a strong, capable man like Liam Cassidy carry it for me."

A second ticked past, then another. He would be confused by her abrupt reversal. No more confused than she, in truth. Then he shook his head and swept his arm wide with a dramatic flourish. "Lead the way."

Saskia had taken no more than three steps before she experienced certain effects, presumably from the whiskey. Effects that shared a striking similarity to the time she'd imbibed a few glasses of punch at a ball only to discover some lordlings had added spirits. Effects that somehow made her lighter on her feet and in her body and in her head. Namely, giddy effects.

With those giddy whiskey effects flowing through her, she and Cassidy edged around the taproom and up the stairs. Then it was a quick journey down the dimly lit corridor to the door bearing a brass number three in its center. "This is me." She tapped the number plate for good measure.

"And the key?" asked Liam Cassidy.

She pointed toward the satchel he yet held.

Within an impressive efficiency, he'd retrieved the key, had it turned in the lock, and the door opening on silent hinges. "Arabella, it's been a pleasure spending an evening in your company." An amused glimmer in his eyes, he bowed.

A vertical line formed between her eyebrows. "You're not coming in?"

But...but...but she hadn't felt his strong, capable hands on other parts of her yet.

He shook his head. "I'm not."

How in control he looked.

How *frustratingly* in control.

"But, Mr. Cassidy?"

"*Liam.*"

"Liam?"

"Aye?"

"I'm such a very good girl and don't good girls deserve to get what they want every so often?"

She spoke the words playfully, as Arabella. Yet secreted behind her playfulness lay a truth. For all her intellectual and business pursuits that were viewed askance by the *ton*, she *was* a good girl.

Liam Cassidy, arrested in place, searched her eyes. Gone was his lopsided smile and his charm. He was trying to understand her.

Well, she could help with that… "I'm four-and-twenty."

"And?" If anything, he looked as if he understood less.

All right, then… "I've never been kissed."

He blinked.

It was the truth.

She had never been kissed—and in this moment, it was all she wanted.

She couldn't remember ever having wanted anything else in her entire life, only *this*—a kiss from Liam Cassidy.

It struck her groggified mind that while she wrote theoretical romantic words, she had no experience of them in practice—and here she stood on the precipice of necessary, empirical experience.

Not as Arabella.

But decidedly as Saskia.

"I must be kissed."

"And someday—"

"*Tonight.*"

"—you undoubtedly will be."

"By *you.*"

A bemused laugh escaped his beautifully formed lips that her gaze had been lingering on too long for politeness.

"Four-and-twenty is far too advanced an age to have never been kissed." She lifted her gaze. "Wouldn't you agree?"

He had the look of a man who'd been struck speechless. Still, he managed, "I…would."

"*There.*"

His brow furrowed, as if he'd been tricked into confessing what was only the truth.

And Saskia felt not one whit sorry as she lifted onto the tips of her toes, slipped her hand around his neck, and pressed her mouth to his. A flurry of impressions cascaded through her—of the feel of his mouth…his scent of salt and citrus…the solidity of him against her. Yet though she'd never been kissed—or kissed anyone, more like applied to this situation—a sense tingled through her, setting off little alarm bells.

This kiss wasn't all it should be.

His lips, though perfectly formed, weren't as soft as they should be. And his solid body… It was *too* solid. *Unyielding* would've been a more accurate descriptor. And his hands… They weren't upon her. In the novels she wrote, for instance, the hero took the heroine into his arms. But Liam Cassidy's arms remained rigidly at his sides. So, though Saskia's mouth was determinedly pressed against his, she still felt like she'd never been kissed.

Her eyes fluttered open and found his upon her, watching her as if from a remove. Those alarm bells began clanging wildly inside her. She broke the kiss, but not fully away. "Aren't I…" She searched for a word. "*Kissable?*" Tears threatened—or perhaps they'd already sprung to her eyes. She could no longer account for herself.

"Of course you are." The words emerged from his mouth with all the ease of an extracted tooth.

"Then prove it, Liam Cassidy."

Her mouth separated from his by a scant inch, so close his sweet, whiskey-scented breath whispered across her lips, she watched a war wage behind his eyes and waited. From the edge of her vision, she perceived movement, and the breath caught in her lungs. It was his hand…reaching up…caressing the side of her face…then pulling her spectacles off and slipping them into the front pocket of his coat. A shiver traced through her. If he was removing her spectacles, then…

His warm, calloused hand found the back of her neck and held her steady as she swayed forward onto the tips of her toes… as he angled his head…as his lips met hers.

From the first moment, this was an altogether different kiss from the one she'd given him. This kiss was firm and soft and… *purposeful.* A force inside this man drove this kiss. A force that something inside her responded to with exuberance…with heat…with urgency. Both her arms had now twined around his neck, her body stretched up the length of him. His hand found her waist, squeezed, and guided her around so the doorjamb pressed against her back, so he was firmer against her as his tongue skated across her bottom lip, the tip touching hers, pulling a delighted groan from her.

So, *this* was a kiss.

Or, rather, what a kiss should be.

And, *oh*, it wasn't only the hard length of his body against her, but the hard length of something else, too—*his manhood.* She wasn't such an innocent that she didn't know *that.* And, really, by the second, she was becoming less and less an innocent, for all her body suddenly wanted was that hard length inside her. This body of hers…how newly awakened it felt—and ravenous. Within the space of one second and the next, a woman could transform into a wanton, it seemed.

Her hand, bold and curious, traveled down his body, all those hard, corded muscles tensing and releasing beneath her touch. Then her hand was upon *him.*

She nearly gasped.

It was so…*big.*

Really, classical statuary had a lot to answer for, for she hadn't expected this…this…*girth.*

And yet the knowledge of his size did nothing to diminish the hunger her body felt to have him inside her. If anything, she wanted him more—and not from curiosity. From the wantonness that had awakened within her…from desire, pure and urgent.

Gold-flecked green eyes flew open, then his hand was covering hers, halting its bold exploration, and removing it from…*him.* His mouth tore away from hers, angling so his breath blasted hot against her neck. He pulled back enough to meet her gaze. She opened her mouth to speak…to ask him to stay…to join her in the bed that beckoned beyond the threshold…

All this she wanted to say—*to beg.*

He pressed his finger to her mouth and shook his head as he reached into his front coat pocket for her spectacles and carefully returned them to their customary perch upon her nose.

Then he wrapped a hand around each of her upper arms and guided her beyond the threshold and into her room, whereupon he released her and backed away—and shut the door in her face.

Leaving her stunned.

Leaving her to her bed—*alone.*

CHAPTER THREE

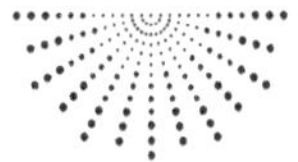

SOMERTON MANOR, NEXT DAY

As her hired coach rolled into the wide, gravel forecourt of Somerton Manor, Saskia slipped the kid gloves off her hands and dug her fingernails into her palms in an attempt to distract her thudding heart and her racing mind with the sharp bite of pain.

It didn't work.

Nothing had since the moment her bleary eyes had slitted open on this too-bright morning and memories of last night assailed her from every angle.

Liam Cassidy...Arabella...the kiss.

Whiskey lied.

In the brisk, unforgiving light of morning, she understood that.

Except she couldn't fully blame the whiskey.

The whiskey had come *after* her fateful decision to become Arabella for the night.

She dug her nails in deeper and groaned—for the hundredth time today. As she'd only managed to roll out of bed an hour ago, she'd surely reach a thousand groans before this day was done. For here was the thing: she was arriving to interview Liam

Cassidy as herself—as Lady Saskia Calthorp. She had no choice in the matter.

And the aching head she was arriving with...

She had no choice in that, either.

Too soon, the carriage stopped and a Somerton footman rushed to open the door and hand her down. Her feet firmly on crushed granite, she took in the house before her. Nay, not a *house*. The imposing Portland-stone structure before her wasn't simply a house; it was a *manor*. But that word was too small, too. This *house* was a palace with its wide Classical portico and grand Palladian façade of three stories of windows staring down at her.

A duke's *house*, lest she forget.

Through the front door stepped the butler, his face arranged in the studied passivity of a servant of his rank. "How may we be of assistance to you?"

Saskia cleared her throat. She wasn't one to become flustered by stiff servants. "I'm Lady Saskia Calthorp." This butler would know his Debrett's, and that Lady Saskia Calthorp was the sister of the Duke of Acaster. "I have an appointment to meet with Mr. Liam Cassidy."

Ice wouldn't melt in her mouth.

She was rather proud of herself, in truth.

If this butler felt the faintest hint of surprise, his face didn't betray him. "Of course, my lady."

Saskia followed the servant into the receiving hall that was no less grand than the house's exterior with its gleaming black-and-white checkered marble floors and high domed ceiling.

A duke's house, indeed.

"If you will wait here, my lady." The butler offered a bow, pivoted on his heel, and disappeared down one of the five corridors extending from the receiving hall.

In truth, Saskia would have preferred to accompany him and remain in his dour company, for it was when she was alone that her mind felt free to wander and remember...

Last night.

Last night, she'd had her first kiss—and it wasn't at all what she'd expected.

Which had her rattled.

The thing was, that kiss—what it had evolved into—was nothing like the kisses she wrote in her books. Those kisses kept within proper, nice...*restrained*...boundaries. But the kiss Liam Cassidy had delivered was none of those things. It had involved tongues...and panting...and cockstands...and feelings tracing through her body that pooled low and deep within her hidden places...feelings that had her inviting him into her room...into her bed.

That kiss had been the very opposite of proper, nice, and restrained.

She'd only just had her first conversation with the man, then after a single hour, she'd kissed him and invited him into her bed.

And he'd said *no.*

Well, he hadn't said it.

He'd shut the door in her face.

Oh, the humiliations just kept layering on, didn't they?

Her eyes squeezed shut on a mortified groan.

"And you are?"

Her eyes popped open to find a tall, dark-haired man clothed in riding attire at the far end of the receiving hall.

The Duke of Rakesley.

Her groan must've caught his ear as he was passing through.

But wasn't he an unflinching, commanding sort of man? One could tell from a glance that he was accustomed to having his way and his questions answered.

Right.

"I'm Lady Saskia Calthorp."

His near-black eyes narrowed. "One of Acaster's younger sisters?"

"Aye."

"We're a little way from London." His head cocked. "What's your business at Somerton?"

Here was the direct approach Rakesley was known for. She appreciated it. "I'm here to begin writing your brother by law's memoirs."

Straight black eyebrows lifted toward the skylight. "*Memoirs? My brother by—*" His brow furrowed. "Do you mean *Bran?*"

"Your other brother by law."

"*Liam?*"

She nodded. "Liam Cassidy, yes."

"First I'm hearing of it."

Saskia held her tongue. It wouldn't do to tell this arrogant, commanding duke that his brother by law hardly needed his permission to write his memoirs.

Her face might've said it anyway, for Rakesley started walking. "Best you follow me, then," he tossed over his shoulder.

Saskia's feet scrambled into motion, one corridor opening onto another, then yet another, until she found herself exiting the house into all-encompassing sunlight. She held a hand to her forehead and squinted against the onslaught. Late-night whiskey and morning sunshine didn't make for happy company.

Rakesley's pace, however, didn't slow for stragglers as the Somerton stables came into view. They were rumored to be England's finest stables. *Glorious*, they'd been described, and Saskia saw why as they passed through a wide iron gate, beneath an imposing stone arch, and entered the stable yard. Built of the same Portland stone as the house, no expense had been spared in the construction of these stables that rivaled the manor house itself for palatial.

When the duke stopped to speak with a man who was certainly Somerton's head groom, Saskia took in the hive of industry all around her. Horse stables were busy places at all hours of the day, but especially in the morning—lads and grooms hustling to and fro, walking horses...scrubbing cobbles...

mucking stalls...hauling water and hay... The keeping and tending of horses was no small enterprise, especially when done at the superior level of Somerton, the duke's capable hand evident all around. So, too, she couldn't help noticing how all deferred to Rakesley. Not out of fear, but rather respect. The duke was a fair, if exacting, employer.

The head groom set off to attend another task, and Rakesley returned his attention to Saskia. "Liam is on the practice track. This way," he said, already on the move.

As Saskia followed, she remembered something.

Namely, why she was here.

To collect information.

Further, she didn't have to follow Rakesley like a subordinate.

She could walk beside him—and converse.

"So," she began, once she'd drawn abreast with him and earned an irritated glance for her efforts, "you're married to Cassidy's sister?"

"Aye."

"His *twin* sister, correct?"

The duke's purposeful stride covered yards of ground at a rate that communicated his wish to be rid of her. "Aye."

Saskia had already known those two facts, for she, like all society, had heard of Rakesley's scandalous marriage to Liam Cassidy's twin sister, Gemma, who had once been the duke's jockey. But she'd asked not to inquire about Rakesley's duchess, but rather to lay the ground for her next question. "Where do the Cassidy siblings hail from, anyway?"

Without slowing his step, Rakesley shot her another questioning glance. "Why do you need to know about my wife's upbringing?"

Saskia felt her brow lift. Rakesley's defensiveness intrigued... "It's Cassidy's upbringing, too, isn't it?" Into the silence that met her question, she ventured further, "And as it's a memoir we're writing, readers will have a reasonable curiosity regarding the subject."

The duke's jaw tensed. "You'll need to ask Liam. It's his and Gemma's story, not mine."

Saskia's brow creased.

How odd.

Before she could follow that line of questioning, however, Rakesley said, "You'll be staying at Somerton, I suppose." He sounded none too happy about the prospect.

"I have a room at the Drunken Piebald."

The duke gave a curt nod, and that was the subject closed. He wasn't a man known for his sparkling conversation, and she now saw why.

Ahead, the practice track came into view. Saskia always forgot how massive racecourses were, and though this one was for training, its circuit could've been no less than a mile, its verdant, close-cropped turf immaculate…the white railing pure as snow. When racehorses closed their eyes and dreamed of heaven, it was Somerton's practice track they dreamed of.

A few horses and riders were spread across the track, none of them at a full gallop, but taking exercise. Rakesley's attention was again pulled by his head groom, leaving Saskia at liberty to look about. Quickly, her gaze found itself fixed upon a large, muscular black colt all the way on the opposite end of the track. She knew little about horses or racing, but her sister by law, Celia, owned quite the renowned racing stable herself, as did her brother by law, Julian, and she'd attended enough horse races over the years to know a fine piece of horseflesh when she saw it.

And the rider on the colt's back…

Her heart drummed a hard thump in her chest.

Liam Cassidy.

Her cells had known it before her mind.

Dressed in a crisp white linen shirt and buff trousers, rather than colorful race-day silks, he was so light in the saddle, bent over slightly, floating just above the horse's back as he rode. His mouth moved, as if he were engaged in conversation with the horse. The colt clearly liked the attention, for his body held a loose, relaxed quality. While Cassidy held an authority over his mount, he didn't command the horse. Rather, he rode as if he and the horse had an understanding.

How talented and capable was Liam Cassidy.

If she were prone to hyperbole, she might characterize him as a god of the turf.

And, last night, she'd kissed him.

Except she hadn't kissed him.

Arabella had kissed him.

Arabella had invited him into her room.

Utter recklessness, that.

Utter madness, too.

And he'd said *no*.

Really, he'd saved her from herself, and she should be grateful and relieved.

She was neither.

As rapidly as those thoughts had whirred through her brain, Cassidy reached their side of the track, jumped from his mount, and handed the horse off to a waiting lad with a list of instructions. This was a different Liam Cassidy from the one she'd observed in society and the one she'd encountered last night. This Liam Cassidy was all business when it came to the care of his horseflesh.

Saskia made herself small against the railing and retrieved journal and pencil from her reticule. As she jotted a few notes, Cassidy's easy smile graced all with its presence as he greeted Rakesley and the head groom, a man he called Wilson. She wrote the name down. Not that Wilson was likely to make an appearance in the memoir, but anything to keep busy.

For she was a bundle of nerves.

Any moment now...

Cassidy tossed an idle glance in her direction—and as quickly away.

In that split of a second, no light of recognition entered his eyes.

She wasn't sure if she was relieved or insulted.

She was considering the possibility that she might've got away with it—were spectacles truly that disguising?—when he went still.

Really, really still.

Stone still.

Too still.

Her heart thudded hard against her ribs—*pounded*—indicating it might just succeed in breaking free of her chest.

His gaze shifted…landed on her…and *narrowed*.

She registered the instant recognition flickered to life within his eyes.

Rakesley glanced between them. "Do I need to make introductions?" He sounded utterly unconcerned. "Or have you met in society?"

Cassidy's brow crinkled.

Saskia's mouth refused to move.

Rakesley exhaled an impatient sigh. "In case you don't know, Liam, this is Lady—"

"Arabella, correct?" asked Cassidy.

"—Saskia Calthorp," finished Rakesley.

As clear as the cloudless sky above, two choices appeared before her.

She was always finding herself faced with choices when it came to Liam Cassidy.

She could acknowledge a previous acquaintance and let Rakesley believe they had met in society.

Except between her and Cassidy, such an acknowledgment would be acknowledging last night.

Which would be acknowledging Arabella.

And she didn't want to acknowledge Arabella.

Because if she acknowledged Arabella, she would be acknowlededging all that had transpired as Arabella.

Namely, their kiss—and his *no*.

Blessedly, a second option lay available to her—*deny, deny, deny*.

She was under no obligation to acknowledge last night or anything that had transpired.

Here, beneath the bright morning sky of a new day dawned, she and Cassidy could start over.

Denial offered them a blank slate—a *tabula rasa*.

All she had to do was *deny, deny, deny*.

All she had to do was lie.

She stuck out her hand. "I don't believe we've met." She ignored the uncharacteristic scowl her words had provoked on Cassidy's charming, handsome face. "I'm Lady Saskia Calthorp."

Never had a lie felt so good.

Or necessary.

CHAPTER FOUR

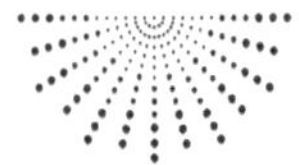

*F*lummoxed.

That word would just about accurately describe Liam at the moment.

Bewildered would, too.

While he didn't know exactly what was happening here, he knew one thing: Arabella was telling bald-faced lies.

Or *Lady Saskia Calthorp.*

Or whoever the bloody woman purported to be today.

Head cocked, he took in the woman standing before him. In broad daylight, she presented herself as an altogether different woman from the one he'd encountered in the Drunken Piebald. This woman's hair was pulled back in a tight chignon. Her mouth was tighter, too. In fact, everything about her was *tight*. He'd known her light hair to have been strawberry-blonde, but the sun burnished it more gold than red. Watchful behind round spectacles, her blue eyes held a silvery quality. But her mouth…

It was the same—*kissable.*

That mouth was undeniably Arabella.

Yet the woman, when taken as a whole, was undeniably *not* Arabella.

Last night, he'd suspected it, hadn't he? That Arabella wasn't who she said she was?

And when he'd rested his head on his pillow, with the immediacy of a lightning strike, it had come to him precisely who Arabella was—a lady.

How had he known?

Only a *Lady* lady made it to her four-and-twentieth year without ever having been kissed.

But she wouldn't be making it to her twenty-fifth year in her unkissed state, for they'd kissed.

Well, she'd kissed him.

Then…

He'd kissed her back.

Where was the harm in a kiss, anyway?

Except he kept thinking about that kiss.

She hadn't known what a kiss was. She'd thought it one mouth pressing against another. Of course, that was all an outside observer of a kiss between two other people would see, so it followed said observer would think that was all a kiss was.

But a kiss was no minor thing.

A kiss, done right, was so much. It was hot and breathless and physical. And beyond the physical, a kiss done right revealed one person to another.

His kiss with Lady Saskia had been passionate and pure and oddly sweet.

Yes, though barely begun, that had been a kiss done right, for it had revealed that below her falsity, what they'd shared last night was no simple game of pretend.

Which was why he was so irritated that she was standing before him with her hand extended as, not Arabella, but…

Lady Saskia Calthorp.

Through the wool in his ears, Liam heard Rake take his leave.

Still, the woman who wasn't Arabella was waiting for him to shake her hand.

He let her hand go unshaken. He had something to say. "About last night—"

Her unshaken hand took up her pencil and tapped it against her open journal. "Shall we begin?"

Exasperation flooded through him. "Shouldn't we talk—"

"About your first horse race?" She nodded eagerly. *Too* eagerly. "It's starting the story in the middle, which is generally a good place to begin a narrative. We can always circle back to your earlier life once we've hooked the reader."

Liam wasn't sure if they gave out awards for acting, but this woman deserved one, as her silvery-blue eyes remained guileless behind her spectacles and her pencil hovered above paper, ready to record his every word.

She almost had him doubting himself.

Could last night have been a dream?

His gaze slipped to her mouth—lips that weren't plump as some, but not thin, either.

He knew the taste of those lips…the feel of them.

Last night had been no dream.

In fact, it was turning into something of a nightmare.

"Yes." Her nodding picked up pace. "The middle is where we shall start."

It had been some number of years since Liam had felt this unsettled. Like the ground beneath his feet was sand during an earthquake. No hope of it firming. One simply had to ride it out.

Right.

He cleared his throat. "I started racing five years ago."

"*Five years ago,*" she repeated as she scribbled words across the page. "Is that before or after you broke your leg?"

Again, the ground shifted beneath his feet. "That's not common knowledge." His forehead was likely arranged into a scowl. Did the blasted woman have to record every word he spoke?

"It was mentioned at the inn where I'm staying."

"The Drunken Piebald." A strange feeling of triumph surged through him.

There.

She'd admitted she was staying at the Drunken Piebald.

Her gaze lifted. "Molly mentioned it."

Something intriguingly unknowable passed behind her eyes. But it was the note that sounded in her voice when she spoke the name—*Molly*—that had his head tipping to the side.

That *Molly* sounded tart—and not like the sweet cherry sort.

His mouth curved into an unapologetic half-smile, the sort of smile one might characterize as charmingly roguish.

And why shouldn't it?

He had nothing to apologize for.

Except those dealings from five years ago in combination with his dealings with *Arabella* last night might've created an impression in this woman's mind.

An impression that might not shoot too wide of the mark when it came to his dealings with the opposite sex.

Still… "The broken leg doesn't go in the memoir." He wasn't asking.

Lady Saskia exhaled sharply through her nose. If he wasn't very mistaken, she was annoyed.

He liked that.

Let her navigate some shifting sands beneath her feet.

"I understand you are ignorant of the concepts of crafting story, but conflict drives narrative." How magnificently and unabashedly condescending she was. "Readers like to see characters fall, then pull themselves back up."

He spread his hands wide in faux apology. "But you're forgetting one thing."

If she were a horse, she would've snorted. "And what is that?"

"I'm not a character, Lady Saskia. I'm a flesh and blood man."

And didn't she know it, he didn't say.

He didn't need to.

She'd heard it.

Her throat bobbed as she swallowed, and he experienced a thrill of triumph. At last, he'd broken through her infuriatingly cool hauteur.

He seized his moment. "If my injury became common knowledge amongst owners and jockeys, they would see it as a weakness."

"But you're not weak."

Something in him liked hearing her say that. "They would go after my leg on the turf."

"How so?" The sincerity of her interest showed in the subtle narrowing of her eyes. She was so intrigued, in fact, that she'd forgotten to keep writing.

"Jockeys would urge their horses' bodies into my left side to get at me during races."

Her brow darkened. "But that's…that's dangerous."

"Aye, it is."

"It's unconscionable." The woman was proper outraged.

"Perhaps." He wasn't quite willing to go that far. "The fact is everyone seeks an advantage on the turf." He shrugged. "That's how the game is played." He waited while she scribbled down his pearls of wisdom. "So, we're agreed, then?"

"What are we agreeing to, exactly?"

"The broken leg doesn't go into the book."

A slow tick of time loped past, then she nodded. "Does it still hurt? Your leg?"

The question took him slightly aback. "Sometimes, after a race," he admitted. "But everything hurts after a race for a few days."

"I suppose it is a physical sport."

He wasn't sure when it had happened, but a shift had occurred—an alteration to the elements between them. As if, somehow, the genuine was peeking through the plain deception of the woman before him. As if, at last, the true version of Lady

Saskia Calthorp had introduced herself, a woman who was intelligent and genuine.

He found his gaze slipping toward her rose-pink mouth. He'd kissed that mouth. And interestingly, he wanted to kiss it again—even after all the lies it had spoken.

Lies.

That mouth belonged to the woman who was denying their kiss.

That mouth wouldn't be kissing him again.

A pity, that.

There had been something different, something especially alive, in her kiss.

In the near distance, the lad returned with his mount. "There's my three-year-old for the season—*Morningstar*," he said, pointing. "You might want to write that down."

Lady Saskia's pencil began moving.

"Shall I give you a foretaste of what he can do on the turf?"

Her gaze startled up. "I, *erm*, I think…" Her journal snapped shut. "I think I have all I need to get started."

"Oh?" That couldn't possibly be true.

Still, she nodded.

"Well, it was a pleasure meeting you, *Lady Saskia.*"

The flicker in her eyes said she'd caught the irony in his voice.

He pivoted and strode onto the track, where he grabbed the pommel of Morningstar's saddle and jumped onto the Thoroughbred's back smoothly and efficiently. As he urged his mount into motion, he knew…

She was watching.

A charge sizzled through him.

If she was going to watch, well, then he would give her a show.

Once Morningstar had trotted half a lap, Liam urged him into a canter. It wasn't just his body that went lighter in the saddle when his mount increased speed. When riding a superior animal like Morningstar—one possessed of perfect conformation and smooth action—a feeling of freedom took wing inside him as if he and the thousand pounds of power and strength below him were at one in purpose and drive. Though he wouldn't be opening up Morningstar properly right now, this feeling had to be what birds experienced as they soared through the air, unbound by gravity.

He loved being a jockey.

It was a gift to be able to do this every day—to win at it.

He loved that, too.

But today was different. While he was well accustomed to riding for an audience of thousands, today he was performing for an audience of one—*Lady Saskia Calthorp*. Showing off for her, really. Not for what her pencil would record of him.

For *her*.

Too soon, however, the time arrived to cool Morningstar down. A smile not just on his face, but running the length of his body, Liam returned to the stretch of railing where he'd last spotted Lady Saskia—only to find her gone. His smile fell, leaving a wake of disappointment. He'd wanted to meet her in the eye and find that look ladies got when they watched him ride—*appreciation...desire*. He wanted to see if his prowess on the turf brought out the Arabella inside her.

He snorted. No small amount of arrogance and pride in that want. So be it. He was a competitor at the top of his sport. He enjoyed being acknowledged as the best. And, aye, he'd wanted to see that acknowledgment in Lady Saskia's eyes.

"Morningstar is looking sound for the Two Thousand Guineas."

Liam twisted in the saddle to find Rake approaching. "We need to train his starts with other horses."

Rake nodded. "I'll have Wilson assemble a field tomorrow."

From the way Rake was looking at him—head cocked...a bit

of distance in his night-dark eyes—Liam intuited a conversational shift coming and steeled himself.

"Word has it you're publishing a memoir," said Rake, as if offhand. "How did that come about?"

"It's a long story."

Rake's brow lifted. "And you'll be spending the racing season in Lady Saskia's company?"

"Something like that."

Rake wouldn't long tolerate these non-answers Liam was giving, but truly, he hadn't yet worked out for himself how those questions and their inevitable answers fit into his life.

"Why did you think her name was Arabella?" asked Rake. He would've caught that.

Liam had hoped he hadn't. He tried for dismissive. "I got her confused with someone else."

A sardonic smile lifted the corners of Rake's mouth. "There can't possibly be two women in the world like Lady Saskia Calthorp. I would think her one of one."

One of one.

The woman was certainly that.

Rake turned serious. "She asked about your childhood."

Muscle by muscle, tension traced through Liam. If he'd been mounted, the horse would've sensed that unease and shaken his head. "What did you tell her?"

"I told her to ask you."

Liam nodded slowly, his mind racing.

He would need to have another chat with Lady Saskia Calthorp.

A rule-setting chat.

Sooner, rather than later.

Tonight.

CHAPTER FIVE

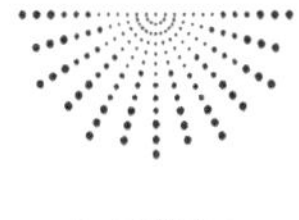

LATER

Saskia had intended to venture down to the Drunken Piebald's taproom for only as long as it would take to grab a swift evening meal of chicken and leek pie.

She'd—*rightly*—begun thinking of the ten-mile radius of surrounding countryside as Liam Cassidy territory, and she wouldn't be settled until she was back in her library in London—*her* territory.

However, she'd made a critical error in the execution of her plan.

She'd brought her writing materials to keep her company.

And, as ever, when her writing materials were at hand, an idea rushed toward her.

Of course, she jotted it down—as one did.

Then another idea came, and another, and she was no longer jotting, but *writing*, one idea following another in the flow that had become familiar to her these last few years. This flow mustn't be hindered. She'd learned ideas must be committed to paper the moment they were had. Particular arrangements of words, too, as sometimes the muse gifted her not only with the idea, but the perfect order of words with which to express that idea. Words so perfect they would surely be unforgettable.

But they were forgettable, she'd learned from hard experience. If she didn't write them down immediately, they would dissipate and float away into the ether. The idea would remain, but the words she was left with would always be poor substitutes. Sure, these new inferior words would suffice in getting the idea across, but they would always be mere echoes of their former selves.

Now, it was an hour later, and Saskia had a pencil in her right hand and a fork in her left and a plate of chicken and leek pie long gone cold. However, she did have five pages to show for that hour. A fair tradeoff in her mind. She'd eaten her share of cold meals since she'd become a writer, and it wasn't the worst thing.

Except, what she'd written during this last hour, well, it wasn't what she should've been writing.

She'd written a scene for a novel she had no business yet beginning.

A scene where the heroine happened to meet the hero in a taproom remarkably similar to the Drunken Piebald's, down to the dense, fuggy air, the knife-scarred tables, and the close-knit patrons. Further, the heroine gave the hero a false name. *Araminta*. And, oh, how Araminta and the hero flirted and bantered and flirted some more before they…*kissed*.

And the kiss Saskia had spent the last hour writing… It was like no other kiss she'd ever written.

In fact, the kiss she'd just written likely couldn't be included in this or any other novel—not in its present configuration of words.

For the kiss she'd just written resembled diary entry more than fiction.

Criminy.

The sudden, strident scrape of a chair being dragged across grime-sticky pine floorboards screeched through the air. A racket that was growing…*closer*. Irritated, she glanced up—and froze. Before her mouth could gather itself to greet or protest or even gasp, Liam Cassidy was seated in the chair on the opposite side of the table.

Speechless, she was rendered.

A too-charming smile tipped at the side of his mouth. "Hello, Arabella."

Her mouth resisted the impulse to offer a greeting—or even a protest.

His gaze lowered to take in the contents of the table between them. "What are you working on?" His head tipped to the side as if he were reading upside down. "My memoirs?"

Saskia's brain, at last, caught up with the moment. "*Erm…* yes." Frantic hands gathered pages, paying no heed to their order.

She and he reached for the last page in the same instant. "Can I see what you have so far?"

"No," she said.

She may have shouted.

His brow lifted, but the page yet lay contested between them.

He couldn't read this.

He *couldn't.*

If he did, she might actually expire of mortification.

He released the page, and Saskia wasted not the split of a second shoving it into her satchel, which she closed with a decided snap. When she glanced up, it was to find him settled back in his chair, arms crossed over his chest, observing her steadily.

She gathered her wits about her. If there had ever been a time in her life in which she should be entirely herself—the formidable and unyielding Lady Saskia Calthorp—this was the moment. "I take it you will state your business imminently?"

His too-charming smile didn't alter an iota. My, but wasn't Liam Cassidy on the formidable and unyielding side of the scales himself? "Oh, we have plenty of business to state between us. Really, the question is where to begin?"

What was the saying about curses and chickens roosting? For seated across from her, in the form of one exceptionally handsome and formidable and unyielding man was a curse come home to roost. No one would mistake him for a chicken.

He would have to be dealt with, that was what his formidably charming and determinedly unyielding smile said. "Shall we begin with last night?"

She didn't answer; she waited.

As if he'd expected as much, he continued. "Last night, you were—"

"I don't want to talk about last night," sprang from her mouth. "Or who I was."

Now it was him not answering; him waiting.

Over the years, she'd learned a little trick. A bracing of oneself on the outside tended to shore one up on the inside, too. "Our relationship," she began and instantly regretted her choice of word—*relationship*. It wasn't only that it wasn't the correct word, but it was a word that implied solidity. She cleared her throat. "Our *association*"—a far superiorly vague word in the circumstances—"must be kept within professional boundaries."

Humor sparked in his eyes.

Professional boundaries.

Where had those been last night?

What a hypocrite she was, but she saw no other way out of this impossible situation than through.

He nodded, as if giving the idea of *professional boundaries* serious consideration. "May I ask you a question that might hold some relevance?"

"You may," she deigned.

Oh, criminy, had she retreated so far into her internal fortress that she was now *deigning*?

"This morning," he said, "why did you act as if we'd never met?"

"I haven't the faintest idea what you're talking about."

Oh, she was doing nothing to right this ship.

Nothing.

Though she couldn't say his charming smile altered, it did, somehow, shift into what could only be characterized as *wicked* as he leaned forward. Though a table stood between them, it was as if he'd erased all distance. "Shall I refresh your memory?" he asked, his voice pitched low, for her ears only.

The feeling that suggestion produced inside her...

Unsettled wouldn't be the correct word. It was too firm and held dark implications. No, this feeling was far less certain. It resembled more of a wobble.

A *seismic* wobble.

She reached for a retort—something witty and cutting that Lady Saskia Calthorp would say—and found one. "I suppose you would think yourself that memorable."

He shifted back in his chair and looked at her as if he were taking the measure of an opponent.

Gone was the charm.

Gone was the wickedness.

She almost regretted that retort, for it was a falsity, wasn't it?

Almost.

False words had gotten her into this situation, so how about they got her out of it?

It was a decent enough logical leap.

But it was he who spoke the next words. "Then how about we venture even further back into the past?"

She blinked. *Further back into the past?* They'd only met last night. What was the man on about?

"You see, I've given last night a long and thorough think," he continued, "and I find something interesting about it."

"What's that?"

"I didn't know who *you* were, but…" A few ticks of time sped past. "But you knew who *I* was."

Saskia had never been punched in the gut, but she thought the feeling reverberating through her was how it would feel—lungs winded, heart racing, blood rushing through the veins and roaring through the ears. She now understood at a physical level the meaning of the word *gutted*.

He wasn't finished, either. "The thing is, we should've encountered one another by now. After all, I've met all your other siblings." He began counting them off, one after another. "Your brother, the Duke of Acaster. Your sister, Lady Ormonde. Your other sister, Lady Viveca. In fact, it was Lady Viveca who used her considerable skills of persuasion to convince me to agree to the memoir in the first place. She said someone else would do the writing. Presumably, she meant *you*." He tapped the table, his gold-flecked green gaze steady. "At some point during the last few years, I should've met you. And last night, at the very least, I should've known you on sight." His eyes searched hers. "So, why didn't I?"

Could he not hear her heart hammering against her ribs? The blood roaring through her veins? "Does this truly matter?" Was that breathlessness in her voice?

"That's what I'd like you to tell me, Lady Saskia."

Never had she seen this man this serious.

"Does it?" he asked.

It didn't and…it *did*.

But she was under no obligation to tell him that.

Those were her private thoughts and reasonings.

They belonged solely to her.

Right.

An idea came to her.

An idea that might just come to her rescue.

She reached down, opened her satchel, and dug pencil and journal from its depths. Pencil in hand, she opened the journal to a blank page. Suspicion entered Cassidy's eyes, and a frisson of relief pulsed through her. She was on the correct course.

At last.

"What are you doing?"

"What I'm here to do." So lightly had she spoken the words that a breeze might've taken them.

"Which is?"

"To write down your every word."

Open exasperation shone in his eyes. "Can't we talk without you having to record everything?"

"But isn't that the point of me? Lest you forget, Mr. Cassidy—"

"Liam."

"*Li-am*," she repeated. "Lest you forget, I'm writing your memoir as *you*. So, I need to record your manner of speaking so it will translate onto the page."

It wasn't exactly a lie.

It was, in fact, true.

Except…it wasn't factually true to this moment.

But that didn't stop a small thrill of triumph from whizzing through her.

She'd upset his balance—for once.

And it felt good.

It felt better than good.

It felt *safe*.

She'd always been good at this—at guarding herself.

For the first time since last night, she felt certain and firm and…

Safe.

And if making herself safe meant unsettling Liam Cassidy, all the better.

CHAPTER SIX

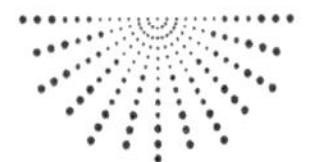

On the turf, Liam had battled many a formidable foe.

It was simply the nature of horse racing.

But none held a candle to Lady Saskia Calthorp when it came to formidability.

And as for the sport they were presently engaged in, it was one he'd never played, its rules murky and unknown to him.

Of course, they would be, for the rules of this game were entirely of Lady Saskia's own making. Just when he thought he had her, she dug into inner reserves and located yet another weapon in her arsenal.

He could've admired her resourcefulness, if it didn't frustrate him so bloody much.

He'd arrived tonight with but a single goal in mind—to have a word with the woman.

A few words, in fact.

He'd spotted her immediately, sitting alone at the same corner table as last night, bent over her journal, pencil moving across paper, a fork held in her other hand, taking an indifferent bite every so often. It was as if her stomach couldn't keep up with her brain.

At first, he thought he would attract her attention as he'd spent the first ten minutes exchanging greetings with every single person in the taproom. A winning jockey was a popular man in any room. Four years ago, after he'd started winning races, he'd been unprepared for the burst of popularity, but these days he was better able to manage the expectations of all those strangers. Both male and female, they thought he could be their bosom friend…or their confidant…or their lover… The list went on.

But, no, Lady Saskia hadn't noticed his arrival, so retreated into her own world she'd been.

Who would she be tonight?

He couldn't help wondering.

Last night, she'd been the bold Arabella.

Today, prim Lady Saskia.

Actually, the more apt question was: who was this woman, *truly*?

It seemed he wanted to know.

Except he wasn't here to know her better. He had other business to attend, and it was best he got to it. "Rake mentioned you inquired about my upbringing."

She nodded, her pencil poised to record his every word. "Is that where you would like to begin?"

He settled back in his chair and crossed his arms over his chest. "My upbringing falls outside the scope of this memoir."

A little frown turned her mouth down at the corners. "But readers will want to know about your early life. This is a memoir."

He nodded, as if he were agreeing with her. "Of my racing career."

"But people will want to know how it started."

He held up his hands, as if helpless to the facts. "This is not a negotiable point."

She let her pencil fall to the table and exhaled a frustrated sigh.

He seized his advantage. "Consider it one of those professional boundaries you mentioned."

She shook her head. "An example of a professional boundary would be that we never—" Her mouth snapped shut, and a blush pinked the tips of her ears.

Liam knew what her next word would've been—and he didn't feel inclined to let it pass unspoken. *"Kiss?"* he asked, all innocence.

She pressed her lips into a firm line.

"In which case," he continued, reveling in the sweet torture he was doling out, "are you saying we definitely should *not* go upstairs and finish what we started last night?"

Her closed mouth muffled a strangled groan. Yet, for the split of a second, he might've detected something pass behind her eyes…

Temptation.

In a flash, it was gone, open irritation in its place.

Irritation at him or herself, he didn't know.

Perhaps both.

Feelings could be two things at once.

Irritatingly.

"What say you, *Arabella?*"

Oh, he was pushing her.

Her brow gathered, and she appeared to snap to. "It's only April and we're to be in one another's company through September, so we need to establish a few rules between us."

"Rules?" He snorted. "Are *rules* different from *professional boundaries?*"

Her jaw tensed. "No more kissing."

"So, one rule, then."

No more kissing.

He found he didn't like that rule.

"Are we agreed, Mr. Cassidy?"

"Liam," he said reflexively.

They'd kissed.

She knew the feel of his cock.

She could bloody well call him *Liam*.

She shot to her feet. "I have an early return to London in the morning. I'll take my leave of you now, *Mr. Cassidy*."

How attractive she was in this moment, all determination and fire.

Lady Saskia Calthorp was more than a pretty lass. She was beautiful. One could almost forget that fact in one's dealings with her, because she required the entirety of one's attention to keep up with the lightning-quick pace of her mind. But when one took a moment to look at her, to really soak her in, one realized she was unquestionably lovely.

With a deliberate unfolding of his body, he rose and just noticed she'd forgotten something in her haste—her satchel. He grabbed it, but didn't offer it to her straightaway.

Impatient, she held out her hand. "My satchel."

She wasn't asking; she was telling.

And Liam found he wasn't finished torturing her yet. "What sort of big, strong man would that make me if I didn't carry your bag up to your room for you?"

Her eyes narrowed.

His reference to her words from last night hit their mark.

She wanted to resist—but she couldn't.

So, it was that Liam found himself following Lady Saskia's brisk stride, annoyance charging her every step as they made their way across the taproom, up the stairs, and down the corridor. Once they reached number three, she faced him and held out her hand expectantly. "My satchel."

The nearly undetectable glint he'd detected in her eyes a few minutes ago yet stirred in his mind.

Temptation.

It was nothing new for him to be a temptation to a woman. Women were always that eager to jump into bed with him and see what sort of ride he had to offer.

But he liked being a temptation to *this* woman.

Especially so.

Instead of loosening, his hand tightened around the worn leather handle of the satchel—though it shouldn't—and he angled slightly into her space, so close he could catch her scent of June roses…hear the hitch of breath in her throat.

His breath might've done the same.

On his honor, his intention had been to set the satchel on the floor beside her feet.

But of a sudden, the space between and around them transformed into an intimate space, as if it were only they two in the world. In this intimate space, how easily intentions could shift. His mouth could find the sensitive skin along the elegant curve of her neck…feel the alive throb of her pulse beneath his lips… the whisper of her breath in his ear…a soft feminine gasp when the tip of his tongue traced the line of her clavicle…sending a cascade of goosebumps rippling across her skin…

All this could happen in this intimate space.

None of it could happen.

Gently, he released the satchel and straightened, breaking that intimate little space. Confusion shone in expressive silvery-blue eyes—and something else, too. Was that…*regret?*

Without another word exchanged between them, he offered her a shallow bow, pivoted on his heel, and didn't stop until he was stepping outside onto the inn's forecourt, waiting for a lad to bring his horse Homer around. Only now was he able to draw a proper breath. That the air hitting his lungs was brisk and crisp fit the moment.

Stirred up was the only way to characterize this feeling.

Lady Saskia Calthorp was a lady to stir one up. For it wasn't only that he was a temptation to her; she was a temptation to

him. Something about her got into his head…got into his blood…
and stirred him.

But this stirred-up feeling that had to do with her wasn't only
about her.

His upbringing.

His warning hadn't satisfied her.

She would pursue the information further, he knew it.

Hers was the sort of mind that would.

And when she went digging, what would she find? She
already knew he had a twin sister, Gemma, who was married to
the Duke of Rakesley. Oh, the scandal that elopement had
provoked, given Gemma had been Rake's jockey. But all that had
occurred five years ago, and the gossip had long since died down,
especially considering Rake and Gemma had already produced
an heir along with one more besides.

A little more digging on Lady Saskia's part would turn up a
few more facts: Liam's mam was Irish, hailing from County
Cork. Her name was Maeve, and she'd been beautiful with
indigo-blue eyes and wild red curls.

And when Lady Saskia discovered those facts, the next facts
would become obvious: that while the beautiful Maeve had
served as the cook for the Earl of Bolton, she'd given birth to
twins—the illegitimate offspring of the earl. Then she'd passed
away over five years ago, and her twins had disappeared.

Those were facts that could be uncovered with some determined digging.

But other facts awaited discovery, too.

Facts of Liam and Gemma's upbringing that belonged solely
to them. No one had a right to those facts. No one had the right
to know of their blood connection to the Earl of Bolton. No one
had the right to know of their unusual upbringing beneath his
roof.

No one had the right to know of his and Gemma's flight after
Maeve's death.

For years, Liam had believed their bid for independence a success. Then several months ago, one night after a race, Liam had been enjoying a pint of ale with a hundred of his closest friends when he'd turned and found himself face to face with the earl.

"Liam," he'd said, "a word?"

One thing Liam had never liked about himself was his close resemblance to Bolton. Sure, he had the red from his mam's hair, but as far as looks and height went, he and the earl bore enough similarity that the discerning eye would've found no trouble taking them for father and son.

As Bolton had a determined set to his jaw, and Liam couldn't trust himself to speak in front of others—*what in the bloody hell was Bolton doing here?*—they found a quiet table in a corner.

Bolton spoke first. "Quite a career you're putting together."

Liam waited.

"I'm proud of you."

He'd snorted, still unable to trust himself to speak. Unable to trust himself not to say, *"You have no right to be proud of me."*

Bolton didn't seem to notice the words not spoken. "I'm dying," he said, blunt.

Liam let the words glance off him. This was the sort of rot Bolton would say. He was manipulative in that way, always needing to control everyone he considered his, and Liam had worked too hard to extract himself from this man's poisonous web only to be pulled back into it.

He'd shot to his feet. "We're done here."

But Bolton wasn't finished. "There is something you need to know. Something about your mam and me."

Liam had hesitated for the sliver of a second. *Mam.* She was Liam's weakness—and Bolton knew it.

Right.

Without another word exchanged, he'd left the tavern without a backward glance. Perhaps Bolton had been telling the truth...or he hadn't. Liam could live without knowing.

Today, with Lady Saskia asking about his upbringing, he'd again experienced that sensation of sand shifting beneath his feet. It was the old way of thinking that wanted to tug at him, leaving him strangely susceptible to the earl's pull. As if in speaking of Bolton, he would conjure the man into this very room.

No, better to keep Bolton locked away.

He needed to be careful.

He wanted nothing to do with Bolton—and he suspected he wanted too much to do with Lady Saskia.

CHAPTER SEVEN

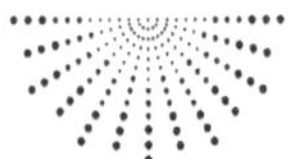

SIRENS CIRCULATING LIBRARY, LONDON, MAY

*S*askia wouldn't have gone so far as to call her life regimented.

Rather, it was structured in a manner that suited her perfectly.

She liked structure—liked it in her writing, liked it in her life.

At five o'clock in the morning, she rose and spent her first two waking hours outlining, plotting, and writing.

At seven, she dressed, then made her way downstairs to the kitchen to break her fast with strong black tea and crumpets.

By eight, she was conferring with Mrs. Dunlevy, who served as both bookkeeper for Sirens and housekeeper for Saskia. They discussed the day ahead and which tasks took precedence. Then Saskia grabbed the stack of recently arrived broadsheets and lugged them into the Newspapers and Periodicals room, where she switched out yesterday's news with today's. Next, she was moving through other rooms, pulling curtains open, Alice the housemaid in her wake straightening and cleaning behind her—a quick sweep of the floors, a swipe of the feather duster here or there, the disposal of the random cobweb.

At nine o'clock, Sirens was ready to open for business.

The number of members lined up at the front door at that hour, waiting to be admitted, never ceased to surprise Saskia. Some came for the day's broadsheets. Others to return a book and check out another. Some wanted silent company. Others wanted long-winded conversation.

Then there were those who came to purchase the books published by Sirens, for their publishing house had several authors exclusively beneath their banner. Seven out of ten buyers —she'd done the math—came to purchase a book by Harriet LaPlume. And every time a customer asked for the latest release by Harriet LaPlume—*every...time*—a lightning-quick rush of pure exhilaration spiked through her. There was something so thrilling about accepting coin directly in hand for the words, characters, and stories she'd committed to paper.

As the morning progressed, she kept busy with the tasks Mrs. Dunlevy set out for her. Then, soon enough, it was midday and Viveca was arriving for them to take tea together before her sister took over the afternoon duties and Saskia returned upstairs and wrote until closing time at four, when she would assist with end-of-day duties downstairs. Viveca would say her farewells for the evening and depart for the home on Tichborne Street she'd shared with Blaze these last few years.

It wasn't the most exciting life that Saskia led, but it had its successes and it fulfilled her.

She couldn't think of any other life she would rather lead.

Five years ago, when the dukedom of Acaster had been sprung on Gabriel—and all their family of four, really—she hadn't exactly been transported with joy by the prospect of becoming a *Lady* and all its attendant societal expectations.

But now, she was able to view that occurrence and this life from a different vantage point. Her life as a lady had brought her opportunities and freedoms unpredicted. So, not only was her life successful and fulfilling, it was lucky, too.

"Hello, sister," came a familiar voice at her back.

Saskia half twisted and squinted through spectacles perched low on the tip of her nose. "Is it noon already?"

"Aye, it is," said Viveca. "What task has Mrs. Dunlevy put you to this morning?"

"She has me taking inventory of Harriet LaPlume's latest release."

It felt strange to refer to herself in the third-person. But it was a necessary precaution, if she wanted to keep her identity as Harriet LaPlume a secret from everyone except Viveca. There was no keeping a secret from Viveca.

"Shall we take our tea upstairs today?" asked her sister.

"Why?" They usually took their tea in the kitchen.

"So we can discuss the Liam Cassidy pages."

Like that, Saskia's heart leapt into a gallop.

Of course, such an occurrence was always the case when her writing was the topic of conversation.

But this feeling was more than simply about her writing.

This was about her writing *about Liam Cassidy*.

She'd given Viveca those pages a week ago and, in the days since, had done her level best to forget them. But here was her heart hammering away against her ribs, revealing a single truth that couldn't be denied...

Dormant didn't mean forgotten.

"Of course."

Several minutes later, she and Viveca were seated comfortably on the sofa in the upstairs sitting room, tea arrayed on the low occasional table before them. Saskia could only watch as her sister drank tea, consumed two pear tarts with gusto, and tortured her with small talk.

"Have you heard," continued Viveca, relentless, even as her words were slightly muffled by a bite of cucumber sandwich, "of a friction match?"

"I haven't." Saskia was holding her cup entirely too tightly.

"They're calling it the *Lucifer.*" Viveca waggled her eyebrows. "Evocative, isn't it?"

Unable to take it anymore, Saskia exclaimed, "Oh, will you just tell me what you think of the pages already?"

Brow lifted, Viveca set her plate down and exchanged it for the stack of papers Saskia had been doing her best to keep out of the edge of her vision—and failing.

"I read the outline." Her sister's voice had gone suspiciously blank. "It's good."

Viveca nodded, and Saskia tried not to read too much into that nod. Because if she did, she might suspect her sister was trying to convince herself that the outline was, indeed, good.

Criminy.

Viveca continued nodding. "Yes, the arc of taking the reader through the racing season is *good.*"

There was something her sister wasn't saying.

"And the first chapter?" Saskia forced herself to ask.

Viveca's gaze held hers. "There's just one problem with the first chapter."

"Which is?" She might just snap the handle off this teacup. She set it carefully on the table.

"It's not good."

The knot that had formed in Saskia's throat tightened, threatening to garrote her. "Pardon?"

"It's dry."

Saskia scoffed, incredulous. "Please tell me how you truly feel about it."

"It's dead boring."

Saskia's mouth gaped open.

Which Viveca took as permission to continue. "It's not engaging in the least." She tapped the cover page for emphasis. "There's no spirit in these words. They're just a relating of facts. Liam Cassidy is a jockey. He's a winning jockey. He trains at Somerton. Speaking of Somerton," she continued, "you were clearly taken with it, for you labor on for pages about *spring green turf* and *snow white railings* and *Palladian porticos*. In fact, I learned more about Somerton in this chapter than I did about Liam Cassidy."

It was almost comical how decidedly unimpressed Viveca was with the chapter—*almost*.

Heat burned through Saskia all the way to the tips of her ears.

And Viveca went on… "It's like you've lost your understanding of character. It's like…" She took an interminable moment to search her mind. "It's like you've never written a book."

Stung, that was Saskia in this moment. Not only by Viveca's words, but by the honesty contained therein. It might not have been her best work, but surely it was serviceable enough. "Well, it *is* an early draft." Oh, how that little defensive note in her voice annoyed the blazes out of her.

Viveca's sea-blue eyes held a steely glint. The truth as Viveca saw it was coming, and all Saskia could do was wait and brace herself for it.

"There's no *life* in it."

Oof.

Saskia could've had any number of reactions to that last bit— *hurt…offense…anger*—but the fact was Viveca intended to provoke none of those emotions.

Viveca's sole intention was to make the book better.

So, Saskia would sit and take the critique and let it make the work better.

Viveca's head tipped to the side. "Aren't jockeys superstitious?"

"I…don't know."

What did superstition have to do with anything, anyway?

"*See?*" Viveca exclaimed. "You *should* know."

"If jockeys are superstitious?"

Viveca only answered her question with more questions.

"What are Cassidy's superstitions? What are his rituals before a race? When did he start them? *Why* did he start them? The number of races he has won is a matter of public record. Anyone can recite those facts. But what makes Liam Cassidy *the* Liam Cassidy? The Liam Cassidy the public adores. The Liam Cassidy who is *the best.*"

Despite it all, Saskia found an overwhelmed smile tugging at her mouth as she held her hands up, palms out. "All right, sister, you've made your point."

Viveca popped the last bite of cucumber sandwich into her mouth. Around it, she spoke. "I don't need to tell you how to solve this."

"You don't?"

"Surely, you know the answer."

Dread filled Saskia's stomach.

The thing was she thought she might know the answer.

But, oh, how she didn't want what she thought might be the answer to be the answer.

It was Viveca who said it. "You need to spend time with Liam Cassidy to make his memoirs spring to life. Facts aren't enough. We must hear him speaking from the page."

And there it was in plain English.

The answer Saskia didn't want to hear.

After her last encounter with Liam Cassidy at the Drunken Piebald, she'd made a decision. She would write his memoirs… from a distance. Why did she need to spend time with the man, anyway? She was a fiction writer. She could easily fill two hundred pages.

But—*of course*—Viveca had seen through the filler and found that at the heart of all those words Saskia had written was little more than air.

And Saskia knew why.

She didn't know Liam Cassidy.

She knew fictional characters of her own creation better than she did that flesh-and-blood man.

"Isn't this week the start of the racing season?" asked Viveca.

Saskia didn't want to answer.

Saskia had to answer… "Yes."

"What's the name of the first pair of races?"

The dread that had settled in Saskia's gut might've become a permanent fixture. "The Two Thousand and One Thousand Guineas."

Her sister's brow lifted expectantly, as if to say, *Well?*

"The Two Thousand was run two days ago," admitted Saskia.

She'd read about the race in the turf rags she now subscribed to. The colorful commentary had been enough for her to be able to imagine the tightly contested race. Reportedly, Cassidy had received an "accidental" whip lashing to the face from another jockey.

And, apparently, that was all part of the sport.

That would definitely go into the memoir.

Viveca's brow lifted with expectancy. "And?"

"And what?"

"Did Cassidy win?"

"He did."

Viveca clapped her hands together. "Oh, this book is going to be such a success. But only if you…" Her eyes narrowed. "Sister, get yourself to Newmarket *now*. You can take my carriage."

And that was the matter settled.

Within the half hour, Saskia found her bags packed and strapped to Viveca's carriage and herself seated inside the luxury conveyance as it wove its way through London and toward Suffolk. Tomorrow was the running of the One Thousand Guineas, and it seemed she would be there to witness it.

To witness Liam Cassidy in his element.

To put life into the page.

And here she'd thought she could read about his season in the turf rags and write a memoir. She'd been wrong—and she had only herself to blame.

She should have expected this.

That Viveca would see through her fluff.

That she would have to spend time with Liam Cassidy.

The simple fact was she couldn't trust herself around him.

Yes, all right, she'd harbored an infatuation for him for years.

She should've anticipated her response to him.

But she hadn't.

That infatuation had existed in the realm of fantasy.

It had provided fuel for her writing.

That was all.

How could she have known meeting him in the way she had would put flame to fuel?

And what happened when flame hit fuel?

Conflagration.

But they'd agreed upon professional boundaries, hadn't they?

They even had agreed-upon rules.

Well, *a* rule.

No kissing.

And, really, shouldn't that one rule be enough to keep them each to their side of the professional boundary line?

She hoped.

She doubted.

CHAPTER EIGHT

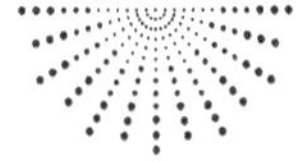

NEWMARKET, NEXT DAY

Race mornings weren't like any of the other mornings in Liam's year.

Every other morning began with his eyes popping open and him rolling out of bed the very next instant and getting on with the day ahead of him.

Race day, however, took on a different cadence from the moment he woke.

He didn't immediately roll out of bed.

He lay still and *pictured*.

That was his term for it.

He pictured every step he would take on this day.

He walked himself through the minutes—his feet hitting the floor...the splash of cold water to the face...donning his race silks...his walk to the stables, keeping himself to himself all the while...the rhythm of the brush across his mount's coat. Even Rake knew not to speak to him. The finalization of all their strategies and tactics occurred the night before.

Then the groom would fold and layer the blanket beneath Liam's watchful eye before placing the saddle. Liam saw to the straps. Then, all secure and as he liked, he would mount the Thoroughbred.

The quiet part of his day complete, he and horse ventured from the stable and out into the fray of the crowd. Today, all would be straining and clamoring to take the measure of Liam Cassidy and his mount Daylily, bouncing on the tips of their toes, some eyes narrowed, others wide, as they decided on whom to place their bets. Liam would continue keeping himself to himself as they walked to the Rubbing House for the weigh in, then out again into the crowd as they entered the racecourse and took to the turf to warm Daylily's muscles for the race. Then they would approach the start...jostling for position, feet prancing, waiting for the firing of the gun, Liam's heart in his throat, anticipation roaring through his veins...

On race day, all this sat in his mind before he ever ventured from bed.

It settled him.

It focused him.

It solidified purpose.

Up to a point.

He never pictured the race itself. For the outcome of a race wasn't predetermined and couldn't be predicted. Between the weather and the condition of the turf, and the other horses and jockeys, there were too many variables, too many competing wants and desires. And everyone trying to attain the same prize —first place.

To picture that outcome, to predict the race, only locked Liam into a fixed direction.

He'd done it before—to disastrous results.

He'd envisaged the race going one way—his way—and when it hadn't, he hadn't been able to adjust.

Still, he'd learned a few important lessons from the loss. One must remain fluid, nimble, and in the flow once the starting gun fired—and one must never, ever try to predict a horse race.

These were details Lady Saskia might want to include in the memoir.

If he ever saw her again.

Which was no sure thing.

It had been a month.

A month since he'd left her at her bedroom door.

A month and a day since she'd kissed him—and he'd kissed her back.

In reality, they'd known each other for only a single day. And while he couldn't precisely say he missed her, strangely, he felt an absence in his life.

A few days ago, he'd raced the Two Thousand Guineas on Morningstar—and won.

She hadn't been there.

And, odds were, she wouldn't be here today for the One Thousand Guineas, the fillies race.

But now—like all other concerns unrelated to the horse below him as a lad led them through the boisterous crowd toward the Rubbing House—he put Lady Saskia from his mind. He held all his energies carefully banked inside him. A passable smile curved his mouth. Monosyllabic responses to any questions asked. A nod to all well-wishes given. He would need every last bit of that energy, for today promised to be a fight to the end.

It was the Duchess of Acaster's filly, Lady Midnight, who would bring the fight to Daylily today. The turf rags had already run with the narrative of day versus night, and the betting around the post was ferocious. It wasn't all unmerited puff, either. The odds were, in fact, tipped heavily in favor of Lady Midnight.

However, he was Liam Cassidy, and that counted for something. His winning record spoke for itself. Further, he held a knowledge that a winning record couldn't reflect: a skilled, intuitive jockey could take a less perfect or talented horse and ride it to victory. A belief that had had him and his mount crossing the finish line first on more than one occasion.

Today didn't have to be any different.

Weigh-in complete, the lad led him and Daylily toward the racecourse. Liam surveyed the grounds. The crowds were massive, of course, with all the attendant laughter, shouting, and all-around general gaiety on a day like this. Later, after the race, there would be a few tears, too. But this was race day at Newmarket, and every emotion available to mankind was to be expected.

What Liam liked about Newmarket more than any other course in England was that pure racing was its *raison d'être*. Dry, hard, and straight, the Rowley Mile, the track where the One Thousand Guineas was run, was blazing fast. The fastest course in England, in fact, as it ran flat for the first mile. But that mile wasn't where the course tested horse and rider. The true test came in the final two furlongs, the penultimate of which was a blistering downhill that bottomed out at "The Dip." Then, from the lowest point, came the final uphill furlong, which was a true test of grit, strength, and resolve. Newmarket wasn't a lovely course, like Epsom Downs or Goodwood, but it dug into the soul, this course. It pulled the fight and the heart from all who raced it.

He found his gaze scanning the crowd with an intensity that could've only been characterized as single-minded.

Lady Saskia Calthorp.

That second night at the Drunken Piebald, he'd miscalculated and scared her off.

Disappointing, that.

But as Daylily stepped hoof onto the dense green turf of the Rowley Mile, Liam tucked all thoughts of Lady Saskia into a back corner of his mind and brought his energy into this moment. A skill he'd developed that was vital to his style of racing. For he didn't use whip or spur to assert his will over his mount. Instead, he employed a number of tactics over the three or so minutes of a race.

He couldn't explain it with words, but a feeling passed from him to horse as he urged him or her to their fastest. A cellular messaging that they were in this race together. Their race wasn't about the domination of jockey over horse—or man over beast. Rather, it was a communion. A mutual goal—to cross the finish line ahead of every other horse.

Two tactics, in particular, were the difference between a win and a loss: that he conceal his intentions and that he remain attuned to pace through every furlong. The stamina of his mount depended on this, especially in a race like Newmarket where the final furlong was an uphill battle.

As they reached the starting line, Liam muscled Daylily through horses and jockeys resplendent in their liveries, aiming for a place nearest the railing as they could manage. As the filly was the unrufflable sort, she kept her cool head in the tetchy scrum of the twenty or so other Thoroughbreds. "Good girl," he cooed into her ear.

None of the other jockeys spoke to him. They exchanged simple, silent nods. They could raise a glass and have a grand, old wassail later, once this race was at their backs.

His strategy for Daylily was simple—start her from the inside and use her quick feet to get out ahead before anyone could notice. For Lady Midnight, however, Liam noted, a different strategy was at play. Her jockey, Clifton Ames, angled her toward the outer edge of the pack. As she was rumored to be a high-spirited filly, keeping her clear of the fractious fray was the better part of wisdom.

But so, too, did that strategy speak of complete confidence. With her perfect conformation, talent, and grit, said that strategy, Lady Midnight could make up the disadvantage of an outside start. She'd run at Great Yarmouth in the two-year-old race last summer and had bested every filly in the field, so Liam had no doubt about the threat she posed. In fact, he fully expected to see her run the Oaks in June and the St. Leger in September. She looked the sort who would take to the longer races as the season wore on.

Once the field was assembled at the starting line, their positions fixed, the crowd went as quiet as a crowd of thousands possibly could. Here was the moment that got the blood up and rushing through the veins...the breath shallow with anticipation...muscles tensed with readiness.

It was up to this exact moment that Liam had pictured this day.

Beyond the imminent firing of the starting gun lay the unknown.

After all, he wasn't the only one out here with a strategy.

Everyone had a plan.

And how often was it that the outcome of a race was determined in the very first step?

Every jockey on this turf knew that to miss or falter on that first step was the end of their race before it could even begin.

Liam's breath held—no part of him moved, in fact—as he waited...waited... The gun fired.

Daylily lurched forward and took her first step...

And it was a good one.

In the space between one instant and the next, the filly bolted into the lead, her lightning quick speed doing precisely what Liam hoped. Yet, though she wasted no time putting a length between herself and her nearest competitor, this wasn't one of those races where Liam could relax all the way to a victory. The work of this race would be coming for them in the second half, he felt the certainty through to the marrow of his bones.

For now, he sank into the ride, the thrill that only one thousand pounds of superior horseflesh thundering below could produce. He and his mount unified in purpose...bound by trust... his teeth gritted against the wind blasting across his face...the ferocity of battle…the exhilaration… All this was possible to feel at once—a surplus of feeling as they had no choice but to give over and to give all.

At his back—*too soon*—Liam heard it… What he'd been waiting for: the inevitable, rhythmic pounding of approaching hooves.

Lady Midnight was coming.

Blast.

He'd hoped to have made it to the ninth downhill furlong before she caught them. So be it. The battle would commence at the sixth. The truth was Liam didn't prefer racing from the front and only did so rarely. His style of riding was better suited to sitting back in the race, while keeping within striking distance of the leaders. It allowed his mount to conserve energy for the final furlong.

Of course, Ames was well-acquainted with Liam's style, which was why he wasn't allowing Daylily to dictate the pace and was, instead, bringing the battle early by imposing Lady Midnight's pace on the field.

Liam dug in for the fight as they thundered toward The Dip, neck and neck. In the final uphill furlong, however, he sensed it— Daylily was fading. Sure, from a spectators' point of view, she would appear to be in the thick of it. But Liam knew differently. Which wasn't to say he was about to concede the race, but it had become Lady Midnight's to lose. Sometimes that happened. Sometimes, the better horse fumbled the finish, whether it be from distraction or lack of heart.

But that didn't happen today.

Today, just as they reached the finish line, Lady Midnight pulled ahead by half a length, making her the clear, undisputed winner of the One Thousand Guineas.

Blast.

Liam didn't like losing.

He'd never developed the knack for taking it in his stride.

Through the ferocity and will-to-win roaring through his veins, it was a hard fact to accept in the heat of the moment. One second, it was the bloodlust of battle...the next, gut-wrenching defeat.

But he never took his frustrated ambition out on his competitors—who he immediately congratulated—or on his mount, who he thanked and praised as he cooled her down. "You gave your all," he said, patting Daylily's neck. "And that's all I could ask for, my sweet."

But he couldn't count the day as a total loss. He now possessed information for the rest of the season. If he were a betting man, he would lay odds that Lady Midnight would not be running in the next fillies' race, the Oaks. The Duchess of Acaster would run her in the premier event of the season—the Derby.

Aye, Morningstar would have his hands full with that filly come June. It was rare for a filly to win the Triple Crown—or Triple Tiara, as some liked to say for fillies—but Lady Midnight had the stuff.

A thrill of anticipation for the coming fight pulsed through him.

Let her bring her best.

Once he'd cooled Daylily down and handed her over to Cal, Rake's most trusted stable lad, a feminine voice different from all the others throwing greetings, commiserations, and curses at him sounded at his back. "You didn't win."

He froze.

The chaotic world of race-day Newmarket fell away, and a new variety of anticipation pulsed through him.

If he wasn't mistaken, the possessor of that voice was...

He turned.

Lady Saskia Calthorp...silvery-blue eyes bright above spectacles perched on the tip of her nose...tendrils of strawberry-blonde hair escaping from beneath a wide-brimmed straw hat, its sunshine-yellow ribbon fluttering in the light breeze…her cheeks flushed…her breath shallow…

Liam's brow creased. "Have you been running?"

She pushed her spectacles up to their rightful resting place on the bridge of her nose, in the process collecting herself.

He wished she wouldn't.

He liked her like this—a bit out of balance.

"More of a brisk walk," she said in that cherry-tart voice he remembered.

A smile twitched at the corner of his mouth, demanding release. "Did you *briskly walk* all the way from the grandstand to inform me of my loss?"

He caught the instant she registered the tease in his voice, for a sheepish smile sparked in her bright eyes. A dry laugh drew his attention to her rose-pink lips. His gaze lingered there a few ticks of time too long. Perhaps it was the blood yet het up in his veins, or perhaps it was pure and simple inclination, or perhaps it was habit that longed to be formed, but he could kiss Lady Saskia.

Here…now…for all to see…

Again.

And he knew the instant the thought struck him.

It was definitely the third *perhaps*.

CHAPTER NINE

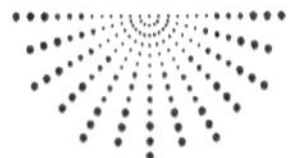

It occurred to Saskia that she might've been standing a hair too close to Liam Cassidy.

Ridiculous thought, really.

They were conversing.

People stood close when they conversed.

All right, maybe not within touching distance, as they were standing now.

For within touching distance lay another sort of distance...

Kissing distance.

A lopsided smile curved a corner of his mouth. "Even winning jockeys don't win every race."

Charming, that smile.

But she could hardly pay it any heed.

Something else had caught her attention. "You have a..." She touched her own left cheek to mirror his right. "You have an injury."

"Battle wound," he said, the notion of battle wounds having no effect on his lopsided smile.

"From a few days ago, correct?" she asked. "Another jockey struck you with his whip during the Two Thousand Guineas?"

"Heat of the moment stuff." An indifferent shrug followed.

"Is that something you would do to an opponent?"

"I don't use the whip."

Her head tilted to the side. "I thought all jockeys used a whip as a matter of course."

"Not me." His smile tipped into the unapologetic. "Not that I don't get physical on the turf. Large bodies in motion and everyone striving for first, one's inner brute rises to the surface and fights if he's to have any chance at winning."

She didn't know how to respond. It wasn't his words that were foreign to her way of thinking, but the light in his eyes as he spoke them.

Nay, not uncomplicated *light*.

Fire blazed within as he spoke.

And though Saskia's mouth had no response, her body did. As if the heat in his eyes sparked and connected to a heat inside her —*conflagration.*

That word again.

"Cassidy!" came a shout. "Get yer arse to the Running Horse. Least you could do is spring for the first round."

Cassidy good-naturedly waved the man and his band of fellow revelers on. "Aye, right you are."

Saskia's brow lifted. "First round?"

"Of ale," he said. "As the loser."

"You came in second place." A surge of unexpected defensiveness rose inside her. "That hardly makes you the loser."

"Ah, there you're mistaken." His eyes glinted with a flash of steel. "Second place is the worst sort of loser."

Criminy.

Behind that charming smile, this man was serious about winning.

She cleared her throat. "Well, then, I won't keep you from your celebrations. I should be—"

"Leaving?"

She nodded.

He appeared to be searching his mind for something to say, and Saskia half hoped he would find it, because, well, she wasn't ready to take her leave.

His smile suddenly brightened. "But aren't you here for research purposes?"

She nodded, slowly, as one who sensed a trap being laid, but couldn't yet see it.

His smile released into full brilliance.

She might need to shield her eyes.

"Then you'll be wanting to come with me."

A disbelieving laugh sounded through her nose. "For research purposes?"

"Aye, most definitely."

Oh, the charm that glittered about him.

And something else, too.

Something that willed her to say *yes*.

She couldn't help but be infected by it. And, really, wasn't he correct? Wasn't what happened off the turf just as important as what happened on it for the purposes of the memoir? Or, if not just as important, *almost* as important?

Which made it still important.

Necessary, even.

Further, congratulations and commiserations had been flooding in from every direction as they conversed. While Cassidy had ignored them, Saskia now saw they could no longer be held at bay. Everyone wanted a piece of Liam Cassidy, and the time for revelry was nigh.

Understanding came to her. A horse race was composed of three phases—the tense lead-up to the race; the race itself; and the aftermath, a release of emotion that flowed toward jollity and the need to revel. The need to release all that excess emotion with one's fellow man and a mug of ale—or several.

At last, though she likely shouldn't, she nodded her assent,

Liam waggled his eyebrows, and they were shouldering their way through the intensifying crowd, off to revel.

These last five years that she'd been a lady, she'd attended every manner of function society had on offer—musicales, recitals, soirées, salons, midnight suppers, hunts, balls—but never had she *reveled*.

One of the leading activities of a post-race revel, she fast learned, was a great number of toasts.

"Here's to a swift horse and a slow bailiff!"

"Here's to you as good as you are, and here's to me as bad as I am!"

And in a pinch, a shout of, "Wassail!" would do.

All these toasts were made by owners, jockeys, and any random celebrant willing to purchase a round of ale or whiskey and hold up their glass.

Lots of laughter in a revel.

Shouting, too.

And women.

Women of all sorts, from high to low, graced the taproom of the Running Horse—*Lady* ladies to ladies of the night and every other sort of woman in between. Women who didn't bother to acknowledge the quiet, bespectacled woman at Liam Cassidy's side in their haste and determination to be near him...to catch his eye...to win his smile.

This rankled, Saskia didn't mind admitting. She was both a woman and a *Lady*, and it was almost as if she didn't exist as she detached herself from the Liam-Cassidy orbit and away to the periphery of the taproom. All the better so she could observe the phenomenon, she told herself, even as that small part of her yet prickled with irritation.

Did spectacles render a woman so entirely invisible and... and...*sexless*?

Liam Cassidy, on the other hand, was neither sexless nor invisible. His second-place finish on the turf today did nothing to diminish his public's appetite for him, which he hardly appeared to notice.

Which wasn't to say he didn't like the attention. He did, very clearly. But he didn't notice his place in the center, because it was expected. It was the usual. It was the place he always occupied.

Saskia edged toward the doorway that led to the staircase that took one to the upper rooms. One of those rooms was hers for the night, as she'd arranged at no small expense when she'd arrived with her hastily packed bags. After all, she'd collected ample information for *research purposes* tonight and had become quite obviously superfluous to events.

She'd made it halfway up the stairs when a voice sounded at her back. "An early night, then?"

Her foot froze mid-step, and she twisted around. Though a few steps lower, Liam Cassidy's gaze met hers nearly eye-to-eye. A butterfly fluttered through her stomach. "I'd hardly call half ten an early night," she found the voice to say.

A ready laugh eased from him. "Half ten is most definitely an early night at Newmarket. It's even morning for some."

She supposed she sounded like a prig. So, priggishly, she went on. "I've an early morning."

The words had the opposite of their dismissive intent by impelling him up the stairs to join her. "Then I shall escort you to your room, milady."

He looked disinclined to take *no* for an answer.

And when she dug deep, she found herself disinclined to give him that answer.

Still, she was irritated, and though she couldn't precisely express *why*, her next question hit the air on a decidedly tart note. "Have you always liked the attention?"

His head whipped around, and his expression could've been characterized as nothing less than taken aback. "Pardon?"

"*Attention*," she repeated. "You appear to thrive on it."

Perhaps she'd expected him to react defensively—perhaps she'd wanted him to—but he shrugged, unoffended. "Not at first."

Curiosity had her asking, "Why is that?"

"I wasn't always keen on being known."

"Were you hiding?"

Opaque emotion passed behind gold-flecked green eyes, and his brow crinkled subtly, his air of carefree reveler gone in an instant. "Why would you ask a thing like that?"

She blinked. What was this conversation they were now having? How had they arrived here?

Were you hiding?

That was how.

But *why?*

Liam Cassidy was one of the most famous men in England. It wasn't possible for him to hide, even if he wanted to. But...

Fame hadn't always been his companion.

She opened her mouth to pursue this improbable conversation when his smile reappeared. "I simply meant the attention can be overwhelming."

He was lying—and he wasn't.

The attention his fame brought him could be overwhelming— *the truth.*

The lie, however, was located in the word *simply.*

A word that could deflect from that which one would keep hidden.

Behind that *simply* lay *more.*

He'd been hiding.

For reasons to do with his past...

To do with the upbringing he refused to discuss.

Saskia felt that certainty deep in her gut.

The brilliance of Cassidy's smile returned tenfold, all opaque emotions and obscuring *simply*s secreted away. "Then I saw the life all the attention affords me..." Another shrug.

"And you like that life?"

"There are worse lives to lead."

There.

Within those words sounded the voice of experience.

Liam Cassidy had led a worse sort of life—and had no intention of revealing or revisiting it—not for her and not for his adoring public.

They reached door number seven. "This is me."

A specific glint entered Cassidy's eyes—one she knew. "Shall I see you safely inside?"

The breath suspended in her lungs.

Yes.

Her body demanded she say *yes*.

Perhaps he was being gentlemanly; perhaps he wasn't. Either way, no safety lay in that *yes*.

She dug inside her reticule, then held up her room key. "Enjoy the rest of your evening, Mr. Cassidy. Your public waits."

Then she inserted the key into the lock, entered her room, and shut the door behind her.

Alone...

Safely.

Safely, that was, until she opened her eyes, noticed the figure in her bed, and promptly screamed bloody murder.

CHAPTER TEN

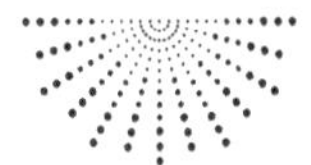

*L*iam had made it halfway down the corridor, still shaking his head—at Lady Saskia or himself, he couldn't say—when the scream pierced the air.

His feet stuttered to a stop.

If he wasn't mistaken, that scream had come from—

The door to number 7 slammed open and out flew Lady Saskia, her eyes wide and wild. She swiveled and stabbed an accusatory finger toward the open doorway. "In my room…it's a naked—" She gulped. "*Man.*"

Liam had already made up most of the distance back to her door, but those words in combination—*naked* and *man*—had his hands clenched into ready fists and him charging into the room like a bull seeing red.

The sight greeting his eyes, however, had him stopping dead in his tracks.

There was, indeed, a naked man inside Lady Saskia's room.

He was even on her bed.

But he was also sprawled face down on top of the coverlet, snoring, milk-white bottom bare to the breeze.

Liam lifted a single eyebrow. "Not who you were expecting in your bed tonight?"

Saskia snorted. "One would hope for better options in bed partners."

There was her usual unruffled self recovered.

"You don't mind sharing?"

She glared up at him, eyes narrow slits.

"Not with him," chuckled Liam. "With me."

Her eyebrows made a break for the ceiling.

Apparently, he hadn't made himself clearer with his second attempt. "Come to my room, Lady Saskia. We'll find a suitable sleeping arrangement."

Her eyes harbored doubts, and her feet remained as unmoved as the rest of her.

"You cannot stay here." He said this firmly. He wasn't leaving her with a strange man.

At last, she sighed and nodded, then gathered her belongings, which totaled two unpacked leather satchels. The lady traveled light.

In no time, Liam was ushering Lady Saskia Calthorp into his room and shutting the door behind them. They were alone. Had the bed always been that big?

He gave himself a mental shake and ignored the bed as he crossed the room and deposited her bags near the corner wash-stand. She stopped in the center of the room looking as if she had a grand speech to deliver.

"I shall sleep on the floor, of course," she proclaimed.

He'd thought she would say something like that. "You're welcome to the bed," he offered. "I've slept on worse floors."

Unmoved, she held out a hand. "All I need is a pillow and a blanket."

If Liam understood one thing about Lady Saskia Calthorp, it was that one gained little ground by arguing with her once her mind was made up. He grabbed the pillow and stripped the heaviest blanket off the bed and handed them over.

With a curt nod of gratitude, she began assembling her pallet for the night, which he observed from the periphery of his vision while he set to his own nightly ablutions, beginning with the removal of his boots. He only realized he'd groaned with pleasure when he felt her gaze hit the side of his face.

"I have a question for you." She'd lowered to a seat on her pallet. "For the memoir."

"Ask away."

"Do you have any race-day superstitions?"

He reclined in the straight-backed chair, rickety wood creaking beneath his weight. "Like a putting-my-left-sock-on-first superstition?"

She nodded.

"Aye, I have a few."

Her head canted. She was waiting.

All right, he would indulge her. "Let's see. I don't eat or drink anything on race morning."

"Not even coffee or tea?"

He shook his head. "I don't talk to anyone if I can help it. I always brush my horse. I check the straps three times."

"*Three?*"

"*Three.*" He rolled up his left shirtsleeve and extended his wrist for her perusal, revealing a thin leather band. "I score a new hash mark onto this band."

"Win or lose?"

"Before I even race," he explained, not because he had to, but because he wanted to. "It's a way of marking the day, but also showing gratitude for it."

"*Win or lose.*"

"Aye, win or lose, I'm grateful."

"But you don't like to lose."

"I don't." He could acknowledge as much. It wasn't a secret. "But I'm ever thankful to my mount for giving their all, win or lose." He hesitated. "And I'm thankful for this life I've somehow attained."

Understanding lit within her silvery-blue eyes that could be inflexible steel one moment and soft calm sea the next.

A feeling stole through him.

He liked being understood by this woman.

She reached for the pillow and began determinedly fluffing it. "Now, if you will extinguish the candle before you retire to bed, I'll bid you a good night."

"I would be happy to give you the bed." He had to offer one last time. What he didn't need to do was add cheekily, "Or I could share it with you."

She flipped onto her side and faced away from him. A dry snort floated over her shoulder.

The thing was it wasn't all cheek.

Though such behavior fell well wide of their established *professional boundaries*, he would happily share a bed with this woman.

"Good night, Mr. Cassidy."

It was only then he noticed something… "Lady Saskia?"

"Hmm?"

"Are you planning on sleeping with your spectacles on?"

"Of course not," she tossed over her shoulder with no small amount of scorn, even as he noted her discreetly sliding them off her nose.

"And your clothes, too?"

"I am."

"Your boots?"

"Aye."

"Your corset?"

"Aye."

"You cannot possibly sleep in a corset and boots."

"I can manage myself very well," came her cherry-tart retort.

"Then I shall, too."

A second ticked past, and utter stillness reigned on her side of the floor.

Another second, and more stillness.

But the next second, she rolled over to face him. "You shall, too, *what* exactly?"

"Sleep in my clothes."

"You cannot possibly sleep in your clothes."

"I can."

"But you rode in a horse race today." Her matter-of-fact tone suggested it would brook no argument. "Don't you have bruises? Won't you be sore?"

He shrugged.

Three ticks of time passed, then she exhaled a blustery sigh. "All right."

"*All right?*"

He was being disingenuous.

He'd won—and they both knew it.

She sat up. "But you can't watch."

"Wouldn't dream of it."

He flipped his chair around so it now faced the opposite direction—away from her—then began tugging a sock off his foot and giving every appearance of a man paying no mind to the woman currently undressing in his room. But while he couldn't see her, he could hear her. The rustle of wool and muslin…the flick of one bodice button after another…the whispery shush of her dress being shed and tossed aside…the slide of corset strings coming loose and undone…the inhalation of a relieved breath… the fall of the corset onto pine floorboards…

She would be down to chemise and stockings now.

It wasn't only logic that had followed her every movement.

His cock had, too.

Lady Saskia in naught but chemise and stockings.

Stillness filled the air.

She was finished undressing.

Right.

He slipped his race shirt over his head, its spring-green and midnight-blue stripes coated with a film of turf grime, and before he could continue, her voice sounded, "What is that...*garment?...* affixed to you?"

Ah.

So, she'd been watching him—and had given herself away.

It was that curiosity of hers.

It couldn't help itself.

"It's a leather breastplate," he explained. "It protects me if I fall."

A few seconds passed. "Clever."

He loosened the ties fastening the breastplate to him, then set it on the table. He reached for a small pot of salve and dug out a healthy dollop, which he began smoothing into various sore spots on his torso.

"Now what are you doing?" She sounded slightly exasperated.

So...

She was still watching.

"This will help calm tomorrow's aches."

Her eyes surely upon him, he continued rubbing the salve into various places known to give him trouble the day after a race— his shoulders...the small of his back...the muscles of his neck. What he didn't have to do was take quite as much time and care with the task.

She was watching—and possibly liking what she was seeing.

Her voice pierced the quiet. "There's a bruise you missed."

For the first time since she'd undressed and since he'd undressed, Liam allowed himself to look at her. She was propped onto her side, strawberry-blonde hair loose and spilling around her, silvery-blue eyes unflinching upon him behind her spectacles.

Her spectacles had returned to her face.

"Can't get them all." A habit, his affable flippancy to matters of seriousness.

That flippancy had no effect on her. Before another second could tick into the next, she pushed to her feet and was across the room, her hand extended for the pot of salve. "Here, allow me."

He extended the salve, despite the refusal that should've issued from his mouth.

She moved behind him—and the world went still.

Yes, the celebration to end all celebrations was presently roaring in the taproom below, bouncing through floorboards, but that world fell away, distant and muted. In this room, his skin awakened with anticipation…alive to the inevitability of her touch.

It wasn't only his skin that had gone alive to possibility.

His cock, half-mast and poised for full turgidity, also held aspirations.

A fingertip that held the hint of a tremble touched the center of his back, just to the left of his spine. He sucked in a rough breath. She stilled. "Does that hurt?"

"No," grated across his gravelly throat.

Her finger resumed its progress, and the entirety of his consciousness lost its ability to concern itself with anything other than that half-inch pad touching him—*skin against skin.*

He groaned.

Her finger stopped.

He nearly groaned again.

Temptation beckoned. To beg her to keep going, to use the entirety of her hand, while she was at it, to dig in deep…

No.

He gave a loud, abrupt clearing of his throat. "Thank you." His voice still sounded like it had been dragged down a long, gravel drive.

Her hand fell away.

And here was another groan that wanted airing—from the loss of her touch.

He remained still while she returned to her pallet. Then he extinguished the candle and took himself to that too-large bed, where he lay on his back, arms behind his head, and stared up at the ceiling, midnight shadows frolicking across the whitewash as the downstairs carousing raged on.

But it wasn't the night's revelries or sore muscles or his lack of a pillow that would keep him awake all the hours that remained of this night.

It was the woman presently occupying a six-by-two patch of his floor.

Well, her effect on him.

And his stubborn erection.

That, too, would hold him hostage to the sleepless hours that remained between now and dawn.

CHAPTER ELEVEN

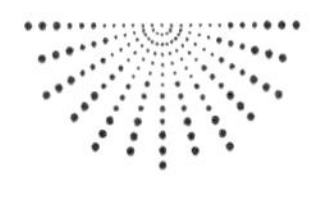

NEXT MORNING

*S*askia's eyes managed to slit open a paltry sliver, only to find a shaft of sunlight shining directly on her face.

Against all probabilities, somehow, she'd slept.

Soundly.

So soundly that this shaft of sunlight wasn't a soft golden ray of dawn, but one of cooler mid-morning.

Further, she was alone.

Liam Cassidy was gone.

Gone back to London or Somerton or wherever it was he went when he wasn't racing, training, or reveling.

Which, of course, was for the best.

Last night...

She could groan.

She did groan.

She'd watched him undress down to his trousers. Midnight candlelight had made a glory of lean, hard muscles of back, chest, and arms, casting each individually in mellow shadow and light. Then he'd begun rubbing salve into those muscles, and from her pallet on the floor, she'd watched, transfixed, her mouth gone dry as parched desert sand.

She shouldn't have noticed it, but she did—the bruise.

She should've kept her mouth shut and left it.

But it hadn't been possible.

Further, she'd rubbed salve into that bruise…touching him…feeling him—his heat, his strength.

Again, she groaned.

Oh, how was she to get through this summer?

She gave herself a firm mental shake.

There was only one way she would get through it—*routine*.

Her routine upon waking was to write, so write she would for a couple of hours before taking herself back to London.

She pushed to her feet and reached for her clothes. A few minutes later, she was dressed, teeth scrubbed, and seated at the room's only table, her journals stacked before her, pencil poised in hand.

Already, she felt better.

She should start with the memoir, for she had yesterday's race and Cassidy's list of superstitions to record. Instead, she reached for the journal containing her novel-in-progress. Certain details of the hero demanded to be written—his masculine scent of salt and citrus…the hot, alive feel of his skin…the hardness of muscles below…the tremble of those muscles beneath her touch… The room grew unbearably hot, and she had to slip the two topmost buttons of her dress free to cool herself.

She'd sunk herself deep into a description of the green of the hero's eyes—not quite emerald…not quite moss—when the door burst open, startling a surprised yelp from her. Into the doorway stepped Liam Cassidy, as if her thoughts had the power to conjure him. But, of course, they didn't, for if they did, he certainly wouldn't have been wearing a shirt.

"Milady," he said, then stood aside for the retinue of servants who followed, each bearing a tray—this one with teapot, cream, and sugar…that one with plates and silverware…yet another with all manner of breads and pastry...and still another with meats and cheeses... Then there was the sweets tray.

She shook her head, bemused and charmed, despite herself. "You've brought a feast."

"I'm always ravenous the day after a race."

He propped a shoulder against the doorjamb as the servants set up a makeshift buffet on the dresser. Meanwhile, Saskia sat stunned in place while they finished up and vacated the room. Cassidy shut the door behind them.

She was alone with him.

Again.

He grabbed the teapot and two cups before lowering into the seat opposite her. "Lady Saskia," he said brightly, "how have you been occupying yourself this fine morning?"

"As I do every morning."

"And how is that?"

"I've been writing."

His gaze fell to the journal open before her and the pencil yet clutched in her hand. "Ah, the *Memoirs of Liam Cassidy*, is it?"

"*Erm...*"

But before she could gather either her bearings or his intentions, with one swift movement he reached out and snatched the journal away.

No, no, no...no!

Under no circumstances could he be allowed to read what she'd written.

She jumped to her feet and extended her hand. "Those pages aren't for your eyes."

He settled back in his chair—and held onto the journal. "But they're supposedly my words, so why wouldn't they be for my eyes?"

"Cassidy—"

"Liam."

"*Liam*," she began—and further words refused to issue forth.

The fact was she couldn't tell him why he couldn't read those pages without giving something of herself away.

She drew up to her fullest height and leveled her fiercest glare at him. "Any gentleman would have already returned my property to me."

Something opaque and unknowable flickered behind his eyes. It was gone the next instant, leaving in its place his good humor and determination. "Let's have a look at what *I* have been writing about myself, shall we?"

Saskia could sink through the floor...fly out the window...sprint through the door...*anything* to get away from what was surely coming.

Oh, the humiliation of her own thoughts, musings, and words repeated back to her.

Words, thoughts, and musings about *him*.

She wouldn't be able to bear it.

He cleared his throat, his eyes searching the pages for a starting place.

But he didn't begin reading aloud.

He was reading to himself.

And that was worse.

Much worse.

His eyebrows gathered.

His eyebrows released.

His head cocked.

It was as if he couldn't believe what he was reading.

A groan escaped her. She reached for the chair-back for support before her legs gave out from beneath her. Surely, the thunderous race of her heart couldn't be favorable for her health.

At last, his gaze lifted. "What am I reading?"

She cleared her throat. "It's, well"—the throat-clearing hadn't taken—"it's the beginnings of a novel."

There went his brow creasing again. "About *me*?"

"No!" she exclaimed too quickly and altogether too loudly. "I write novels." For some reason, she couldn't stop talking… "About other men."

That last part was too slow, for Cassidy—*Liam*—looked more confused than ever.

Still, he extended the journal, which she snatched out of his hand and held tightly to her chest. Yet relief was slow in coming, for a question lingered in his eyes.

A slew of questions.

"You write novels," he said, deliberately. "About men…*other* men."

She sighed and slumped into her chair, her journal still clutched tight. "I write novels about men *and* women."

He nodded, slowly. "So, you write novels about *people*."

She laughed. She had to. Otherwise, she would cry. "Yes, I write novels about people."

A smile tipped about his mouth. "About their scents…and the feel of their skin."

She groaned. "That won't make it into the novel."

"Is this your first novel?"

"It isn't."

"No?"

Now, the inevitable point of this conversation had arrived, and she had no choice but to say… "I write under a pen name."

His brow lifted, his mouth turned down at the corners. "Which is?"

"Harriet LaPlume."

His eyes went wide. "*You* are Harriet LaPlume?"

"Have you heard of her?" That wasn't quite right… "*Me?*" That wasn't right, either… "*Her?*"

And here was her heart threatening to break free from her ribcage again.

He nodded. "I purchased your latest book for my sister last Christmas."

"You did?" Sudden heat flushed through her. "You can't tell anyone."

"Your secret is safe with me."

She believed him.

For some reason—well, lots of reasons, likely related to his handsomeness and his warm eyes and her longstanding, private admiration—she trusted him.

And while she understood her reasons for trusting him weren't at all rooted in experience, she simply couldn't prevent herself from wanting to trust him.

Which had gotten many a woman into many a tangle with many a man.

But there was no help for it.

"Now," he said, coming to his feet, "let's eat."

As he served himself from the makeshift buffet, she followed, only now realizing she, too, was ravenously hungry.

When once again seated across from him, though, she felt a slight imbalance.

He knew her greatest secret.

Yet he'd revealed nothing of his.

An imbalance that couldn't stand.

She took a slow sip of tea and watched him load his fork with beans, sausage, egg, and ham. He could really tuck into a meal, couldn't he? She cleared her throat. Questioning gold-flecked green eyes met hers. "Turnabout is fair play, you know," she said.

"*Turnabout?*" he spoke around the bite.

She nodded, feeling more sure of herself by the moment. "You know a secret of mine. Now you must tell me a secret of yours."

Must.

A word that instructed and commanded.

A word he had every right to ignore, if he so chose.

A seriousness entered his eyes. He was weighing the imbalance between them and whether it was in his interests to correct it. Likely, it wasn't. But he was a sportsman, and the rule of fair play would appeal to his better self.

She hoped.

At last, he said, "What I tell you can't go into the memoir."

Anticipation lit through her veins. She nodded.

He held her gaze. "I'm a bastard."

She blinked. "In the general sense or…"

He caught her humor and chuckled dryly. "I'm the illegitimate son of an—" A beat. "Aristocrat."

"Oh." That would explain his refusal to discuss his upbringing. It might also explain the hiding. Still, she had to ask… "And you won't tell me who that aristocrat is?"

He shook his head. "I won't." He shrugged. "He doesn't matter, anyway."

She doubted that very much, but let it pass. It would've been an additional secret revealed, which would've left *her* owing *him* a secret.

And she wouldn't be giving up any more of those today.

So, each keeping to their side of the table, they ate on, a surprising agreeability in the air.

And it was in this space that Saskia realized a truth.

She liked Liam Cassidy.

Not for his handsomeness or good humor or fame.

She liked him for himself.

Once his plate was all but licked clean and hers as empty as it was going to get, he asked, "Do you require an escort back to London?"

She shook her head. "I've my sister's coach waiting for me."

A question yet lingered in his eyes. "I'll see you at the Derby next month?"

"Perhaps."

Though she'd never spoken a flirtatious word in her life—her night as Arabella notwithstanding—that *perhaps* hit the still morning air with an inflection that could only be characterized as coquettish. Later, surely, her boldness would inspire after-the-fact mortification.

But not now.

Not with him catching that hint of flirtation and responding with a glint of wickedness in his eyes as he came to his feet. "Until the Derby," he said with a bow. *"Perhaps."*

He grabbed a sticky bun on his way out the door, then was gone, leaving Saskia alone with her thoughts.

Oh, so many thoughts to be left alone with.

She and Liam Cassidy were coming to know one another, weren't they? It could be likened to the analogy of an onion peeling back its layers, but onions stank and made her cry. She preferred to liken the experience to an early-summer rosebud releasing its petals, one by one, until it reached full bloom. With every interaction, she and Cassidy—*Liam*, he'd insisted—peeled back another petal...another slender layer of distance removed between them.

If they kept on like this, soon, nothing would remain between them.

And where would that leave them?

CHAPTER TWELVE

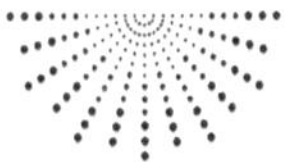

LONDON, A FORTNIGHT LATER

These last five years, Liam had attended his fair share of gatherings hosted by the high and mighty *haut ton*—soirées, salons, musicales, suppers, picnics, hunts, balls…

Take this ball—a ball being thrown by no lesser personages than the Duke and Duchess of Acaster. As one would expect, it was a sumptuous affair with chandeliers casting brilliant crystalline light, illuminating the ballroom from frescoed ceiling to gleaming mahogany floors and all those in between who danced to lively waltzes, laughed with genuine delight, conversed in all seriousness, drank with abandon, and generally gave over to a night of conviviality.

And he understood why he counted amongst their number. First, his sister had married a duke. That was one reason for the pile of invitations back in his flat of rooms. Second, he was a winning jockey, which was the primary reason for those invitations. People liked a winner.

Plainly, for the aristocrats populating this room, he was entertainment. After all, he was a luminary of their favorite sport. Further, he held no illusions that the instant he was toppled off that mountaintop—an inevitability, of course—the river of society invitations would slow to a trickle before altogether drying up.

"You cannot be serious, Cassidy," said the lord—an earl or a viscount or some such elevated being—who'd edged just a hair too close to him, a glint of desperation in his eyes.

Liam gave an indifferent shrug. He allowed that shrug and the casual smile accompanying it to do much of the heavy labor on nights out in society. "I am serious, in fact."

"Of course, you're not." On a scoff, the lord glanced around the room for effect. "It's horse racing, and you're a jockey, of course you influence the odds."

Liam could only speak the truth. "I have no dealings with that side of the sport."

"Just tell me, Cassidy." The lord was growing more fractious by the moment. "Who are you betting on for the Derby?"

"I don't place bets." Liam knew some jockeys who did, of course. But that didn't make it right. "Now, if you will pardon me." Without waiting for an answer, he pivoted neatly on his heel and made for the periphery of the ballroom.

He experienced a version of that conversation at every society event he attended.

But it wasn't only the lords who cornered the ever-so-popular Liam Cassidy for their own interests—the ladies did, too. And Liam couldn't honestly say he'd minded that particular effect of fame all that much.

Take the lady who'd appeared in every room he'd entered tonight ten seconds after him. She would stand directly in his line of sight, her dark sultry eyes meeting his before sliding away, the shadow of a coquettish smile playing about her mouth. *Seduction*, that was what the woman was about. And in that way, she looked at Liam Cassidy and ultimately saw the thing most everyone else in this room saw when they looked at him—*entertainment*.

And as his star had ascended and his popularity had grown, hadn't he been only too happy to provide a night's entertainment to those ladies in search of a little not-so-innocent fun?

But neither that reason nor any of the others were his motivation for having accepted the invitation to *this* ball *tonight*.

He was here precisely because the invitation had come from the Duke and Duchess of Acaster. Sure, it was true the duchess's stable of Thoroughbreds numbered amongst the best in all England. She even owned Lady Midnight. But it wasn't their connection through horse racing that brought him here tonight.

It was the duke, actually.

Well, not him, strictly.

It was his connection to the woman Liam hadn't been able to put from his mind this last fortnight—*Lady Saskia Calthorp*.

The logic was simple.

The duke was her brother, which meant she would have been invited.

Which had the odds tipping in favor of her attendance.

Which meant, even now, he might at this exact moment be sharing the same air as her.

The blood had been jittery in his veins all night with the possibility.

The thing was, in all their interactions, he'd played it light and breezy. He'd given nothing away at how deeply she affected him. A skill he'd cultivated early in life—out of necessity. A skill that had carried him on to the highest levels of success.

But Lady Saskia struck a chord through him that sat deeper— that yet resonated.

He wanted to see her again.

He *needed* to see her again.

Perhaps.

Her answer when he'd asked if she would attend the Derby.

That answer had been sitting at a sideways angle inside him since.

He wanted—*needed*—something surer.

So, here he was, attending her brother and his wife's ball.

"If it isn't *the* Liam Cassidy himself," came an unapologetically East-End voice at his back.

Liam turned to meet the direct gray gaze of a tall, rangy man dressed beyond the first stare of fashion into the realm of the extravagant with his velvet aubergine evening attire and pebble-sized diamond stud winking in his left ear.

Blaze Jagger.

"Jagger," said Liam, sticking out his hand, which the man took.

The fact was Liam had never spoken to Jagger—he kept away from the betting post, in truth—but he had no qualm with the man. After all, he and Jagger were viewed on the same level by the eyes of society—providers of entertainment.

But Jagger, enterprising rogue that he was, had done society one better. He'd gone and married one of their own—Lady Viveca Calthorp, as she'd been. A lady who just so happened to be the sister of the Duke of Acaster and…Lady Saskia.

A small world, the *haut ton*, and never had Liam been so grateful for the fact. If Blaze Jagger was here, his wife was here. And if his wife was here, then the odds increased that her sister would be here. In the tick between one second and the next, anticipation lit through Liam's veins.

"Now," said Jagger, "an interesting rumor pricked my ears concerning *the* Liam Cassidy. So, you can imagine my utter delight at seeing the man himself gracing this resplendent ball with his presence."

"Rumors ever abound concerning turf matters," Liam dismissed.

Jagger's mouth curved into his rogue's smile. "Little persistent whispers. And those little persistent whispers have it that you will ride Morningstar in the Derby, but not Daylily in the Oaks."

A line formed between Liam's eyebrows. "That so?"

Jagger's eyes narrowed to slits. "Any truth in it?"

Though Jagger no longer ran the betting posts at the race-courses, he did operate The Archangel, an exclusive gentlemen's gaming club that took bets on the season's major races. Liam understood his next words would influence the betting that had already started. But as word had already leaked, he saw no harm in saying, "Aye, there's truth in it."

Jagger's head cocked. "And what truth is that?"

"I'll be riding Morningstar in the Derby, and an up-and-coming jockey will ride Daylily in the Oaks."

"That so?"

"Aye."

And they'd reached the end of the truths Liam would be divulging to Blaze Jagger tonight. Jagger could find out with the rest of England that the Duke of Rakesley had not one, but two talented jockeys in his stable. The stable lad, Cal, who had been at Somerton nearly his entire life, had expressed an interest in trying for a jockey. Not an unusual dream for a lad. So, Liam had worked with him, to see if talent would rise—and it had. In fact, Cal had talent to spare.

So, after the Two Thousand and One Thousand Guineas, once Liam and Rake determined it likely the Duchess of Acaster would race Lady Midnight in the Derby instead of the Oaks, they decided the Oaks would be Cal's debut on the turf. The field there would provide the lad with a solid challenge, but he also stood a chance of winning.

"Husband," came a feminine voice.

Along with Jagger, Liam turned to find two ladies approaching, one of whom was Jagger's wife, Lady Viveca. The other of whom was…

Lady Saskia.

Until now, Liam had never beheld her in the finery befitting the sister of a duke: her silk gown the hue of a blush-pink rose, overlain with gauzy net threaded through with silver, which caught the light and glittered. Hair arranged half up and half down, a long thick tendril artfully arranged over her shoulder, leading the eye toward décolletage more abundant than her typical buttoned-up-to-the-chin attire had suggested. And her usual spectacles sat perched upon her nose. He found he liked that. Those spectacles spoke to who she truly was. She would see. Practicality above all other considerations.

"A waltz has struck up," said Lady Viveca to her husband, her eyes for no one else. "And I find myself in dire need of your hands upon me."

Liam's eyebrows threatened to lift clear off his forehead. Had Lady Viveca said what he thought she'd just said?

The subtle sigh issuing from Lady Saskia's parted mouth and the roll of her eyes toward the ceiling said her sister had and that such proclamations weren't a novel occurrence.

Roguish smile curving Jagger's mouth, he took his wife in his arms and waltzed her onto the dancing floor.

Leaving Liam alone with Lady Saskia.

He should greet her.

Or inquire about her health since they last spoke.

Or even ask how her writing was faring.

But all those conversational possibilities lacked urgency and immediacy.

What felt urgent and immediate were the words that had formed in his mouth and were now spilling out... "Lady Saskia, would you do me the honor of this waltz?"

The fact was, though Lady Viveca's words had been saucy and inappropriate, they'd held the urgent and immediate ring of truth.

An urgent and immediate truth that yet resonated through him.

He wanted Lady Saskia's hands upon him.

He wanted his hands upon her.

And a waltz was a perfectly socially acceptable means of achieving both ends.

She didn't promptly place her hand in his or say the expected, *"I would be delighted."* Instead, silvery-blue eyes gazed up at him from behind brass spectacles, her head slightly tilted.

The ground beneath his feet went shaky. In these five years of having attended many a ball, he'd never once been refused a dance. Hadn't even considered the possibility. Ladies were only too thrilled to dance with the dashing Liam Cassidy, if for no other reason than to share a giggly gossip with their friends and sisters later.

But Lady Saskia wasn't like any other lady.

She was her own person with her own ideas about life.

She would make up her own mind, and the possibility existed that she might say *no*.

Surely, she *should* say *no*, for the feeling rioting through him—the want...the *need*...to touch her—shared a kinship with madness.

Then she placed her silk-gloved hand in his and stepped forward. It wasn't only relief that pulsed through him as he led her onto the dancing floor and set his other hand properly above her waist, but another feeling, too—a greater, fiercer feeling—that twined alongside it...

Determination.

He wasn't sure where this determination would lead, but he understood fundamentally the dance wasn't the goal.

The dance was only the beginning.

He swept her into the *one-two-three* of the waltz and whirled her across gleaming mahogany, air beneath their feet for all he knew, with such ease did they mirror each other's steps in the ebb and flow of the dance. He should've predicted this—that, of course, Lady Saskia would be a natural dancing partner.

They'd made it halfway across the ballroom when he realized he must say something. He cleared his throat. "Are you enjoying the night?"

"I am."

"You're an exceedingly graceful dancer."

Exceedingly graceful?

"I've had a few lessons."

"Ah."

It was a perfectly suitable conversation. A conversation he'd had a hundred times on a hundred dancing floors.

And that was the problem.

Frustration roared through him.

This perfectly suitable conversation wasn't the conversation he wanted to have.

Yes, it was the correct conversation for the social setting, but it wasn't the correct conversation for…*them.*

He and this woman had shared secrets.

They'd shared a room.

They'd shared a kiss.

And here he was, saying, "Lucky for the duke and duchess the morning's stormy weather cleared up by the afternoon."

A single eyebrow subtly lifted, as if she knew this for socially acceptable conversation, but couldn't understand why in the blazes he was subjecting her to it.

Well, she wasn't the only one.

What happened to that feeling of urgency…of immediacy?

It yet rioted through him…scorched through his veins…and he was discussing the weather?

And it further occurred to him that the lift of Lady Saskia's right eyebrow might not only signal confusion.

It might signal disappointment.

She would harbor her own expectations of what it would be like to be in his arms—and he was disappointing her.

Sometimes the universe delivered exactly what one needed at the precise moment one needed it, and at this precise moment the universe delivered an open door. A literal open door to allow cooling night air into the ballroom. And when the universe provided an open door, one would be remiss not to waltz straight through it.

Which, Saskia in his arms, Liam did.

Though the air was cooler out on the terrace, Liam burned with intention as he led them beyond the ballroom's arc of golden light, until their feet found grass and the only illumination came from the mellow moon high in the night sky. A light breeze carried the music, but out here in the furthest reaches of the duke's garden, it was the music of night that forwarded itself— the chirruping of crickets…spring-green leaves soughing through the canopy above…the rasp of breath in his lungs…and hers.

Beneath the wide canopy of an English oak, her hand still in his, she pulled them to a stop. He turned and met her searching gaze. "Why are we outside?"

A fair question.

"I've been giving some thought to secrets and rules." They weren't the words he'd expected to say, but they were better words than he'd spoken in the ballroom.

"Have you now?"

"We have a few of each between us now, don't we?"

"We do."

They spoke with voices lowered. These words wouldn't catch on the air and carry beyond them.

"One rule, in particular, has been turning over in my mind."

"Oh?" she asked, a breathless exhalation, really.

"The no-kissing rule."

Her head tipped to the side. "I would think it a rather straightforward rule."

"One could easily be fooled into thinking so," he allowed. "But…"

"*But?*"

He released her hand and lightly grazed his knuckles across her cheek. "What are our parameters for a kiss?"

"Parameters?"

He nodded. This was serious business, in its way—and also fun. "The parameters remain ill-defined. You work with words all day, Saskia, surely you can see the lack of definition."

"I'm…" Her brow crinkled. "I'm not sure I can."

"Shall I illustrate my point?"

The air went still. Her eyes searched his. He was asking for permission beyond the simple surface of his words. He was also asking for something more—*trust*. And though urgency and immediacy fired through his veins, he could act on nothing without her permission or her trust.

The tip of her tongue swiped across her bottom lip. "In the interest of clarity between us, I believe you must." Her voice wavered with a most gratifying tremble.

The hand not caressing her cheek slid along the indent of her waist, and he angled so his mouth nearly met her ear. "For example, does it count as a kiss if I press my mouth *here*." A subtle shift forward and his lips were touching her earlobe, the skin soft and downy, and she was exhaling a light sigh. "Or," he uttered, his breath grazing across delicate skin, producing a spray of goosebumps up her arm, surely tightening her nipples into peaks, "*here*." His mouth trailed down her neck, and this time it was a trembly groan that accompanied her sigh. But she wasn't the only one affected. The blood rushed hot through his veins. His cock gone hard as iron, demanding he push farther… "Or…"

His mouth drifted lower…his hand tugged her bodice…and there was a plump breast revealed through her gossamer chemise…and a peaked pink nipple straining against muslin… leaving his mouth no choice but to test this parameter, too. He sucked the taut bud into his mouth, one hand cupping her breast, the other clutching her waist, steadying her as she gasped and emitted a tiny, feminine, "*Oh.*"

He should stop.

He *needed* to stop.

Or he would go lower… He would press his lips to every inch of her until he had her cunny in his mouth and she was screaming her pleasure toward the stars above.

But she hadn't given him permission for that.

She hadn't given him permission to transform her from innocent to experienced.

With the suddenness one ripped a bandage off a wound, he removed his mouth from her breast and took a large step back, separating from her completely. Panting, they stared at each other with new eyes. He reached out and touched her one final time—to adjust her bodice to its rightful position…above her pretty plump breasts.

"Is that the matter clear between us?" he had the presence of mind to ask.

Though a breathless laugh escaped her, her silvery-blue eyes remained serious. "I'm not sure. I reserve the right to seek further clarification in the future."

A laugh of his own startled from him.

No small measure of relief in that laugh.

Lest he forget, this woman was Lady Viveca's sister. They might just be cut from the same daring cloth.

He had but one more question to ask… "Will you be attending the Derby?"

Perhaps.

That had been her answer when he'd last asked the question.

And he hadn't liked that answer.

"Yes."

"Then until next week."

No small amount of triumph pulsing through him, he offered a slight bow, pivoted on his heel, and made his way from the duke's garden through a side gate.

He hadn't come to the duke's ball merely to see Saskia, or talk to her, or dance with her, or even to touch her.

He'd come here with a single intention.

An intention to turn her *perhaps* into a *yes*.

And he had.

But that wasn't all, was it?

He'd wanted to hold a match to her…to see if she would ignite into flame.

And, oh, how she had.

CHAPTER THIRTEEN

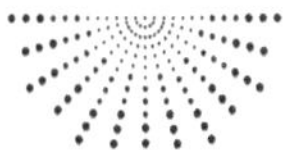

EPSOM DOWNS, A WEEK LATER

As a member of the *haut ton* these last five years, Saskia had attended many a horse race.

This horse race, however, was the first one she'd ever given a toss about.

It was Derby Day, the biggest racing day in the sporting calendar, given its proximity to London and the public's ability to watch the race for free from the hill. Saskia couldn't help feeling infected by its energy, even from her elevated place in Prinny's Stand, which was occasionally made available to those high-ranking aristocrats who had achieved favor with the King. It just so happened the King had taken Gabriel's advice regarding a few investments and earned a pretty penny. As an expression of his gratitude, the King had granted Gabriel access to the stand for the Derby, along with any family and friends he chose to invite.

Which was how Saskia found herself celebrating Derby Day from the most exclusive viewing point at Epsom Downs, alongside Gabriel and Celia, of course, but also Viveca, Blaze, and Mr. and Mrs. Lancaster. One of the most popular ladies of the *ton*, Mrs. Lancaster was Celia's cousin and best bosom friend, and known to her closest intimates as Eloise. She'd been instrumental to introducing Saskia and Viveca into society five years ago, and they held a deep affection for her. Everyone who met Eloise felt that way, in fact. Her smile was that warm and gracious and genuine.

Eloise slid into the chair beside Saskia, who was using her field-glass to scan the grounds. Only a few Thoroughbreds had made their way onto the turf, and none carried a jockey wearing the spring-green and midnight-blue silks she sought.

As Eloise took in the grounds alongside Saskia, she said, "It's so wonderful to see you outside of Sirens."

A slight frown turned down the corners of Saskia's mouth. It couldn't help itself. "Don't you like our library?"

Eloise gave her hand an affectionate squeeze. "I adore Sirens. But it requires so much of you, doesn't it?"

Saskia lowered her field-glass, unsure how best to express her feelings on this subject… "Sirens is the most worthwhile part in my life that requires anything of me."

In other words, she left unspoken, being a lady wasn't an occupation. It was merely a title, and while a title had its uses, it wasn't *enough*.

Eloise's eyes shone with understanding for all Saskia left unsaid. "You're young, my dear, and we're deep into the season. Attend a few balls and musicales. Let yourself be young and beautiful and gay. Let yourself be the belle of the ball."

Saskia playfully shoved her spectacles up the bridge of her nose. "Does the belle of the ball wear specs?"

Eloise nodded. "In your case, yes."

Saskia shook her head, even as she smiled. Oh, the loyalty of a friend. "I see you're very close to becoming quite occupied yourself."

Eloise's smile somehow grew warmer as her free hand rubbed her much-swollen belly. "The physician estimates this little one will arrive next month."

Before Tessa started producing babies a few years ago, Saskia hadn't considered herself a baby person. But the birth of her first niece, Clara, changed that. The fact was Saskia adored babies—their chubby legs…their slobbery kisses…their bright, curious eyes—and the prospect of another baby entering her orbit filled her with both anticipation and joy. "Do you have a preference whether the babe is a *he* or a *she*?"

"My only preference is good health."

Such a typically Eloise answer. *He* or *she* would be fortunate to have her as a mother.

"But, Saskia"—Eloise had more to say—"Sirens has been operating for four years. It's become one of the most popular circulating libraries in London. You're publishing the novels of that writer Harriet LaPlume, which must be bringing in a mint. Hasn't the time arrived that you can allow Mrs. Dunlevy more responsibility in the daily running of it? And you can get on with being a lovely young lady?"

"A lovely, young, *marriageable* lady?"

"Well, *yes*."

On the other side of Eloise, Viveca lowered into a chair and angled forward, joining the conversation. "Saskia isn't only spending all her time running Sirens. She's writing, too."

Saskia only just didn't gasp. But her stomach did plummet to her feet. She suspected her brow of darkening into a thundercloud. "Viveca—"

Eloise's luminous brown eyes went wide. "Is that so?"

Viveca continued in her breezy-as-she-pleased manner. "Oh, yes, she's writing Liam Cassidy's memoir."

Saskia could somewhat breathe again. While Viveca hadn't exposed her as Harriet LaPlume, she had introduced Liam Cassidy into the conversation. She supposed her involvement in his memoir wasn't precisely a secret, and Eloise was all but family, but still…

Viveca continued. "Sirens will be publishing his memoir next year."

Eloise glanced back and forth between Saskia and Viveca, her smile broadening with delight. "Truly?"

"Aye," said Saskia, her tone flat.

The frothy giggle of a debutante trilled from Eloise. "I must confess to finding him terribly dashing." Another giggle. "We can keep that between us ladies, of course. And, Saskia, have you met the famous Mr. Cassidy?"

"I have."

"And what have you learned?"

She should've been prepared for this moment with a list of appropriate details that she could rattle off at a moment's notice.

Instead, it was the *in*appropriate details that pushed to the forefront of her mind.

He snored.

When he was engaged in a conversation, his pupils flared so the hazel-green of his eyes disappeared and all that was left was a golden ring.

It happened in the instant before he delivered a kiss, too.

His mouth… It was divine, whether pressed against her lips or her earlobe or her neck or her breast…

Even today, a week later, her body was still alight from his exploration of the boundaries of a kiss upon her.

But that last part was more about her than him, wasn't it?

And, anyway, none of it was anything she could say.

Blaze strode up and tipped his sky-blue silk hat, as he lowered into a chair. The man grew more sartorially ostentatious by the year—and Viveca loved it. He angled forward, his head cocked. He was listening. Saskia's audience had grown. She'd never been one for audiences attending her every word. That was more Viveca's territory.

She cleared her throat. "Well, Liam Cassidy is the greatest jockey of his generation."

They all waited.

Specifically for her to tell them something they didn't already know.

"He has a few superstitions."

Viveca's eyes lit up. "I knew it."

"He doesn't eat or drink on race morning." She didn't feel she was betraying his confidence with these revelations. After all, they would be going into the memoir. "He doesn't speak to anyone, if he can help it. He brushes his mount and checks the straps himself."

"I have another morsel for that memoir of yours," offered Blaze.

"Oh?" asked Saskia.

"You'll never catch him at the betting post or any other den of iniquity you can think of."

"You're saying he's not a gambler, then?"

"A stand-up fellow to my way of thinking," said Blaze. "I can spot a rotter from a mile off."

While Saskia had no doubts about the latter, she would form her own opinions regarding the former. Blaze tended to adhere to his own system of values when it came to "stand-up" folk.

Before she could relate more on the subject of Liam Cassidy, the rest of their party arrived and everyone shuffled around so Celia could sit closest to the corner, as she was the most avid horseperson amongst them and had a contender in the race, Lady Midnight. Gabriel lowered into the seat beside his wife, and Viveca and Blaze moved down one seat each so Mr. Lancaster could sit beside Eloise.

"Oh, look," said Viveca, pointing, "they've assembled at the starting line."

Saskia's head whipped around, field-glass already affixed to her face. At the far end of the U-shaped track scrambled a great scrum of Thoroughbreds, their riders brightly fitted out in the owners' silks, every color in the rainbow accounted for in a wide assortment of patterns ranging from solids to stripes to polka dots to cross-hatch. But it was spring-green and midnight-blue stripes she searched for...

There, close to the railing, muscling into what was clearly his preferred starting place. Gone was Liam's usual smile. Even from here, she could see how serious he was in this environment—*focused...determined...all business*—the entirety of his attention on his horse and their mutual goal of winning this race. How attractive it was—*his seriousness...his capability...his confidence.*

A hush swept across the crowd, the collective breath bated with anticipation. Every muscle in Saskia's body knotted with tension, she waited...

The starter's gunshot cracked through the air and the pack lurched forward, urged on by the jockeys and their own competitive drive. The crowd's collective hush roared into a collective frenzy. As the horses thundered up the ascent to the top of the rise, Morningstar was in the lead pack, but not running first. Saskia intuited this would've been by design, for Liam had a race plan and he would surely execute it.

She felt as if she were split into two people: the self who watched with near primal excitement, that urged Liam and Morningstar faster...*faster*...to *win*. Then there was her other self. The one whose fingernails were digging half-moons into her palms with anxiety and no small amount of fear. The thing was while she'd attended several horse races, she'd never known a jockey personally. She'd never conversed with one or shared a room with one. She'd never kissed one. She'd never explored *personal boundaries* with one.

She wanted Liam to win, yes, but, more, she wanted him to be safe. She wanted to share more conversations with him. More kisses, too, if she were being honest.

Funny how such moments provoked honesty with oneself.

Lady Midnight, meanwhile, hung at the back of the lead pack. Saskia didn't know much about horse racing, but even she could see that Lady Midnight wasn't a great starter. But what she lacked at the start, she was making up for in the middle as they blazed toward Tattenham Corner. She had heart, Celia's horse. It was difficult not to cheer for her, but Saskia found she wasn't. It was another horse, in her heart of hearts, that she wanted to win.

One of the best things about watching a race from Prinny's Stand was that it enjoyed a close, unimpeded view of the infamous Tattenham Corner with its sharp left turn that formed the bottom of the racecourse's U. This turn had felled many a horse and rider over the years. In fact, Saskia couldn't remember having attended a single Derby where several horses didn't get tangled up and tumble to the turf, all the day's hopes and dreams gone to dust in an instant—and this Derby was no different.

Yet, somehow, Morningstar and Lady Midnight came through the chaotic fray with their legs still thundering beneath them for the final half mile. Here, in the downhill, was where the horses who had stamina picked up speed and showed what they were made of. And it was Morningstar in the lead, but only by half a length as Lady Midnight stayed right with him. These two horses had met their match in each other.

Saskia wasn't sure when it had happened, but she'd come to her feet. Everyone else had, too, as the horses entered the final hundred-yard uphill stretch to the finish, neck and neck now as Lady Midnight closed on Morningstar's half-length lead.

Two blinks of the eye later, the horses were across the finish line. From several hundred yards away, however, it was impossible to tell who finished victorious. The roar of the crowd diminished in volume as all awaited the announcement of the winner. Saskia's hands clenched into tight, nervous fists, her heart battering away at her ribs, as she waited for the longest three seconds of her life.

At last, a strident voice cut through the din. "It's Morningstar by a nose!"

Instantaneously, the crowd burst to life. Bright, startling jubilation took wing inside Saskia, which she instantly tamped down.

As she offered Celia a consolatory hug, she felt like a little traitor. Lady Midnight was Celia's horse, and second by a nose was a tough loss.

Eloise took her cousin's hand. "But, Celia, my dear, the universe has to balance itself out."

Her cheeks flushed and her eyes overbright, Celia's blood was clearly up as she asked hotly, "What on earth do you mean, cousin?"

Eloise remained her ever unbothered self. "Simply, you cannot win at everything. It wouldn't be fair to us mere mortals. You're a beauty of great renown. You're married to possibly the most handsome duke in all of Christendom, who also happens to be one of the wealthiest."

"I hardly see how those factors play into a horse race." Celia was resisting Eloise's soothing.

"You have two beautiful, healthy children," Eloise went on, unperturbed. "Your stud has gained a reputation as one of the best in England."

"All right, cousin," said Celia, finally giving over with an exasperated laugh. "You've made your point."

Viveca, who had been following the exchange, chimed in. "Actually, it makes the case for the existence of the Greek gods, as their system of governance very much played by those rules. Everyone must be properly humbled every so often."

"Or *quite* often," agreed Saskia, unable to resist. She and Viveca could make a wholly unassailable argument when they put their minds together. Besides, she thought Viveca was onto something with this line of reasoning. "The Greek gods tended to be rather enthusiastic with their humblings."

Eloise clapped her hands together with a delighted laugh; Gabriel rolled his eyes; and Blaze bussed an approving kiss onto his wife's cheek.

Viveca reached out and grabbed Saskia's hand. "Come, sister, let's congratulate our future bestselling author."

Before Saskia could open her mouth to protest, she was swept into the flow of the hordes of spectators all streaming in the same direction—toward the racecourse. And though it was a raucous, jubilant crowd they navigated, the saving grace was that their group consisted of a duke, a duchess, their family, England's preeminent barrister, his popular wife, and the one-and-only Blaze Jagger, so the crowd parted for them like the Red Sea.

Then Saskia, along with thousands of her fellow Londoners, was on the trodden turf of the track, once pristine grass churned into brown clumps from thundering horse hooves. Each of her senses felt incredibly alive—the earthy, juniper-and-thyme scented turf…the enlivening roar of the crowd…the light breeze lifting the hairs at the back of her neck—as if she were both at one with all around her *and* so deeply inside herself that she could feel the individual cells of her being.

Ahead, a horse moved left and another right, then a clump of spectators suddenly dispersed and the way cleared. At the end of that clear way stood Liam—sweaty, dirty, raw energy cascading off him in waves. The whip lash to his cheekbone was mostly healed, but a faded red mark remained. If anything, it made him look even more dashing as he offered a smile to all and accepted congratulations from every direction. She suspected half the bruises on his body tonight would be from all the congratulatory slaps on the back.

His gaze shifted and the roar of the crowd and the sweet scent of churned earth and the touch of the breeze faded into insignificance as he locked eyes with her. She would've sworn the world had gone still—her and him included—but then she was standing before him. She'd been moving all along, toward him.

Of course, *toward him.*

That was the *only* direction she moved these days.

His smile went lopsided, as if concentrated fully upon her. "Lady Saskia."

When she opened her mouth to respond, she could only hope and pray her voice didn't fail her. "Mr. Cassidy."

She was rather proud of herself. How proper and correct she sounded. Anyone from the outside would see two people very correctly, very properly maintaining professional boundaries.

Those people wouldn't know they'd kissed.

That he'd placed his mouth on places that were neither proper nor correct.

Those places that yet craved him.

His mouth.

She was staring at it.

A throat cleared beside her. Saskia snapped to and found expectant eyes upon her, waiting. "I, *erm*, I suppose everyone knows Mr. Cassidy."

It was Mr. Lancaster who galloped into the breach, hand extended. "Michael Lancaster," he said. "Pleased to make your acquaintance, Mr. Cassidy. The performance you put on for us was nothing short of a marvel."

"Ah, well," said Liam, "all credit to Morningstar."

Some people put on a show when it came to expressions of humility. Not Liam. Saskia happened to be in the position of knowing that for a fact.

"Looking to take the Triple Crown?" asked Blaze. "Have I got that right?"

"I think Lady Midnight will have something to say about that." Liam offered a bow toward Celia.

Celia lifted her brow. "Indeed, she will."

Liam nodded, slowly, though there was no mistaking the spark of competitive fire in his eyes.

"Now," said Blaze, "the first dram of whiskey at the Royal Reform Club is my treat. Join us, Cassidy."

And that was everyone moving to partake in the madness of Derby Day, for though the race was run, this day wasn't done. In fact, the day wouldn't be ending until dawn tomorrow morning.

That was everyone moving along—except Saskia.

"Sister?" Viveca had been watching Saskia a mite too closely these last few minutes for her comfort.

A hasty search of her mind just so happened upon the perfect excuse. A rarity these days. "I need to return to the inn and record the race while it's still fresh in my mind."

Viveca gave her a long, penetrating look. "If you're sure?"

"I am." And she even managed a smile.

Viveca gave her hand a quick squeeze before moving on to join her husband and the rest of their party, who had already disappeared into the crowd. Her head and her heart irritatingly conflicted, Saskia turned her feet in what she guessed was the direction of the King's Head.

Then she felt it—a hand close around her upper arm. She attempted to shake it off—she supposed she *was* an unchaperoned and unprotected lady—as a familiar voice said, "*Saskia.*"

She stopped in her tracks, even as her head whipped around —*Liam.*

"You're not joining us?" He was all but shouting.

"I have some writing to do," she shouted back.

His eyes searched hers. "Then you're back to London?"

"I'm staying the night at the King's Head."

Of course, she'd owed him an answer, but she hadn't owed him *that* answer. A straightforward, *"I'll be returning to London tomorrow,"* would've sufficed. Instead, she'd told him not only that she was staying, but *where* she was staying.

Should she offer him her room number, too?

He looked disinclined to relent. "You could join us later."

She shook her head. "It'll be an early night for me."

He nodded, slowly, as if only accepting her answer with great reluctance. "Shall I escort you to—"

"I can manage on my own," she cut in. "A good day to you."

And she, again, pointed her feet in the direction of the King's Head, this time determined to stop for nothing and no one.

Not even for Liam Cassidy.

Especially not for Liam Cassidy.

The thing was she didn't need to record her impressions of the race straightaway or retire early tonight.

Those had been lies—necessary lies.

The truth was simple.

She couldn't trust herself around him.

He appealed too greatly to an untamed part of her.

The part of her who was Arabella, the reckless wanton at the mercy of her desires.

Nay, not desires in the plural sense.

Desire—singular…*him*.

Liam called to some place inside her that had no choice but to respond.

No, she couldn't trust herself.

His look of disappointment when she'd declined his invitation to celebrate with him had nearly undone her intention.

She didn't like the idea of disappointing him.

In fact, she might want to please him…too much.

And then what?

It wouldn't only be her intention undone, but herself, entirely.

CHAPTER FOURTEEN

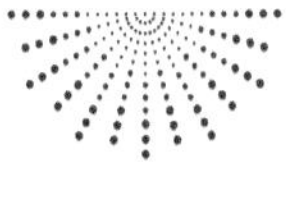

LATER

Liam crossed the threshold of the King's Head and tugged the wide-brimmed laborer's hat he'd acquired sometime during endless rounds of carousing low on his forehead. Nothing compared to the singular earthy fug of a taproom at midnight—of spilled, hoppy ales…of sharp, sickly sweet whiskey…of bodies that hadn't bathed in days.

Somewhere around the ten-thousandth congratulatory slap on the back, he decided it was to be a rare early night for him.

Still, he understood what all the excitement was about, for it had been the most tightly contested Derby in a generation. The ruling on the turf had been no exaggeration. Morningstar had literally won by the tip of his nose.

What Liam knew and what no one else did, however, was that Morningstar should have taken second. But out there in the heat of the race, Liam had ridden like he'd never ridden in his life. He'd ridden like a man possessed—and he knew why. Instead of focusing on his connection to Morningstar like he usually did on race day, he'd been connected to a single thought—Saskia was in the crowd, watching him, and he would make sure he gave her something worthwhile to see.

Morningstar hadn't been the superior horse on the turf today, but Liam had been the most determined jockey.

Under no circumstances would he have lost the Derby with Saskia watching.

He stepped past the inn's front desk where a gent stood complaining to the proprietor about the drunkard presently sprawled across his doorway and snoring loud enough to lift the roof off the inn. "You must do something about the lout."

"It's Derby Day." The proprietor's tone rang heavy with world-weariness, resigned to the inevitabilities. "You came here expectin' a nunnery?"

That provoked several guffaws from those gathered round and taking bets on who would prevail.

Into the taproom Liam strode, his face pointed to the floor as the merrymaking ratcheted into full swing all around him, his feet making a straight line for the staircase that led to the first floor. By all rights, he should still be deep into a carouse, but his heart wasn't in it. He'd wanted to celebrate with one person—and she'd taken herself off to read and write.

He snorted.

Only Saskia would attend the Derby, then excuse herself not only to read a book afterward, but write one, too.

What a beauty she'd been today, with her pinked cheeks and her eyes bright silvery-blue with exhilaration behind her spectacles.

His heart had leapt at the sight of her—*leapt*.

He was mad for her.

That was all there was to it.

By exploring the boundaries of a kiss upon her, he'd thought to bind her to him in some way. But he rather thought his gambit might've accomplished the opposite effect, and it was *he* who had bound himself to *her*.

There was no hope in it, though, was there?

He might've been famous and at the top of his sport and, plainly, bloody wealthy as a result, but he was a bastard. He needed to stop playing these games with her before they went too far. The woman was the sister of a duke.

A hopeless madness was what he'd gotten himself into.

A first, actually.

His madnesses, in the general sense, had always been the opposite of hopeless—consummated to everyone's satisfaction, to be specific.

As his foot touched the bottom staircase step, a voice, feminine and reedy, cut through the taproom's receding roar of merrymaking. "Liam."

He froze in place. A shiver slowly prickled up his spine.

He knew that voice.

He twisted around to find a petite woman of no particular beauty, hair pulled tightly into a middle-parted chignon and a severity of expression to match, staring up at him with no liking in her small dark eyes.

"Countess." Out of long-established habit, he offered her a bow.

The Countess of Bolton.

Here, at the King's Head...on Derby Day.

And the reason for her presence struck him. "Bolton is dead."

He didn't ask.

He knew.

And all he felt was...*nothing.*

She swallowed and gave a curt nod. "Find us a table, Liam."

If he'd been leaning toward offering his condolences, the inclination evaporated. Here was the Countess of Bolton he knew—*steely, imperious, demanding.*

Though he was no longer under her command, he found them a table in a tucked-away corner and settled into the chair opposite hers. "You didn't have to come all this way to deliver that news." He didn't owe this woman anything but the most minimal civility—and he'd already given her that. "So, if that will be all…"

He made it halfway to his feet before she hissed, "Sit down, Liam."

His head cocked. A note sounded in her voice that he'd never heard before. The usual chill frosted each syllable she spoke, yes, but something else, too…*a tremble*. And within her eyes sparked recognizable emotion—*fear*.

He lowered into the chair, crossed his arms over his chest, and waited.

Her eyes searched his. "Did you know?"

"That Bolton was dying?" Liam nodded. "Aye, he tracked me down last year to deliver the news."

Barely suppressed emotion glinted in the countess's dark eyes. Emotion that bore a close resemblance to barely suppressed fury. This woman was fearful and furious, and he couldn't understand why. As a recently bereaved widow, shouldn't she have been sad and weepy?

"And that was all he told you?" she pressed—*demanded*.

A feeling traced through Liam. Bolton had told him he was proud of him, too. A memory that continued to produce a spray of conflicted emotions inside him.

Without waiting for a reply, she said, "You don't know." A laugh, bitter and lacking any humor, snuck past ungenerous lips. "Of course, you don't. You would've wasted no time evicting me from my own house."

Had she come unhinged with grief? He'd heard of such happenings. "I'll procure a room for you for the night, and we can continue this conversation on the morrow."

Or never.

With another bitter emission—a deep sigh, this time—she slumped back into her chair and halved in size, like a balloon suddenly deflated, as if her fury had been the only thing keeping her going. "They were married."

Liam's brow crinkled. "Who were married?"

The countess released another sigh. She shook her head. She sighed again. "Bolton and Maeve." Another shake of the head. "Your parents."

Liam stared at her for a solid three seconds. "Impossible."

The woman had sailed around the bend.

"Oh, too possible, it seems." The countess's eyes narrowed into thin black slits. "And you didn't know?"

"Know *what*?" he all but exclaimed. "Whatever Bolton told you, it was a manipulation and a lie intended to deliver nothing but hurt."

Though a truth they both knew, the truth didn't feel as cathartic to speak as he would've reckoned.

Unmoved, the countess dug inside her reticule, her hand eventually emerging with a sheet of parchment, which she slapped onto the stretch of table between them. "Three days ago, *this* was found in his safe." Another bitter snort. "A safe I knew nothing about." Her eyes glittered with that suppressed fury. "But his solicitor did."

Liam made no move to take the paper. "What is it?"

"A certificate of marriage." She tapped the parchment. "Thirty years ago, Bolton took Maeve Cassidy's hand in marriage." Her hand retreated as if stung. "It's all there."

Liam remained utterly, utterly still. He hardly dared even breathe. His heart, however, had other ideas—it pounded like a hammer. "Impossible."

"Oh, possibilities abound in that backwater they call Ireland." She shook her head as if acceptance had yet to find purchase in her mind. "Like the ability to marry by couple beggar."

"*Couple beggar?*" The countess kept speaking words that refused to make sense.

"A defrocked minister who performs church rites for a fee and asks few questions." The blaze of fury within her dark eyes tempered not a whit. "But he records those rites in his register and even leaves a little piece of paper for the blissful couple certifying the marriage."

Belief refused to take hold inside Liam. "But he was married to *you*."

"They knew each other as youths, apparently, when Bolton visited his mother's family. And one of those summers, they married. He must've immediately thought better of it, but then he couldn't dissolve the marriage without appearing the fool, so he locked the marriage certificate away in a safe—and took his chances."

And took his chances... "You mean"—though unwilling, Liam's mind was piecing the puzzle together—"he married you."

"And he married *me*, a proper Englishwoman." Bewilderment traced alongside her fury. "A proper Englishwoman who couldn't give him a child. So—" She lifted empty hands. "He remembered he had another wife and tried his luck with her. And, lo, how Maeve delivered. Not one, but two babes at once. But Bolton only needed the one, didn't he? *You*, the boy. The *heir*."

Another puzzle piece fell into place... "That's why he had us living under his roof."

"There's something you need to know, Liam. Something about your mam and me—"

No.

He shoved the parchment toward the countess. "Burn it. I don't want it."

Her eyes... They almost held pity for him—*almost*. "It doesn't matter if you burn it or destroy it in any other manner you please, Bolton's solicitor witnessed the document and has already set matters in motion. You'll be presented to the King as the Fourth Earl of Bolton." She scoffed, as if unable to believe it herself. "You've been the heir all this time, Liam. You're Bolton now."

Even as his mind refused to accept anything the countess was telling him, his bones knew otherwise. This was the truth. For if this woman could've got around this truth, she would have. *She* herself would've burned the document if it would've made a lick of difference.

Right.

Animal instinct had Liam shooting to his feet. He wasn't sure where he was going, but he had to get away—to think or to drown, he wasn't sure. "I take it you can find your way back to…" *To hell* would've been impolite to say. He settled for, "To your quarters."

Malice glinted in her dark eyes. "Your lordship."

As Liam staggered through the taproom, the roar in his ears had naught to do with the raucous gaiety surrounding him, every other man offering him a clap of congratulations. He couldn't account for what they said to him or what he replied in response. He needed to move and keep moving. The feeling streaking through him felt exactly like sheer, sweat-inducing panic.

Blessedly, his feet led him to the bar, where he promptly lifted his hand and shouted over the din. "A bottle of your finest."

The barman gave a brisk nod and returned with a bottle of some brown substance or another. It really didn't matter. He needed to drink about half of its contents in the next five minutes. He slapped a guinea onto the bartop's spirits-sticky surface. He was free to leave—except he wasn't.

A question wanted to be asked.

A question he shouldn't ask.

So, he went around the question and shouted, "A lady is—"

Expecting me.

He couldn't speak those words. Not about Saskia in a public place. If the wrong curious ears picked them up, he would expose her to scandal.

As he combed his mind for a proper way to proceed, he went to run his hand through his hair, but couldn't, for perched atop his head was a… "*Hat.* I need to return her hat to her."

The barman cast a skeptical eye over the straw laborer's hat that had two holes that Liam knew of. "That a new style of ladies' hat, is it?"

If Liam's next words weren't going to be precisely wrong, they weren't going to be precisely right, either. He leaned halfway across the bartop and signaled the barman to move closer. Reluctantly, the man did. He'd seen it all before. "Her name is Lady Saskia Calthorp," he said, low, so his voice wouldn't carry.

The barman cocked an eyebrow. "Wears specs?"

Liam nodded. "Aye, that's the one. You know her room number?"

"Aye, I know it."

Without another word, Liam plunked another guinea onto the bartop.

The barman gave Liam a thorough up-and-down. "You're Liam Cassidy, aye?"

"Aye."

The man nodded. "No shortage of ladies leaving their hats with you every day of the week, I reckon."

Liam knew his role in this sort of conversation well enough to grin waggishly—which he did. "A man doesn't like to brag."

The barman snorted and palmed the coin. "Room Four is the one you'll be seeking."

Liam nodded and, not a minute later, found himself upstairs, dodging other guests in various states of celebration and inebriation and passing by his own door. He didn't stop until he reached the door with a large brass four affixed in the center.

It wasn't as simple as he didn't want to be alone.

He wanted to be around Saskia.

She had a way of making the world feel right and sane.

The hand not holding the bottle of whiskey lifted and hesitated.

He shouldn't knock.

He should leave her be.

Leave her to her reading and writing.

Leave her to her life.

Yet, knowing this, his fist tapped out three light knocks—consequences and hopeless madnesses be damned.

CHAPTER FIFTEEN

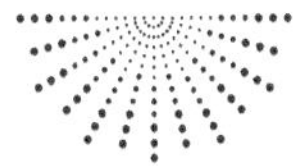

Tap-tap-tap.

Saskia kept her gaze firmly affixed to the book before her and kept reading.

Well, her eyes remained on the book, but she couldn't truthfully say she was comprehending a word of it.

That *tap-tap-tap*, in fact, marked the ninth time someone had come knocking on her door tonight.

She'd been counting.

She'd stopped answering the door after the third *tap-tap-tap*.

A long-suffering sigh issued from her parted lips, and she kept resolutely reading, settling her bottom deeper into worn sofa cushions long since gone flat and hard.

Tap-tap-tap.

She should've returned to London. Why had she stayed?

Oh, she knew why.

Because Liam Cassidy was here.

But to what end? To invite him to her room?

Well, she'd fumbled that opportunity.

Tap-tap-tap.

"Go away!" she shouted. She was finished with the niceties. They didn't work on the determined and inebriated.

"Saskia," came a muffled masculine voice that sounded as if it were pressed to the crack between door and frame.

Her head cocked. She might know that voice…

"*Saskia*," came the voice again, urgent and insistent.

She *did* know that voice.

Her legs paying no heed to the caution her mind advised, she was off the sofa and across the room in a trice, her ear pressed to the door as she cinched the sash of her nightrobe tighter.

"Saskia," the voice implored, "come on and open up."

Liam.

Still, she hesitated.

If she opened this door, the stroke of midnight gone well past, she wasn't sure she could account for what might proceed. The turn of the lock was yet in her control, but what followed, wasn't.

Yet, knowing all this, she opened the door.

Before her, arm propped high on the door frame, stood Liam, a charming smile tipping one side of his mouth. At some point, he'd changed out of his racing silks and was now wearing proper, fitted gentleman's attire and an incongruous laborer's wide-brimmed straw hat.

Derby Day.

That was how one accounted for such a contradiction.

He lifted his other hand, and she noted the bottle of whiskey. "Celebrate with me?"

His smile… It wasn't its usual charming self, but rather an echo of it. And within his eyes lurked something…*new*. A word came to her—one she'd never associated with this man.

Desperation.

That which lurked within his eyes was *desperation*.

She crossed her arms over her chest. "I was just reading before bed."

He looked unconvinced. "I suppose you can sleep through raging thunderstorms and howling blizzards, then?"

"And I suppose you'll state your business?"

He waggled the whiskey bottle, the playfulness at odds with the glint of desperation that yet lingered within his eyes. "Just one drink? Between friends?"

Knowing full well she shouldn't, she stood aside and allowed him into her room. He lifted the hat off his head and tossed it onto the table where the day's pages were strewn. She hadn't been untruthful on that account. She had come back to the room and written into the evening, only stopping when her stomach's growling had become unbearable.

But Liam paid her scribblings no mind as he made for the sofa beneath the room's wide window long gone dark with night. He lowered onto its hard, unforgiving cushions and settled back, one arm resting on the ridge of the sofa and an ankle crossed over a thigh. How elegant and masculine and utterly at ease he looked.

She needed to say something appropriate, she understood. "Congratulations on your win today."

There, that was most appropriate.

"Thrilling, wasn't it?" He didn't sound all that thrilled.

"Thrilling wins must be commonplace for you, I suppose."

He shrugged an indifferent shoulder. "That going into the memoir?"

"Would you like it to?"

He didn't answer her question. Instead, he asked one of his own. "Bring a couple of cups on your way over?"

He patted the sofa, indicating she join him.

She shouldn't.

Yet there were her feet moving of their own accord again, and she'd grabbed a pair of teacups and soon found herself lowering onto the opposite end of the sofa.

"Actually," he said, pouring whiskey into the teacups, "you and I aren't too dissimilar on that front."

"What front is that?"

He held out a teacup for her, which she accepted. "We both like to win. Only horses are my vehicle and words are yours."

"Writing isn't a competition."

He snorted. "Your books are selling like hot gingerbread during Christmastide." He wagged a finger at her. "I know competition when I see it."

She smiled, despite herself.

He lifted his teacup, and she followed suit. The sharp, sweet scent of whiskey hit her nose, and she winced. "To winning," he said and took a large gulp.

Though she held her breath to brace herself, the spirit went down her throat like fire. But unlike the first time she'd tried it as Arabella, this time it warmed, rather than burned.

Liam settled back into his corner of the sofa, as if he were observing her from a great distance—which she didn't much care for. "Have you a question to ask of me?"

"I do."

She found her muscles tensing, as if preparing themselves for impact at high speed.

"Would you mind very much telling me of your life before you became Lady Saskia Calthorp?"

Her eyebrows drew together. Unexpected, that question. "When I was merely Miss Saskia Siren?"

He nodded, as serious as he ever was on the track before a race. "Aye."

Of course, Saskia didn't owe this man any insights into her life. After all, she was writing *his* memoirs, not the other way around. But this wasn't about debt or even fair play. It was about the desperation she'd noted in his eyes. He needed to hear about her life, and she was powerless not to give him that which he needed. "My papa made a decent living as a barrister's clerk in Gray's Inn, and my mum kept a clean, efficient household. Both facts I learned from Tessa and Gabriel, of course, as I was three years old when they perished."

Liam's brow furrowed. "They died at the same time?"

"Papa was struck down in the street by a dray horse, and Mum died six months later from a fever."

"I'm…so sorry."

"I don't remember that first life," she continued. "I only remember the life that came after. Of Tessa taking care of Viveca and me while Gabriel was off at Eton on scholarship, then Cambridge."

"Tessa must've been a child herself."

Saskia nodded. "She was nine when our parents died. She managed through various means she's never fully confessed to Viveca or me, but our fortunes took a turn for the better when Gabriel realized he could use his brilliance with numbers to charge all those aristocratic lordlings at Eton a fee for doing their work for them."

A sudden grin lit up Liam's face. "Truly?"

"*Truly.*" She couldn't help smiling right along with him. "So, our fortunes rose, and we got on. Tessa and Gabriel protected Viveca and me from the brunt of it, and by our teen years, we had private tutors and unfettered access to a fine education." She exhaled a sigh that still held a note of disbelief to this day. "Then, five years ago, it happened."

Liam nodded, but held his tongue. He would know what was coming.

"Gabriel was informed that he was a duke."

"How did that come to be, anyway?"

"The short of it is that our grandfather didn't get on with his father and decided to make his own way in the world. The long of it is that his father was, in fact, a duke, and while our grandfather was a younger son, his brother died without legitimate issue, which made Gabriel the new duke."

"And you a lady."

She nodded. "And me a lady."

The fact still confounded her.

Liam's head subtly tipped to the side. "Don't you like being a lady?"

"In some ways, I can't say I especially do." For some reason, she was telling the truth—and couldn't seem to stop. Was whiskey a soother of truth? "But in other ways, I have to acknowledge that having our brother Gabriel as the Duke of Acaster and our sister Tessa as the Marchioness of Ormonde, not to mention Celia as our sister by law and Mrs. Eloise Lancaster as our close family friend, have all been instrumental in the success of Sirens. It's not only money that greases the wheels of success, but connections, too. It's the way of the world, isn't it?"

"Aye, it is." He looked as if he would say more, but wasn't sure if he should.

"What is it?"

"Yet you write under a pseudonym, Saskia. Wouldn't it follow that your books would be even more successful if the world knew Harriet LaPlume was Lady Saskia Calthorp?"

"Perhaps," she allowed. "But I can't write what I write as *Lady Saskia Calthorp*. There's a truer me below her, and it is she whom I must access so I may write."

"So, you have Harriet LaPlume for that self."

She felt suddenly awkward and conscious of herself. "It sounds odd, I know."

Within Liam's eyes, however, she detected not ridicule or even amusement at her self-seriousness. Instead, she found understanding—*connection*. Something in her words connected to a place inside him, and she couldn't help wondering why. Wasn't Liam Cassidy handsome and famous and the best in his sport? Wasn't that all there was to him?

No.

She knew that much.

A smile lit within his eyes and found its way to his mouth.

"And then there's Arabella. Where does she fit into all those layers that comprise you?"

Saskia moaned. "I wish you would forget Arabella."

He laughed. "Oh, I won't be forgetting Arabella."

Another groan escaped her, this one accompanied by a mortified laugh. "She will haunt me 'til the end of days, won't she?"

"I rather liked Arabella."

"You did?"

"Aye."

Again, she experienced it—that feeling of connection communicated by a seriousness in his eyes, even as he spoke light words.

"I suppose Arabella has a few worthy qualities." She could allow that much. "She's lively and bold."

He nodded.

For some reason, she continued. "Arabella knows what she wants—and pursues it."

Without taking his eyes from hers, he asked, "And what does Arabella want…*now?*"

The question, low and rumbly, slid through her like velvet, sparking tiny nerve endings alight—and there was but one answer that came to her.

You, she couldn't speak.

But the air between them vibrated with the unspoken, anyway.

CHAPTER SIXTEEN

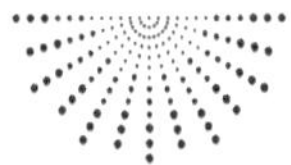

Saskia felt herself suspended inside a weightless void.

As if she'd leapt off the edge of a cliff and was waiting to discover if the rope would hold or if she would dash herself against the rocks below.

Behind Liam's eyes passed the dark and unknowable. "Tonight, we could just be those other selves. *You* could be Arabella, and *I* could be Liam Cassidy."

It took a second for her mind to catch up to his words. "But you *are* Liam Cassidy."

Gold-flecked green eyes remained utterly intent upon her. "And aren't you Arabella?"

They couldn't go on like this.

She couldn't go on like this.

Well, Lady Saskia couldn't go on like this.

Arabella could.

A change of subject was necessary.

She drew herself up, hoping proper posture would influence proper thoughts. "Your ride today was magnificent."

He shrugged a shoulder that could've been interpreted as

indifferent. "It was one of those races snatched from the teeth of Fate. They unfold like that sometimes."

"How do you mean?"

"Morningstar shouldn't have won."

"No?"

"But then, *you* were there."

Her brow furrowed. "What did my being there have to do with it?"

"Well, I wasn't about to lose."

She blinked. "Because *I* was there?"

Liam drummed long, calloused fingers on the spine of the sofa. "There's the fact that you're writing my memoirs."

A strange sense of relief pulsed through her. Here was a place of relative safety from which they could converse. "Oh, yes, of course."

"And there's also the fact that it was *you* who was there."

Her heart beat out a heavy thud. Here was the conversation tipping back into the unknown. "Aren't I simply *me*?"

When he smiled, the charm for the masses was gone. This smile, intimate and true, was solely for her. "Not so simply. You wear more than a few hats, don't you? There's the woman writing my memoir, and there's *you*. A Derby win will help sell some books, but that isn't why I snatched that win from the teeth of Fate."

He'd wanted to win because she'd been watching?

A man could quite take a woman's breath away, speaking to her like that.

She cleared her throat. "No whip lashings to the face today."

He settled back and took a gulp of whiskey, letting his unmarked face serve as answer.

"Are you as beat-up from the Derby as you were from the Two Thousand and One Thousand Guineas?"

"Every muscle in my body is sore." He gave an unbothered shrug. "Will that find its way into the memoir?"

She hadn't realized she was interviewing him, but understood how he would see it so. "Likely."

He shifted to set his whiskey on the side table. "Then you must see for yourself." He shrugged off his coat and lifted his shirt so it came untucked from his waistband, white linen rising above his ribs.

Saskia gasped and suffered an immediate wash of mortification. It was the sight of his ridged stomach, the center hollow fuzzed with golden hair that trailed down to the waistband of his trousers…and below…

He cleared his throat. Her gaze startled up. She'd been staring at his trousers a mite too long—and the amused glint in his eyes said he knew it.

Saskia, she chided herself, *gather your wits, woman.*

But he was pointing to a bruised rib grazed an angry red that was already deepening into purple.

"It's not cracked, is it?"

"Nay."

"How do you know?"

"I can breathe without pain."

An incredulous laugh escaped her. "That's how you gauge whether a rib is broken?"

"It's the easiest way."

She felt her equilibrium returning to her. "There's so much money and beauty in horse racing, but below that glossed surface, it's an utterly brutal sport, isn't it?"

"It can be," he acknowledged. "But everyone in the game knows the rules—or lack thereof."

"Not the horses."

A moment beat past while he considered her. "That's one thing I like about you, Saskia."

"Just the one?"

He snorted. "Of many."

Of many.

Oh, she liked that—too much.

But wasn't it a simple line? A response to her prompt?

Right.

"You always see straight to the main point," he continued. "The horses are the most important part of the entire enterprise, which makes them vulnerable to those with bad intent. That's why they must be treated with the utmost care and respect."

"It's why you don't use whip or spur."

"Aye."

How she liked this moment with Liam, the two of them conversing with openness and honesty. But it wasn't simple, was it? Beneath that uncomplicated surface ran attraction and closeness, not of obvious proximity, but of mind and spirit.

And this point was as far as she knew how to navigate.

Retreat felt impossible; to proceed forward equally impossible.

At least, for Saskia, it was impossible.

"Tonight, we could just be these other selves. You could be Arabella, and I could be Liam Cassidy."

Arabella would know how to navigate the impossible space between them—or if she didn't, she would improvise.

When he released his shirt, without a staying thought, she shoved forward, erasing most of the distance between them on the sofa as she reached out to stay the garment's descent. And that easily, she was touching him…feeling him… "Liam," she said, hardly able to recognize her own voice, "we haven't yet explored the extent of your possible injuries to my satisfaction."

His brow lifted subtly. "Is that so? Well…" He let the moment draw out, and she couldn't breathe as she waited for him to finish, for him to seal her fate. "We can't leave you unsatisfied, now can we?"

There was permission granted.

She shifted so she could pull his shirt over his head. So close that she was nearly on top of him as his scent enveloped her—

salt, citrus, him. She touched light fingertips to a bruise. "Does this hurt?"

"Can't say it does particularly."

"I…I've been thinking about our conversation from the ball."

"Have you?"

"You raised an interesting point."

"Pleased to serve."

"What are the parameters of a kiss? For example…" She eased forward. "Would it be kissing if I press my mouth *here*?" Without waiting for an answer, she angled down and touched her mouth lightly to his bruised rib, his skin smooth and warm beneath her lips.

"*Saskia.*"

Her name a jagged rasp against his throat sent a shiver straight through her. Driven by instinct, she shifted her weight so she moved atop him, her thighs now straddling his. She tilted her head, her hair falling in a curtain around them, her lips brushing his ear. "*Arabella.*"

He reached up and gently caught her chin in his large hand, guiding her incrementally back so their eyes could meet. A whirl of emotions stirred within those gold-flecked green depths—*intimacy...connection...desire...wanting...need.* She'd always been so deep in and of the mind. The characters who ran around her brain felt more than she ever had.

Until she'd met Liam Cassidy.

And, really, until this exact moment.

What she felt now—the intimacy, the connection, the desire, the wanting, the need—was the most real, visceral feeling she'd ever experienced.

It pulsed.

It throbbed.

It urged.

It ached.

She was connected to him in a way she didn't understand—and so, too, was she connected to herself in that very same way.

"Perhaps," he uttered, close to her lips, "we need to refresh our memory."

"Perhaps we do."

He reached up and slid her spectacles off her nose. She'd forgotten them. Then he shifted and, in the space between one heartbeat and the next, pressed his mouth to hers.

This was a kiss.

It was as she remembered and…better.

As his tongue glided across her bottom lip, tangled with hers, this kiss burned with urgency. He groaned into her mouth as he pushed her robe open, reaching around her waist, pulling her body into his. Below her, she felt it—his manhood. Instinctively, she lowered so all that separated her quim from his shaft was her night chemise and his trousers. Of their own accord, her hips moved, his length thick and hard against her soft center. His hands tightened around her waist, grounding her to him.

Oh, this was pleasure and a fire lit.

But a fire held demands.

A fire ever needed *more*.

That was her at this moment—a lit fire—and all she wanted was more of Liam.

Between them, she reached until she found his length.

But it wasn't enough.

She began fumbling with the falls of his trousers. His hand covered hers. "Saskia."

"Arabella," she corrected.

A beat of silence, then, "*Saskia.*"

She understood what he was saying—and what he wasn't. They were one and the same. If they were going to cease this madness, now was the time. For if they were to proceed down this path, at the end of it, she would no longer be a virgin. And if that was the path she chose, the only way she would be doing so was as Saskia.

The logic held.

Still… "I want this," she implored…she begged. "I want *you.*"

He moaned, pain in it. "You're supposed to be the voice of reason."

"*Me?*"

She supposed that was fair. But, tonight, she didn't want to be the voice of reason. She wanted to be *un*reasonable. Reason wouldn't help her get what she wanted—which was him.

And if the price of having him was the loss of her virginal status, what a small price to pay.

"Oh, my sweet," he groaned, "I'm hopelessly mad for you."

And he thought those were the words that would convince her to be reasonable?

She grabbed his face with both hands and kissed him long and slow and thorough, breathing him in, feeling his elements combining with hers. And when her fingers again found the buttons of his trousers, they didn't fumble. They understood the objective—to free him…to *feel* him. *Hard…long…thick.*

Oh, she wanted this with an altogether unreasonable singularity of intent. "I need you, Liam," she pleaded against his mouth, lifting onto her knees so her quim hovered above his exposed length. "I need you inside me."

Questioning eyes met hers. So, too, were those eyes full of open desire. He wanted this as badly as she. "Liam, I must have you," she insisted, her voice breaking on *you.* *Begging,* if she were honest.

"My sweet Saskia, what you must have, I must give."

He took himself in hand, and the crown of his shaft grazed her slick quim. Slowly, testingly, *instinctively,* breath held, she lowered, tightly taking him in, inch by inch. The discomfort was to be expected, considering the girth of him. The burning sensation, less expected, but logical.

The disappointing truth was soon unavoidable: the union of their bodies that she'd been so desperate to achieve didn't feel as exquisite as she wanted it to.

Not exquisite at all or, even, good.

"Saskia."

She only realized her eyes were squeezed shut when she heard his voice. And before she could intuit his intention, he'd lifted her off him, pulling a cry of protest from her. *"Shh, my sweet."*

My sweet.

It was the third time he'd said it.

Oh, that he would always call her *my sweet.*

Entirely unreasonable, of course.

"But I—"

"Trust me."

With a few quick movements, he had her in his arms and was carrying her to the bed. Once he'd lowered her onto the coverlet, he said, "There's yet one more place I haven't kissed you."

"Oh?"

He angled down and pressed his mouth to hers…to her throat…to her breasts…slowly, deliberately making his way down her body until he reached…

Oh.

He kissed her quim. But not in the relatively chaste way he'd kissed the rest of her body.

He kissed her quim the way he kissed her mouth—with his tongue.

In her entire life, she'd never experienced anything this sublime. Nothing compared to it, as his tongue slid across her slit before finding a most sensitive spot, firming and, *oh*, flicking. She gasped. She moaned. She spread her legs wider, curled her fingers through his hair, and moaned again, this time deeper, an accessing of some place inside her in tune with the animal. A long, masculine finger slid inside her, even as his tongue continued to work its magic upon her.

As her body took in this pleasure and reveled in it and never wanted it to end, it also began reaching and straining and struggling toward a point unknown. Unknown, that was, by her mind, but, somehow, every cell in her sex knew what it was after. Her fingers, now clenched into fists, pulled his hair, and she was possibly writhing beneath that sure tongue of his. How utterly unlike herself she was in this moment—how *transformed*—but she cared not for the wanton she'd become as her entire being collapsed inward to this place where he pleasured her, even as what she was straining toward teased and pulled and stayed just out of reach.

Then, what she could only have described as a flare bursting into conflagration at that place where his tongue met her quim, all that had gone inward released and flamed through her in that expected exquisite pleasure, her sex pulsing with climax, her cries filling the air.

Mere seconds or timeless eons passed, her entire being floating somewhere between earth and heaven, before she opened her eyes to find his upon her, a smile within. He gave her quim one parting, chaste kiss, then asked, "Now, that was better, wasn't it?"

He rose and, beneath her unblinking gaze, discarded his remaining clothing. Then, slowly and deliberately, he moved over her and kissed his way back up her body. Into the sliver of air between their lips just before he, at last, kissed her there, she said, "I need more of you."

"Haven't you had enough?"

She shook her head, adamant. "I'm greedy and unreasonable and possibly insatiable."

He chuckled against her mouth. "So, you're saying you're the woman of my dreams."

The woman of my dreams.

She would think about those words later. Turn them over and over in her mind, in fact. But for now, she said, "Yes."

She wasn't sure those words would hold up beneath the sharp reality of daylight tomorrow.

But tonight, for now, they could.

She hooked her arm around his neck, pulling him to her, luxuriating in the heavy, solid feel of him on top of her. He positioned his shaft at her sex, and she braced herself as he, again, penetrated her. But, *oh*, she hadn't needed to brace herself. Yes, she was tight around him, but this time deliciously so. How very, very delicious he was buried deep inside her. *This* was what instinct had promised. What he'd done with his mouth and his finger had only been a foretaste of *this*—the physicality...the connection...the intimacy.

I'm hopelessly mad for you.

Words one spoke when in the throes of passion, weren't they?

That was all.

And yet how those words resonated through her and amplified all she was feeling. Further, how they reflected all she was feeling.

Hopelessly mad.

She might've been the writer, but he'd put it perfectly.

"Oh, Saskia, I'm on the edge," he growled into her neck. "I can't...*ahh...*"

It was only when he pulled from her that she fully took his meaning. He rolled onto his side and took himself in hand as she watched him stroke himself to climax on a shout, his seed spilling onto the sheets. She hadn't considered the necessity, but she was grateful for his care, even as she ached from the loss of him inside her.

He rolled onto his side as he reached for her, bringing her head to rest on the crook of his shoulder. "My sweet," he said, kissing her lips tenderly.

As she snuggled into him and drifted into the twilight of

slumber, she considered her long-held daydreams of Liam versus the reality of him. The truth was, in all those years of distant infatuation, she'd never carried yearning over into the realm of the carnal. What they'd done together just now was something she could never have conceived of, and she recognized how superficial her infatuation had been. All surfaces—his handsomeness, his smile, his charm, his ease.

But what she'd just experienced was intimacy and connection *and* physicality. The surface elements of his handsomeness put into practice—the feel of his charming mouth…the confidence and ease with which he moved his beautiful body and used it to pleasure her.

She'd never conceived of *this*.

How much better was the reality of him.

A fantasy could never make her feel thus—only a flesh-and-blood Liam.

*D*AWN

Liam needed to leave while the King's Head was at its most quiet. Now was the time in the quiet gray space before the sun peeked over the horizon and heralded a new day.

He wouldn't allow curious eyes to register his departure from Lady Saskia Calthorp's room and have her subject to scandal.

Of course, he never should have come to her room. He should've taken that bottle of whiskey, gone to his own quarters, and drowned himself in it, alone. But after the news he'd received —news he was riding straight to London to confirm—he'd needed to see her.

Need.

A word he was coming to associate with Saskia the longer he knew her.

Into this quiet hour entered the idea of beginnings and

endings. If what the countess told him was true, then the life of Liam Cassidy as he knew it was at an end—a new life as the Earl of Bolton awaited him.

And Saskia… What did she represent?

An ending?

Or…a beginning?

Across the room, she stirred, one silvery-blue eye fluttering open, then the other. Silently, she watched him pull a boot on. Her brow subtly crinkled, she sat up and reclined against the headboard. "Are you leaving?"

"I must." He tugged his other boot on and stood. He should've made straight for the door. Instead, he returned to her side of the bed. She reached out and took his hand, bringing it to her mouth. A smile generated in the center of his chest where his heart happened to beat. "Are we still exploring the parameters of a kiss?"

Eyes serious, she shook her head. "No."

Though a new day stopped its progress for no man's wishes, he wished last night didn't have to end.

"That was a kiss, Liam."

Unable not to, he bent and said into the scant space between their mouths, "And so is this."

He kissed her, slowly, thoroughly, pulling a moan from her that made him doubt himself and his intentions and his sense of duty and honor, that made him want to follow this kiss where it wanted to lead.

On a groan, he broke away, leaving them both breathless. Saskia's cheeks had gone deliciously pink, her eyes bright with budding desire. He could hardly look at her, not if he was going to leave this room. "I must go."

Though she nodded her acceptance of the fact, her eyes silently questioned it.

"I can't let you become the subject of gossip. It would only attach itself to you and become scandal."

It was *a* truth, if not *the* truth.

"I know."

Still, he couldn't leave yet, not without saying one last thing. "In London..."

"Yes?"

"You might hear an odd rumor about me."

"Oh?"

"And it might turn out to be true."

He would leave it at that until he knew the facts with certainty.

He stored up one parting glance at a beautifully disheveled Saskia—strawberry-blonde hair tousled, lips still kiss-swollen, plump breasts barely covered by the bedsheet—before he strode from the room.

Before desire could get in the way of determination.

Hopeless madness.

He done nothing in the last twenty-four hours to assuage the hopeless madness he felt for her.

As he left the King's Head and set out for London, uncertainty churned through him. He hadn't felt this unsettled in years. Alongside Gemma, he'd escaped Bolton five years ago and established a life for himself—a good life.

A life that came with fame and fortune and certainty.

A life beyond his wildest imaginings.

Now, here was the life he'd built vanishing before his eyes.

Now, in death, Bolton had gotten his way and reclaimed him, hadn't he?

And this new future...what did it hold for him?

CHAPTER SEVENTEEN

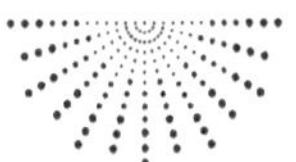

LONDON, A MONTH LATER

*C*omfortably seated inside Viveca's sumptuously appointed drawing room, Saskia took afternoon tea with her sister.

But, really, she was waiting.

Waiting for a certain subject to be broached pertaining to a certain someone.

For the last hour, however, Viveca had been content to go over the Sirens' finances for the week—first the circulating library, then it was on to the publishing house. A few new authors had caught her fancy. "We'll need to bring them out during a month when you don't have a release." Viveca took a sip of her tea. "Speaking of which, when do you expect to have your next Harriet LaPlume novel turned in?"

Harriet LaPlume wasn't the certain someone Saskia had been waiting to discuss. "I, *erm…*"

Viveca's brow crinkled ever so subtly. "Have you been writing?"

"I have."

And she had, truly. She'd been writing steadily this last month, but the fact was Harriet LaPlume was nowhere near to being ready to deliver her next novel. The book she was working on wanted to take a different shape from her previous books, and she wouldn't be sharing it with anyone—not even Viveca—until she understood it better. Likely, she suspected, it would end up in the rubbish bin.

"I could read some pages, if you like."

"I'd rather hold onto them for now." Saskia gave a little shrug. "They may be nothing."

Viveca's bright blue eyes took on that glint of fervor that anyone who knew her knew to watch out for. "Nothing you write, Saskia, is *nothing*."

Oh, that everyone could be loved by a loyal-to-the-bone sister. "I'll share it with you soon, I promise."

Somewhat mollified, Viveca nodded and smoothed clotted cream onto a scone before topping it with a dollop of strawberry jam. "Thank you for bringing Mrs. Stanton's clotted cream. It is *divine*." The last word was muffled by a too-large bite. "I must convince her to share the recipe with our cook."

Saskia shook her head. "Mrs. Stanton doesn't share her recipes."

"Oh," exclaimed Viveca. "I almost forgot to ask."

Again, Saskia found herself on edge, still waiting for that certain subject about that certain someone to be broached.

"Do you have any news relating to the memoir?"

And there it was—the conversation Saskia had been waiting for. "None."

"Have you received any word from him?"

Him.

They both knew who.

"Not since the Derby."

Well, the morning after the Derby.

Information she would keep to herself.

Viveca's head tipped to the side. "What should we call him now, anyway? Liam Cassidy will no longer do."

"*Your lordship*, I suppose." Saskia had given this some thought.

"*My lord*," said Viveca. "The servants will call him *milord*."

"*Bolton?*" suggested Saskia.

Liam, she didn't say.

Even with all those other changes to his name, *Liam* still applied.

Viveca shook her head in wonder. "*Bolton.*"

"*You might hear an odd rumor about me... And it might turn out to be true.*"

And hadn't it?

Within a week, rumor had become fact, which had become the most delicious gossip society had enjoyed in years. The most famous and successful jockey in the land, Liam Cassidy was the by-blow of the Earl of Bolton.

Except...

He hadn't been illegitimate at all. A secret marriage between the earl and his cook had preceded Bolton's marriage to the lady all society knew as his countess. And when the earl died last month, the truth had come flooding out and hit society like a tidal wave.

"No one has seen him since the news became public," said Viveca conversationally. "Where could he be?"

"At an ancient family pile somewhere in the countryside?" That was Saskia's best guess, anyway.

Viveca nodded. "I suppose he'll be learning how to be an earl."

His parting words to her the morning after the Derby...the morning after, *well...* Anyway, those words had intrigued her—how could they not?—but it wasn't until a week later that they'd made sense, and an entirely obvious realization had struck her. The night of the Derby when he'd come to her room, celebratory bottle of whiskey in hand, he'd known of his ascendence into the peerage—and he hadn't come to celebrate at all. He'd come to talk to her about anything else and drink and distract himself.

And how did she know this?

The desperation she'd detected in his eyes, she now understood it.

And she understood something else, too.

The earldom…

He didn't want it.

For him, it wasn't the windfall most would consider it. Liam Cassidy hadn't needed a hereditary title to secure his place in the world. Further, he didn't need a title to prove his worth to the world. He'd done all that on his own, through his own talent and drive.

"There can't be much to being a lord," continued Viveca, "going by how most lords conduct themselves in The Archangel. The stories Blaze can tell. Now, my husband could write a memoir to end all memoirs." She spread her hands wide. *"Licentious Lords and their Lusty Lives."*

"Rather a mouthful."

"A work in progress," allowed Viveca, her mind clearly working on this new prospect. She exhaled a sigh. "I suppose the Liam Cassidy memoir won't happen now." She couldn't hide her disappointment.

"I suppose it won't."

A sharp, little pain needled through Saskia. That very thought had struck her—and kept striking her, sending that sharp, little pain needling through her every time.

"I'll contact him once his life has calmed a bit," said Viveca. "Just to make certain. But surely, he won't be a jockey anymore, will he?"

"Surely not." How glum she sounded.

Viveca angled so she faced Saskia squarely. "Now, I have news." Her eyes sparkled with a secret bursting to be revealed. "Another work in progress, one might say."

Before Viveca could speak her next words, Saskia knew what her sister was about to say.

"I am with child," pronounced Viveca.

Though she'd suspected, instant tears sprang to Saskia's eyes, and she wasted no time gathering Viveca into her arms. "Oh, I'm so happy for you, sister." A wet laugh escaped her as she swiped tears that had already begun streaming down her cheeks. "And for myself."

She loved being an aunt to Gabriel's and Tessa's children, and Viveca's would be no different. Unexpected, that had been, how much she enjoyed her nieces and nephews. She angled back. "I'm surprised it took you and Blaze this long."

Not the most proper observation, but she and Viveca could say such things to one another. It had always been so.

Viveca, of course, paid the impropriety no mind. "Oh, we decided to have a few years of just us. Blaze can be incredibly disciplined when he chooses. Really, you can't imagine the ways he can be disciplined." A dreamy sigh distracted her before she snapped back into the present. "Besides, I wanted to make sure Sirens was firmly on its feet first."

"Oh, sister, you will make the best mother."

"Tessa will always be the best."

"You're right," Saskia allowed. "Second best mother, then."

"I'm content with that."

No one compared to Tessa in the eyes of Saskia and Viveca.

Viveca settled back and pinned Saskia with a long, assessing stare. "I have something else I would like to say to you today."

"How can there possibly be more?" Saskia tried for levity, even as she knew it was no use when Viveca had that look in her eye.

"You should get out in society more often."

Saskia snorted. A reflex, really. "Why on earth would I spend my valuable time socializing with that lot of twits more often than I already do?"

Viveca crossed her arms over her chest. "Which is how often precisely?" Before Saskia could answer the first question, her sister asked a second. "Have you attended a society event since the Derby?"

Saskia had no choice but to admit, "I haven't."

"So, then we're agreed."

Oh, no. Viveca was doing that thing she did when she was determined to have her way. Saskia had ever delighted no end watching her sister perform this conversational trick on others. But never had she been on the receiving end, and she liked it not one bit. "What exactly are we agreed upon, sister?"

"That you need to get out more often."

"I've agreed to no such thing."

"But Saskia…" Viveca reached out and took her hand. "There's no other way."

"No other way?" Irritation flashed through Saskia. "Viveca, will you just speak plainly?"

"I want you to have what I have with Blaze."

"I believe it's safe to say no one on the planet has what you have with Blaze."

But Viveca wasn't inclined to let up. "I want you to have your own version of it, sister. The version that makes *you* happy."

"I am—"

Happy.

But she couldn't speak the word.

It refused to pass her lips.

She could usually say it, because usually she considered herself happy. She was happy with her life—her writing, her business, her comforts. But sitting here with Viveca, hearing her baby news, Saskia understood there was a whole level of happiness she had no notion of.

Yet…that wasn't completely true, was it?

Liam Cassidy—or whatever he was called now.

Their time together…their *night* together… Didn't they offer an inkling of that other level of happiness Viveca wanted for her?

Unbidden, *that night* returned to her. All the next day, her body had felt deliciously used—a little sore, but also *pleasured.*

A thoroughly pleasured body.

But it was more than that, too.

Something else had been both sated and awakened that night. As if she contained another desire alongside the desire of the body. Desires that were both linked *and* separate. One could influence the other, but they could also exist discretely.

And this other desire, what was it?

Not a desire of the mind.

Nothing so flimsy as that.

A desire of the soul…of the heart.

Both desires now awakened within her.

Instinctively, she understood this was what Viveca wanted for her. Someone who inspired those linked desires in Saskia the way Blaze did for her.

Viveca continued. "I suppose you received an invitation to the Duke and Duchess of Rakesley's ball next week?"

"I did."

"Of course, you know who will be attending."

"I do." The duchess was Liam's sister, after all.

But, *oh,* Viveca was too sharp for her own good sometimes.

"I suppose it's his come-out ball." Viveca's head tipped to the side. "Do earls have come-out balls?" She shrugged. "Well, this one is, and anyway, Saskia, you should go." She nodded, clearly liking her idea more by the moment. "And *you* can speak to him about the memoir. After all, you already have a relationship with him."

Saskia gasped—actually *gasped.* "I do *not* have a relationship with Liam…Mr. Cassidy…*Bolton!*"

Within Viveca's subtly narrowed eyes, Saskia detected triumph. "I only meant that you've worked together on the memoir," she said, oh, so sweetly. "The two of you would naturally have an established rapport."

Caught out, that was how Saskia felt—and there was no doing anything about it. Still, she had a fighting spirit and would try. "Oh, *erm*, yes, I…*we* have that."

Would that she could sink into the sofa and through the floorboards below and live through the next hundred years of mortification blessedly alone.

But the universe offered no such sanctuary.

What it offered instead was Viveca's unblinking gaze that possibly—*likely*—saw too much.

Saskia cleared her throat. "I'll attend the ball. Now," she continued, awkwardly coming to a stand, "I must go."

Outside, Saskia's feet marched steadily up Tichborne Street as she made her way homeward. It was a sweltering July day, but no hotter than her cheeks and the tips of her ears, which yet blazed with mortification.

One simply couldn't hide from Viveca and that clever mind of hers. Saskia almost felt badly for her future children. They would get away with nothing. Actually, with a rogue for a father like Blaze Jagger, that might not be true. But one thing was certain— the future children of Viveca and Blaze would be diabolically clever, and there was a tiny, mischievous part of Saskia that couldn't wait to see it.

But that was years into the future, and Saskia had the here-and-now to contend with.

Namely, that she would be attending a ball next week—the come-out ball of the 4th Earl of Bolton, to be exact.

What would he be like?

He was Bolton now.

But was he still…*Liam?*

CHAPTER EIGHTEEN

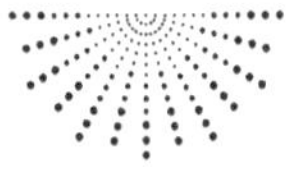

A WEEK LATER

"You have to face them with not a flicker of self-doubt in your eyes."

Gemma pressed her back to the study door, clicking it shut behind her. The gravity of her words were only underscored by the gravity within gold-flecked green eyes that were an exact match to Liam's.

By *them*, Gemma meant the *haut ton*, every last member of which were presently gathered beneath the roof of the Duke of Rakesley's London residence.

Or that was how it seemed to Liam.

Of course, he understood why they'd all accepted an invitation to this ball. They were ravenous for their first look at him. Well, not *him*, as such. After all, they'd seen him about these last five years—at the races and the occasional society event.

But that was Liam Cassidy they'd seen.

Tonight, it was a new man they were gathered to glimpse.

"Sister," he said, summoning his most disarming smile, "I've attended many a society ball."

Gemma crossed her arms over her chest, not disarmed in the least. "Not as Bolton."

Liam's jaw clenched—a recently acquired reflex. Until a month ago, his jaw had only ever tensed during the final stretch of a tightly contested horse race. Now, it happened every time he was addressed as Bolton.

Which was often.

So often, in fact, he might have to accept the moniker as his name.

He snorted with dismissal, hoping to lighten the mood. "A ballroom is hardly a field of battle."

But Gemma wasn't having it. "Oh, that's exactly what it is."

Liam waited for her to continue, for she'd clearly only just gotten started.

"I wasn't the duchess society wanted for Rake," she said, "so I know what I'm talking about. If you don't wish to think of a ball as a field of battle, then think of it as swimming in a sea of sharks."

His brow lifted. "And that's better?"

She nodded. "If you keep a cool head, you'll come out the other side with all your limbs intact."

Before now, Liam hadn't known Gemma's feelings regarding the society she'd begun swimming in since her marriage to Rake. She'd never addressed it with him. But he now intuited she viewed it as a necessary and unavoidable condition of being with the man she loved.

And he understood something else, too—she was only trying to look out for her brother.

He shook his head in both wonderment and bewilderment, something he'd taken to doing several times a day. "Gemma, I'm Bolton."

Silence expanded into the air between their locked twin gazes. Out of everyone in the wide world, only she could understand the weight of those words…the weight of this new reality.

"I don't want it."

She nodded.

The countess hadn't believed him, but Gemma did. She'd been brought up in Bolton's household right alongside him.

She reached out and took his hand. "Liam, you'll be a different Bolton. And do you know how I know? Because you're *you*."

Gemma believed those words, wholeheartedly, and that faith meant more to Liam than he could express. But he understood something else, too, something that prevented him from following wholly into her belief. The might of an earldom was near total power—and near total power was a corrupting force. One only had to look at how it had twisted the Bolton before him, the man who had been their father. The control he'd not only exercised over all within his domain, which had included Liam and Gemma, but the *need* to exert it.

A fearsome thing, that much power in one man's hands.

The door cracked open, and Rake's head poked into the room. "The ballroom is bursting at the seams. It's time."

Liam gave Rake a nod, then returned his attention to his sister, commanding more certainty into his easy smile than he strictly felt. "Gemma, we've made it through everything life has thrown at us thus far, and we'll make it through this, too."

Fervency shone in her eyes. "Me at your back."

"Aye," he said, "and me at yours."

Then Liam was on the move, striding into his new reality as he navigated the many corridors and staircases and more corridors that comprised a duke's London mansion, the crowd growing denser with every step he took toward the ballroom. It was a big moment. But then, he'd occupied the center of plenty of big moments these last five years, as the winningest jockey in England season after season. So, it wasn't that he was unaccustomed to the attention. Rather, the attention that came with winning was attention he'd sought, in a way. It was the attention that came with being at the top of the *ton*'s favorite sport.

The attention now centered on him was a different beast.

Before, he'd simply been handsome, likeable Liam Cassidy,

quick with a charming smile that got him into all the places he wanted to go. The *ton*'s entertainment. Goodwill and jocularity directed at him at every turn.

Now, as he stepped onto the gleaming mahogany ballroom floor, crystal chandeliers sparkling overhead, a path clearing before him as he walked alongside Rake and Gemma, the slaps on the back that accompanied his progress were no less jocular, but he sensed an edge. That odd glint of the eye that communicated envy or competition or both. He'd beheld that same light in many a jockey's eye out on the turf.

He was no longer merely likeable Liam Cassidy.

He was Bolton.

Rake stopped before the massive marble hearth that dominated one end of the ballroom with its intricate Italianate carvings depicting all manner of frolicking deities. As this was the natural focal point of the room, it was fitting that Rake would use this place to lift his glass. The ballroom's collective breath fell into an instant hush. Dukes tended to inspire that effect on a room, particularly a duke like Rake.

Except those two hundred pairs of eyes weren't fixed upon Rake.

They were watching Liam, silently observing him as if he were a newly discovered species of animal. He'd had a bit of Latin from one of the tutors Bolton had brought in to teach him and Gemma, so he reckoned he'd be called something like *Equorum agitator*, which roughly came out to horse driver. In truth, though he'd been offered something of an education and, undoubtedly, some of that learning had sunk in, if it hadn't involved horses, Liam hadn't been much interested.

So it was that Rake raised his glass and introduced the new Earl of Bolton to society, but all those right and proper words fell on deaf ears.

Liam was busy scanning the crowd.

Not in the general sense.

Specifically for a pair of bright silvery-blue eyes behind round brass spectacles.

Was she here?

She would've been invited.

He'd made sure.

Of a sudden, he realized what he was doing wrong.

He was looking in the wrong place.

Saskia wouldn't be in the swell of the crowd. She would be at its periphery, tucked into a discreet corner from which she could observe without being observed.

His gaze wandered farther afield...*there*...staring directly back at him was the pair of eyes he sought. Her gaze neither flinched nor wavered at the contact. Instead, it searched his with an openness and inquisitiveness he hadn't known he'd missed down to the quick of his soul until this very moment. For the first time in weeks—five, to be exact—the wobble that had been his constant companion stilled and he felt...steadied.

A smile—his first unburdened one in weeks—pulled at his mouth and he felt like himself...*Liam*.

The *Liam* he'd been.

The *Liam* she knew.

Himself.

The instant Rake's toast ended and the assembled burst into polite applause, a large blustery man stepped into the empty space before Liam. "So, now you're one of us, let me introduce you to my daughters."

It would've been unmannerly to ask the man to introduce himself first—he was a lord of one variety or another, anyway—so Liam kept the smile affixed to his mouth and endured the ritual of introductions to all five of the man's daughters, each younger than the last, and giggly, too. By the time they'd moved on, Saskia no longer occupied her patch of discreet corner.

Blast.

He said to no one in particular, "If you'll pardon me…" his feet already on the move.

Saskia was here.

That was all the information he needed.

He *would* find her.

But the progress of navigating this crowd was slower going than he liked. It had become a usual part of his life to be the recipient of multiple claps on the back on a given day, not just race day. Such was the life of a winning jockey. If a win, or even a loss, brought a fellow a paltry shilling, he was their favorite person in England—until the next race.

But what had begun irritating him about all the slaps on the back this last month was they had naught to do with his prowess on the turf. These slaps of congratulations weren't for Liam Cassidy. They were for the newly minted Lord Liam Sutton, 4th Earl of Bolton. The man Liam, improbably, found himself to be. These claps on the back were for naught more than the accident of his birth.

A *lord…him.*

He gave his head a clearing shake.

"If it isn't the Earl of Bolton," came a plummy aristocratic voice at his side. And there came the jocular clap on the back that would, of course, accompany such a greeting.

He turned to find the hard, reptilian gaze of the Earl of Bridgewater upon him. Through horse racing, he'd had a few dealings with Bridgewater over the years, and those had been enough to last a lifetime. The reputation Bridgewater had earned —of treating those he deemed below him worse than the dirt beneath his feet—had been entirely true. Those below the earl included his trainers and jockeys…and his horses. A situation Liam found intolerable.

As he nodded and said, "Bridgewater." A mean pleasure that he might take from being an earl occurred to him. He didn't have to smile at a man he didn't like.

He was no longer entertainment.

He was an earl.

In the eyes of society, he was Bridgewater's equal.

A malignant glint flicked in Bridgewater's eye. "How does it feel to be the most eligible lord in all England?"

"Am I now?" Liam kept his tone cool and distant. He had experience in dealing with this sort of man. After all, he'd been raised in Bolton's household.

Bridgewater snorted. "You'll have your pick." Another snort, this one a hair wet. The man was clearly in his cups. "You already had your pick of half when you were naught more than a jockey. Now, you can have any lady you like." Yet another wet snort. "My countess herself would run off with you at the slightest crook of your pinky."

Liam kept mum on that last point—and all the points preceding it, too.

But nothing was stopping Bridgewater, now that he'd got going. He pointed at a lady across the dancing floor. "Take Lady Belinda Cocksey, for instance. She's a country chit, true, and you'll have to forgive her surname—but then you'd be giving her a new one, wouldn't you? She comes with ten thousand pounds on her wedding day." Bridgewater pointed in the opposite direction. "Or Miss Eveline Sharlto. An heiress from the West Indies." He nodded meaningfully. "Sugar plantations, you know."

Liam continued holding his peace.

"Or if you're a lover of beauty, there's Miss Jane Cooper-Dunne. A diamond of the first water, that one." The man practically salivated as he ogled the young miss.

The thing was, Liam hadn't the least use for country pursuits or sugar plantations and, while he held some regard for female beauty, a diamond of the first water was bound to require constant adoration and that sounded like a dead boring life to lead.

"There's another one," continued Bridgewater. "Lady Saskia Calthorp."

Liam's ears perked up. "Pardon?"

The earl extended his arm, nearly ramming his forefinger into the eye of a passerby, who exclaimed an annoyed, "Watch how you go, old man." Bridgewater hardly noticed. "Been on the marriage mart for years, she has."

She stood not twenty feet away conversing with Mrs. Lancaster. But it might as well have been across the Atlantic Ocean, as far as Liam was concerned, for it would take a three-month voyage to get to her at the rate he was going.

"Sister of a duke, and a right knocker, too," continued Bridgewater, appraisingly. "Behind those spectacles, of course."

A right knocker in regard to Lady Saskia Calthorp were the first true words Bridgewater had spoken all night. Strawberry-blonde hair artfully arranged so it was half up and half down, the half down tendrils trailing down her back and over her shoulder, leading the eye toward curves that were unmistakable, though her coral silk dress wasn't scandalously revealing. She simply had that sort of figure—the sort that curved in and out in all the right places.

"You'll want to stay well clear of that one," concluded Bridgewater.

Liam experienced an overwhelming desire in his hands to clench into fists. "And why is that?"

"The fearsome sort of woman, I'm afraid." Another wet snort from the earl. "The uppish reads-intellectual-rot sort."

Saskia would be regarded thusly by the likes of Bridgewater.

In fact, it spoke well of her that she was.

Sure, she possessed an aptitude that many would perceive as *fearsome*, but that wasn't all she was.

She was Harriet LaPlume—and she wasn't.

She was Arabella—and she wasn't.

The true Saskia was woven somewhere in between those identities—but she wasn't located there, either.

The true Saskia was someone only he knew.

Someone he liked.

Someone he'd missed all these weeks.

He still craved her.

Their night together wasn't enough.

So, she was that, too—an unslaked craving of body and mind and, perhaps, soul.

Bridgewater shook his head. "A shame that, really. What a waste of a female—"

"Bridgewater," said Liam on a curt bow and pivoted on his heel. He began walking—*striding*—before he did something rash, like planting his still-clenched fist in the center of an earl's face. Bridgewater shouldn't even have the right to gaze upon Saskia, much less entertain a single opinion about her.

It was only when Liam reached a buffet table that he realized he'd gone in the wrong direction—away from Saskia. A footman dipped a ladle into the wide cut-crystal punch bowl and filled a cup with arrack before extending it. An idea came to him. "And another, if you will."

Armed with two cups of arrack, Liam again entered the breach. This time, he would succeed in catching Saskia. But when he reached the very patch of mahogany floor where he'd last seen her, she was gone. Though his height wasn't a boon as a jockey, he was grateful for it now as he scanned the sea of aristocrats. Mostly, he found an abundance of top hats and brunette-, blonde-, and red-haired coiffures, but none the specific shade of strawberry-blonde he sought.

A frustrated growl had just escaped him when he spotted a fleeting form with the exact shade of strawberry-blonde and figure beneath coral silk that he knew so well. But it was her back he spied, for she appeared to be…leaving.

No, no, no.

His feet were on the move, arrack sloshing in the cups, as he crossed the ballroom and entered the corridor she'd disappeared down. He didn't know all the ins and outs of Rake's mansion, so he wasn't sure what rooms specifically lay behind each door. He opened the first one he came to and immediately found it was the door he would've opened, anyway, if he had known which room was hidden behind it.

The library—and Saskia was inside.

From the opposite end of the room, her gaze startled up from the book she'd already slid from the bookcase. He chuckled. "Of course, this was where I would find you."

A shy smile pulled at her mouth. "I have a confession."

"Do you now?"

He bumped the door with his shoulder, and it swung shut behind him. "Tell me, Lady Saskia," he said, his voice pitched so low and rumbly it could pass for a growl, "what is your confession?"

He was the only one who would be hearing the confessions of Lady Saskia Calthorp.

CHAPTER NINETEEN

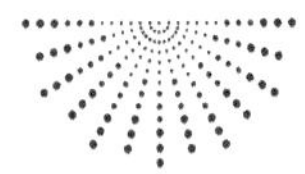

A feeling snaked through Saskia, dark and sinuous, provoked by the sinful register of his voice...the words he spoke as they slid past lips curved into a wicked smile...

Her breath promptly stole away.

He wanted to hear her confession.

And what would she confess?

That wasn't the correct question.

What *wouldn't* she confess?

Her tongue swiped across her bottom lip, pulling his gold-green gaze. To have his attention so enraptured by her mouth...

Well.

It lit places inside her.

Actually, that wasn't true. Those fires hadn't been extinguished in the least. In fact, it had been weeks of endurance with this low flame lit inside her, for it wouldn't subside. Writing only helped so much, as she'd tried to write it into submission—and failed.

Only the man presently staring at her mouth had the power to quench it.

Yet, now, she wondered if that was, indeed, the case.

Wouldn't he only excite it further into conflagration?

She cleared her throat. "I…" She swallowed. "I only accept two of ten invitations I receive for one reason."

A corner of his mouth quirked. "To dance?"

He was teasing, and that playfulness released something inside her.

It was that he knew her.

"I actually attend balls so I can sneak into the libraries of London's finest houses." A smile of her own joined his. "I can't resist." She only now registered that he was holding a cup of arrack in each hand. "I suppose you're expected elsewhere?"

"Why would you suppose that?"

"Isn't someone waiting for their punch?"

"Oh, this." He extended one of the cups. "It's for you."

"For *me*?"

"I thought you might be thirsty."

"Oh." She set the book down and accepted the punch. "That was most thoughtful of you."

She took a sip, then another, an awkward silence expanding between them as he took a sip, then another.

"So," he said, at last, "what do you usually find in the libraries of nobles?"

"Not as many books as you would expect, actually. And the books populating the shelves are usually unopened."

"As in no one has read them?" His mouth turned down at the corners. "How can you tell if a book hasn't been read? Aside from the plain stupidity of its owner, of course."

She laughed. She couldn't help herself. "Aside from that, well, you can tell because the pages are still untrimmed and haven't yet been slit open." She reached for the book she'd set down and extended it. He leaned forward, taking in the unopened leaves. "See? No one has ever read this book."

"Then why have a book, if you don't intend to read it?"

She shrugged, closing the book and replacing it on the shelf where she'd found it. "Books are expensive, so they're a symbol of status, for some. Others like the way books look lined up on a shelf. Some plan on reading the book, but haven't gotten around to it yet." She snorted. "Book collecting might be more popular than book reading, in truth."

She turned to find Liam quietly observing her with his head cocked subtly to the side. "You've made it your business to know everything there is to know about books, haven't you?"

"Quite."

She liked the way he was regarding her—as if he admired her.

She liked it too much.

She needed to steer this conversation in a different direction before she got carried away. "If I'm telling the truth, I had an additional reason for attending this ball tonight."

"To see me?" he asked, lightly…playfully…*flirtatiously.*

"Actually, yes."

"*Actually?*" He clutched his chest. "Was an *actually* ever more lowering? A simple *yes* would've sufficed, milady."

Her mouth twitched. "I was sent as an emissary of Sirens."

His smile didn't exactly fall, but it tempered. "Ah, now that I'm no longer Liam Cassidy."

She nodded.

"Now that I'm an earl."

Relief that he'd broached that word—*earl*—pulsed through her. She hadn't wanted to be the first to utter it. But now that it had been aired, she felt she could ask… "How is it, being an earl?"

He exhaled. No small amount of weariness and acceptance in that exhalation. "A great deal of bowing and milord-ing in my direction. But mostly, I'm busy from sun-up to sun-down. One has to get to know the estates—there are three of them. And the townhouses—there are two of those. One in London and one in Bath, of all places. Then there are the various managers and servants. There are papers and documents and the will with its various codicils that must be followed to the letter. One must make sure everyone is getting paid, and that the earl is getting paid, too." He gave an astonished, overwhelmed shake of the head. "It's a mountain of obligations to manage, and more than you asked to know, I'm sure."

His life now was wholly different from what it once was. It would feel like a lifetime ago to him, but his past life was only a few weeks gone.

"I'm interested in your life," she said.

"As an emissary of Sirens." Understanding shone in his eyes. "You would like to know if the memoir is still on course."

"Aye."

A dry laugh sounded through his nose. "All I did this last month was learn how to be an earl. I haven't given the memoir an ounce of thought."

She resisted the urge to reach out and take his hand and tell him everything would come out all right—even as she wasn't certain of that outcome herself. "You can let us know some other time."

A pang sheared through her. Not for the life he'd gained, but for the one he'd lost. He'd created that other life. He'd loved it. And now... The life of an earl was being forced on him. So, she would ask no more questions, for the natural next question would've been to ask if he would stop racing—and the answer was obvious, wasn't it?

"I met the king," he volunteered.

"Oh?"

"All he wanted to talk about was horse racing." He shook his head and snorted. "Asked me who to bet on for the Great Yarmouth."

She snorted. Unladylike, she knew, but she'd been unable to help herself. "I see his reputation isn't unearned."

A serious light entered Liam's eyes. "I suppose we should return to the ballroom." A hesitation, then, "Would you like to dance?"

"I might, except…"

"*Except?*"

"Except we would be so…*observed.*"

She didn't wish to part company, but she wasn't sure what was holding them together, strictly speaking.

That great charming smile of his flashed. "Come with me." He held out his arm. "There's something I think you would like to see."

Against her good sense, Saskia placed her hand on his forearm. She'd never possessed a whit of good sense when it came to this man, anyway.

He led her from the library, not toward the ballroom, but down the corridor in the opposite direction, then down a staircase and another corridor. She didn't know where he was taking her. She supposed she could ask. Perhaps she *should* ask. But whatever his answer, she knew she would agree.

Not because he was an earl of the realm.

Because he was Liam.

Soon, they were stepping outside, the moon obscured by a low blanket of clouds, the air dense and cloying with unshed rain. The chill inspired a spray of goosebumps up her arms.

"Are you cold?" Before she could protest, or even draw another breath, he'd shrugged off his evening coat. "Here."

Then his jacket was draped across her shoulders. She hadn't it in her to refuse, anyway. She was unable not to slide her hands into the arms and snug into the warmth of his residual body heat and inhale deeply, catching his scent of citrus and salt and *Liam.* When they entered a cobblestone forecourt, she recognized where he'd led her. "I should've known you would bring me to the stables."

A diffident laugh escaped him, but he issued no denial as they entered the building. She glanced all around—the high-beamed ceiling soaring above their heads; the red-bricked center aisle below their feet; and the spacious horse boxes to either side. "The

Duke of Rakesley's London stables are nearly as magnificent as his Somerton stables."

"Yeah, that's Rake for you." Liam stopped halfway down the aisle. "Here's what I wanted to show you."

Saskia poked her head past the low gate of a box to find a chestnut mare lying on her side and a tiny chestnut foal with two white socks on its front fetlocks curled against her. She gasped. "My stars, how adorable."

"This little filly was born yesterday."

Saskia found herself clasping her hands with delight, something she'd only ever described in her novels. "She's so perfect and complete."

The mare pushed up to her feet and ambled over to the gate, nudging Liam's shoulder with her nose. He stroked her muzzle with one hand and reached into his trouser pocket with the other. When it reemerged, he was holding a chunk of apple.

"Do you always carry treats in your pockets in case you encounter a horse?"

"Always."

"Even at a ball?"

"While you're sneaking into libraries," he said, a smile pulling at his mouth, "I'm sneaking into stables."

"Well, that would be going into the memoir." *Would*, not *will*. The fate of the memoir was yet uncertain, wasn't it?

Deciding ten feet were far too many to be separated from her dam, the foal struggled to her feet, spindly legs wobbly beneath her, and closed the distance before dipping her head to nurse.

"You're so natural with horses, Liam."

"Nothing to it, really."

"I don't think that's true." She decided to keep her reservations regarding horses to herself. "Will this filly be a racehorse?"

"Ah, alas, no, as they aren't Thoroughbreds."

"I thought Rakesley only had racehorses."

"This girl will likely be a carriage horse, like her dam. Though you aren't on the wrong track. Most carriage horses have a fair amount of Thoroughbred blood. See how lightly built and elegant these two are? That's from the Arab in the lineage. All sorts of horses for all sorts of jobs."

Saskia shook her head, feeling silly. "Of course. I'm sure I knew that somewhere in the back of my mind." She smiled sheepishly. "I must confess—"

"Another confession, Lady Saskia?"

The words were possessed of the lightness he was so skilled at conveying, but a flame flicked to life in his eyes.

Heat burned through to the very center of her.

CHAPTER TWENTY

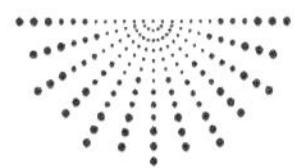

$\mathcal{H}$e'd flummoxed her—and Liam rather liked that.

A man could be most gratified by flummoxing a woman like Lady Saskia Calthorp.

"I…" She spread her hands wide, an abashed smile curving her mouth. "I know nothing about horses."

Well, she hadn't told him anything he hadn't already worked out. "Take the carriage horse as an example," he said. "When one crosses a Thoroughbred with a hardy breed like the Cleveland Bay, one gets any variety of horse types. A carriage horse, like we see with these two girls. Or a hunter, or a hack. It really depends on several factors—size, temperament, conformation."

"Enlightening."

His mouth twitched. "You're dead bored, aren't you?"

"I don't get bored by facts, and you've provided me with one hundred percent more facts than I knew about horses five minutes ago."

He lowered into a courtly bow. "My honor and pleasure, Lady Saskia."

She giggled, and he realized while he'd heard her laugh, he'd never heard her giggle. The soft, feminine, *flirty* sound of it winged through him. Still, he had to ask, "How is it you know nothing about horses? Surely, you've ridden one?"

Her smile didn't precisely fall away, but her giggle did.

He felt a trench dig into his brow. "You *have* been on a horse, correct?"

"Well, if you must know—"

"I must."

She crossed her arms over her chest, which only made her look winsomely small in his too-large evening coat. "I haven't."

The furrow of his brow deepened as his brain attempted to absorb this impossible information. "You can't ride?"

"I can't." Her head tipped to one side. "Well, I'm sure I *could,* but I *haven't.*"

She *would* see that as an important distinction. She was Harriet LaPlume, after all.

He, however, didn't.

"You need to know how to ride."

"I can't say I've ever felt that need."

"There's nothing like it, Saskia. It's fun, and it's freedom."

"And with over a thousand pounds of animal below one, a wee bit dangerous."

"That's part of the fun."

She smiled despite herself. "For some."

How beautiful she was, laughing and talking and just being herself.

Her true self.

Not Harriet LaPlume or Arabella or the fearsome Lady Saskia Calthorp those in the ballroom, like Bridgewater, thought they knew.

Here, with him, she was simply Saskia.

"I suppose we should return to the ball."

Was that regret flickering behind her spectacles?

And though every cell in his body resisted, he said, "I suppose we should."

So, they did as they should and began walking. They'd only stepped onto the mist-slick cobbles of the forecourt when she said, "I have a question for you."

A note in her voice had him tensing. "Aye?"

"Now that you're Bolton—"

And there went his jaw—*clenching*.

"—won't you miss the world of horses and horse racing?"

"No."

"*No?*"

He could see he'd shocked her. "Bolton owns a small racing stable," he explained. "It hasn't met with much success in years, but there is promising stock that can be worked with."

She came to a sudden stop, her head angling so she could get a proper look at him. "*Bolton,*" she said. "You mean *you* own a racing stable."

He blinked. "I suppose I do."

They'd just entered the garden path that would lead them back to the ballroom, waltzing strains of violin and cello reaching out to guide them on their way, when he felt it land—a fat drop of rain on his nose. Saskia blinked, clearly having experienced her own fat drop of rain. "Liam, we need to—"

Her next words were abruptly drowned out when next it wasn't another solitary drop of rain that landed on their heads, but an entire torrent of the stuff that burst free of the clouds above. Instinctively, he took her hand, at first thinking to make a dash for the manse. But it was too far. They would be thoroughly drenched by the time they reached the ballroom. They were already halfway to soaked as it was.

His frantic gaze happened upon a structure, small and indistinct through the dense wash of rain. "*There,*" he shouted, pointing, his feet already on the move.

Within seconds, his shoulder had shoved the door open and he'd pulled Saskia inside with him. "The gardener's shed," she said, using the dim light afforded by the structure's single window to get a look at the cramped room's contents—a square, sturdy table against the back wall…a three-legged stool before it…rows of shelving holding every sort of garden implement known to mankind on two adjacent walls.

But those details hardly penetrated Liam's mind, for he found his hand was still clutching hers—and he'd detected a slight tremble. "Saskia, are you still cold?"

Her gaze lifted. Perhaps she was searching for the right words, as she remained silent for several seconds before she said, "I'm not cold in the least, Liam, and I tremble not from anything beyond you and me."

With such words in her arsenal, it was no wonder Harriet LaPlume sold so many books.

An understanding came to him.

Harriet LaPlume wasn't the secret inside Saskia.

It was the other way around.

It was Saskia, her true self, that provided the fuel and fire for Harriet LaPlume.

He reached up and brushed a sodden tendril of hair from her cheek. Then, carefully, he removed her spectacles and set them aside before he angled forward so only a sliver of air separated his mouth from hers. In the instant before their lips met, he shifted so his mouth grazed her ear. "The thing is," he said, his voice a crushed velvet scrape against his throat, "I might be Bolton, but I'm still Liam."

She released a breath, a light, wavering exhalation he only caught as it skittered across his neck, lifting the fine hairs of his nape as it went. "Bolton holds no sway over me," she uttered. "No title…nothing in this world holds a power over me greater than that which *you* wield."

And there were those words of hers again, inciting him, provoking flame into life. They were the words one spoke in the heat of such moments—he knew it; she was learning it—but those words took possibility and turned it into intention. He tucked a few fingers beneath her chin and slowly traced the pad of his thumb across her plump bottom lip, then he inhaled her next trembly exhalation and replaced his thumb with his mouth. *Soft...sweet...warm...Saskia*—the feel of her...the taste of her... *Nothing in this world holds a power over me greater than that which you wield.* And didn't those words only mirror feelings that stirred inside him? Feelings he hadn't the words to express?

She'd expressed those feelings for the both of them.

These long last weeks of restlessness and ache, he'd struggled. All he'd wanted was to do as he was doing now—to kiss her...to pull sighs and moans from her... His hand moved to her waist, steadying her as he walked her backwards until the small of her back met the shed's only table.

Instinctual, this was.

Madness, too.

Inevitable.

Her arms clasped around his neck, she stretched the full, curvy length of her body against him, deepening the kiss, her tongue no longer that of a shy novice, but tangling slowly with his. She was a quick learner, Saskia. Ardent, too.

This last month, he'd imagined her in all sorts of ways, in all states of dishabille—mostly nude, in truth—and in all sorts of positions—he'd lost count of the number of ways he'd had her in his dreams and how many times he'd taken himself in hand to relieve the ache. But none of those imaginings came close to the flesh-and-blood reality of her in his arms—her desire...her passion.

For the thing about Saskia was when she was in pursuit of a goal, she achieved it. No one matched her for single focus of the mind. And what she was focused on—the goal she was pursuing —was *him*. And how he reveled in that—being the object of desire for a woman like her.

His hands tightened around her waist, and he lifted so she perched on the edge of the table. He gathered her gown and pushed it above her knees, past the frilly garters of silk stockings, exposing creamy thighs. Higher, he slid coral silk until the meager light from the window was caressing tight red-gold curls. His manhood throbbed and ached and demanded he bury himself inside her this instant. *This very instant.* "These weeks without you have been torture, Saskia. I need you so badly."

This need, it might transcend the physical, but the transcendent could wait.

For now, the physical would do.

Her gaze held his. "Then, Liam..." Her hand brushed down the front of his shirt, lower, to the waistband of his trousers... along the hardened length of his shaft. He sucked in a sharp breath. Knowledge shone in her eyes. Knowledge that she held him in the palm of her hand—both literally and figuratively—as she angled forward, her soft lips just touching his as she said, "Take me. I'm yours."

Her nimble fingers flicked open one button, then the next... and the next. His cock sprang free. Trembly fingers feathered along his length, and he thought he might shatter as they explored him. "*Saskia,*" he groaned.

"You're so soft."

"*Not* what every man wants to hear."

"And so very hard."

"Better."

"And long..."

"Much better."

"And so very thick."

"Watch it, or you'll give me a big head."

"Oh, I think I've already done that."

A bold finger traced around the crown of his cock, pulling a ragged groan from him, even as a chuckle rumbled through his chest. "You've redeemed yourself."

He grabbed her sweet, lush arse and brought her to the edge of the table, his length brushing along her warm, slick cunny. Slender, feminine fingers wrapped around him, positioning him at the entrance of her sex. Such sweet torture, this was. Exquisite, really.

"Liam," she said—*demanded*, "take me now."

And while in the normal course of events, he might have a mind of his own, in this moment, he didn't.

In this moment, he was taking orders.

One hand squeezing her arse, the other hooked beneath her leg, he shifted forward and entered her, inch by inch, slowly, her tight sheath adjusting to his girth and his length, until, at last, he'd buried himself inside her. Her breath had gone shallow as she held on to him. "*More*, Liam, I need *more*."

That was all he needed to hear. He began moving while, at the same time, allowing her to control the pace. She was new to this, lest he forget. Lest he give in to the hot demands roaring through him and properly ravish her. Still, his cock held out hope for a proper ravishment of Lady Saskia Calthorp's cunny, but he would allow her these moments to adjust to him.

Soon, he felt her impatience grow as she clutched at him, her hips angling to take him deeper, her legs wrapped around his waist, squeezing and pulling him tighter to her. She whimpered.

"All right, my love."

Again, relentless, he thrust, and she gasped, then she moaned, her pleasure sinking into him, amplifying his own pleasure and his desire, too. His desire to please her. He began moving with steady, deliberate intention, his own satisfaction a distant second to hers, as he moved inside her, his control increasing with every stroke as hers dissolved into mindless abandon. Perhaps this was the height of selfishness in a way, using her desire to gratify him. The presumptuousness of it...the arrogance of it.

He was guilty, then.

He wanted her mindless.

He wanted her enraptured.

He wanted her beguiled.

He wanted her besotted.

He wanted...*her*.

And if his long, hard, thick cock was a means toward the end of binding her to him, so be it.

What wasn't fair in love and war?

So, harder he took her, making her gasp...moan...whimper...cry out, "*Liam*," until he sensed it. Her need turning inward as she reached for elusive climax. He pulled back from her mouth long enough to lick two fingers of his right hand. "What are you doing?"

"You'll see."

He dipped his hand between their joined bodies. Slick, she was, as he found the nub of her sex, lightly grazing that sensitive place, even as he thrust inside her. "Oh," came a long, animal moan from parted lips. "That feels so...*delicious*."

With each brush of his fingers and with each thrust of his cock, she grew wilder, her want and need taking over, transforming her into a wanton. Her breath caught in her lungs, and he knew she'd reached that delicate in-between place, suspended inside her pleasure for one beat of the heart, then another, before tipping over and breaking with climax. She cried out her release into his shoulder, her cunny pulsing against his fingers...around his manhood. His release decided it had waited long enough and was suddenly upon him. He pulled from her, holding himself with one hand and grabbed a handkerchief from a pocket with the other.

She went still, her gaze arrested, as she watched him pleasure himself. "Oh, Liam," she muttered.

She liked that, watching him take himself in hand.

And he liked it too much that she liked it so much.

Too much, indeed, for climax burst through him, piercing white light shooting stars behind his eyes, through his veins, and he was spending into the square of linen and shouting his release. When he opened his eyes, it was to find hers unflinching upon him. "That was…" She shook her head. "I don't have words for it."

"Amazing?" A smile accustomed to charming pulled at his mouth. "The best experience of your entire life?"

Her silvery-blue eyes remained serious. Her mouth, too. "Yes."

He'd spoken the words as a tease, but she hadn't taken them so.

And he thought, perhaps, they hadn't been a tease, at all.

Perhaps they'd been a test.

This evening…the words they'd spoken…the pleasure and havoc they'd wreaked upon each other's bodies…it all held weight, and perhaps he wanted to know he wasn't the only one who felt thus.

"Yes," he said.

"Have I asked a question?"

"I will continue with the memoir."

He couldn't understand how he hadn't seen it earlier.

To continue with the memoir was to continue with Saskia— and *that* he couldn't not do.

Her eyes went wide. He'd surprised her. "You will?"

He nodded and stuffed the used handkerchief into his pocket. Then he stepped back and pulled her dress over her knees. "I shall finish the racing season."

"You're going to ride the St. Leger?"

"Aye."

For the first time in weeks, he again felt the master of his future.

It felt good, and it felt right.

With that renewed sense of purpose, he buttoned the falls of his trousers and adjusted her bodice. He stepped back to get a clear look at her—or as clear as he could manage given the paltry light. But it was difficult to concentrate on how she should look —*proper...virginal*—when she looked so deliciously love-tousled. Such a sight could have a man's cockstand returning to life—as it did now.

He exhaled and steadied himself. He knew what he must say... "You, Lady Saskia, are going home."

"I can't just go home," she protested. "I haven't spoken my farewells."

He pointed in the direction of the manse. "Everyone in that ballroom will take one look at you and think you've just been ravished."

"*But—*"

"And they wouldn't be wrong."

Her mouth snapped shut.

"One benefit that comes with being Bolton is I'm now in possession of a town coach, which will carry you home."

He took her hand, and she hopped down from the table. The rain had, blessedly, stopped. So, as they made their way back to the stables, it was beneath a yet-cloudy, but dry sky. After he'd handed her inside his carriage, she angled forward, "Aren't you coming, too?"

He shook his head. "Rake and Gemma threw this ball for me. I can't leave my sister in the lurch."

She searched his eyes, then nodded. "Goodbye, Liam. I'll see you at the St. Leger."

"London is a small town. You might just see me before then."

With that, he shut the door and called her Sloane Street address up to the driver. Then the horses were in motion, and he was watching the coach disappear around a corner and into the night.

A familiar pairing of words came to him.

Hopeless madness.

A month ago, until this very night, that was what Saskia had been to him—a madness with no hope in it.

Tonight, he'd had that madness confirmed.

But as for *hopeless*… Well, this madness of his might not be as hopeless as he'd once believed.

There might yet be uses for his newly acquired title.

Wooing the sister of a duke might be one of them.

CHAPTER TWENTY-ONE

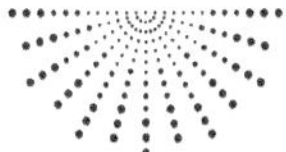

SIRENS CIRCULATING
LIBRARY, NEXT MORNING

*S*irens Circulating Library
    Next morning

It was a morning as ordinary as any other morning as Saskia ticked through the usual steps of her routine.

So, she should've been able to call it a usual morning.

Except she couldn't quite.

She wasn't her usual self.

Not after last night.

She was still alight with sensation—the blood a fluttery rush through her veins...nerve endings yet tingly...the utter, unrepentant ache in her sex...her mind whirring in circles, starting at the moment Liam found her in the duke's library until she was bundled in his carriage and rolling homeward.

Every.

Moment.

She'd awakened this morning—*awakened* might've been a stretch, as lying in bed and staring at shadows dancing across the ceiling couldn't exactly be called sleeping—only to find her pencil eager to fill page upon page with what couldn't accurately be described as fiction. Rambling, incoherent diary entry was more fitting.

It should've done the trick of settling her, mind and body.

It hadn't.

If anything, it had only het her up more.

As she passed through the reception room, arms laden with last week's periodicals to be archived, Mrs. Dunlevy waved her over to the front desk. "Will you have a look at this, Lady Saskia? We've not been open ten minutes and already a new member." New members ever brought that glimmer of excitement to Mrs. Dunlevy's eyes. "Liam Sutton."

Saskia's feet stuttered to a sudden stop.

It was that name.

Not Sutton.

The other one—*Liam*.

He was no longer Liam Cassidy, and Bolton was his title, not his surname. He would have a new surname, and it just might be...

In a trice, she was at the desk, plonking her stack of periodicals onto sturdy oak and leaning across the top, scanning the names in the register book. There it was in black and white—*Liam...Sutton*. "Can you describe him?" she asked, possibly demanded, her heart a hammer in her chest.

Mrs. Dunlevy's brow creased. "You can see him for yourself, Lady Saskia. He's in the Reading Room."

Saskia's lungs could manage neither an inhalation nor an exhalation, but she somehow emitted a squeaky, "Oh?"

Liam...*here*.

She didn't know this empirically—after all, she hadn't yet laid her own eyes upon him—but she *knew* it.

He was here.

She straightened and squared her shoulders. The breath she drew in wasn't as steadying as she would've liked it to have been beneath the watchful eye of Mrs. Dunlevy, who was considering her with a slight cant of the head and a bemused set of the mouth.

Saskia released her breath, somewhat steeled, and pointed her feet in the direction of the Reading Room. With its walnut paneled walls and plush leather wingbacks, this room was the most masculine of Sirens' rooms and its most popular. Though it wasn't yet quarter nine, already five members had settled into their customary chairs with their newspapers and periodicals open for their morning read.

Including their newest member who had chosen a chair close to the corner window.

It seemed *Liam Sutton* was, indeed, *Liam*.

He exuded an air of ease, an ankle idly resting on the opposing thigh, as morning sun streamed through clear glass panes, golden light picking out a few sun-bleached streaks of hair…illustrating the cut angles of cheekbones, jaw, and chin… imbuing the gold-flecked green of his eyes with a near other-worldly glow. A man who stood out in any room.

One couldn't ignore a man like him—or, at least, she couldn't.

And though he wasn't reading a newspaper or a periodical, he was, in fact, reading.

A book, to be precise.

Curiosity pulled her forward.

What would Liam be reading so intently at quarter nine in the morning, anyway?

Through her spectacles, she squinted. The next instant, her mind registered what her eyes were seeing and she gasped, audibly, drawing no few reproachful stares.

Liam's gaze lifted in its own time. No mistaking the mischief that twinkled within—for he read none other than *When a Lady Dares* by Harriet LaPlume. "Lady Saskia."

"Lord Bolton." Too gobsmacked, she was, to say much more.

He held up the book. "I've heard high praise about this author from my sister."

Saskia swallowed.

"Not my usual reading material, mind you." The bloody man was utterly at his ease, and here were her palms sweating. He snapped the book shut and balanced it on his knee. "Harriet LaPlume possesses great skill with the written word."

The tips of Saskia's ears surely glowed scarlet—from mortification or flattery, she wasn't sure.

Actually, she was.

The tips of her ears were equal parts mortified *and* flattered.

"I'm glad to hear you're enjoying Sirens' offerings, my lord."

"Oh, aye." The man was having fun. "Shall I read you a favorite passage?"

Without a staying thought, she closed the distance between them and snatched the book off his knee, "No!"

Her exclamation garnered a few more glares, and even a few smatterings of irritated grumblings, but Saskia had no regrets. Under no circumstances would Liam be reading her words aloud to her.

Simply, *no*.

From his wingback, he continued to observe her, the amusement in his eyes abated not a whit. "Your loss, Lady Saskia."

The cheek!

Though her ears burned and her heart pounded, she recovered herself sufficiently to say, "We thank you for becoming a member of Sirens. Please let us know if we can accommodate any of your particular reading preferences."

Still, he observed her—and she felt so very observed.

Of a sudden, he uncrossed his ankle and shot to his feet. "Will you come with me, Lady Saskia?"

"Come with you?" Her brow dug into her forehead. "Come with you where?"

"Just out front. I have something to show you."

"All right," she said, slowly.

He didn't require any other answer as he led her from the

Reading Room, then through reception and past Mrs. Dunlevy's raised eyebrows, and out the front door. Saskia stepped onto the top step and considered Sloane Street before her with its usual mix of pedestrians, carriages, and tradesfolk with their various conveyances. She hadn't worked out what Liam was trying to show her until he reached a lad holding the reins of a sturdy-looking gray gelding and a pretty chestnut filly. Liam stopped beside the filly and lifted his hand as if he were presenting her. "Lady Saskia, meet Peony."

Saskia's head tipped to the side. "Why am I meeting her?"

"Because she's yours for the day."

"Mine?"

"Yours."

"What am I to do with a horse?"

"Ride her, of course."

"As you know, I can't ride."

"Ah, but that's about to change."

"It is?"

"It is, for you are about to have a lesson."

"I am?"

"You are."

An incredulous laugh escaped her. "Presumptuous."

He shrugged, undaunted. "My sister trained her herself, so Peony is a reliable girl."

The fact remained that a reliable horse was still a horse.

The thought must've shown in her expression, for he said, "You can trust me, Saskia."

"I…" She swallowed against the reflexive response his words provoked. Then she said it anyway. "I do trust you."

The amplitude of his smile increased. "Do you have a riding habit?"

"Actually, I do." Several, in fact, that had never once been worn. Just as all ladies had ballgowns and court gowns and all other manner of dresses that weren't of much use in the general scheme, they also had riding habits.

"I'll wait here while you change. Oh, and wear sturdy boots."

Saskia should've protested or said she had a busy morning ahead of her...*something*...but, instead, she pivoted on her heel and walked—*dashed*, really—straight back into Sirens, avoiding eye contact with Mrs. Dunlevy and not stopping until she was upstairs in her bedroom. In a matter of seconds, she was stripped down to chemise, stays, and stockings and reaching for the deep crimson riding habit she'd always especially liked but never had the occasion to wear. Fortunately, the long row of jet buttons was at the front of the bodice, and she was able to dress without the assistance of Alice.

It was only after she'd tugged sturdy boots onto her feet that she hesitated. Slowly, she made her way to the dressing-table mirror and met her eyes in the reflection.

What was she doing?

This was madness.

She should remove this riding habit, don her morning gown, march herself downstairs, and inform Liam that she had matters to attend and a day to get on with.

But she knew she wouldn't do any of those things.

What she knew she would do was march herself downstairs, inform Mrs. Dunlevy and her raised eyebrows that she was in charge of Sirens for the rest of the morning, and agree to anything and everything Liam had planned for her.

Even if that meant riding a horse.

CHAPTER TWENTY-TWO

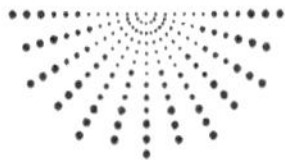

The longer Liam stood on Sloane Street, holding the reins of two horses—he'd sent the lad back to Rake and Gemma's manse on Grosvenor Square—he wondered if he'd done the correct thing in coming to Sirens unannounced and uninvited.

Saskia was a lady who had her life ordered just so and she liked it that way. Surprise visits from men bearing gifts in the form of horse-riding lessons had likely never once figured into her day.

But after last night, he hadn't been able to stop thinking about her. For the obvious reason—he yet ached for her with a ferocity that bordered on desperation—and for another, altogether different reason.

She couldn't ride.

And that couldn't stand.

He had a suspicion that if Saskia ever sat a horse, she would immediately take to it. For though he wasn't sure she was aware, she had a fair bit of daring inside her.

In the clear-eyed light of morning, it had all come together in his mind. Saskia needed to learn how to ride, and he needed to see her again, blast the duties of the earldom. They could wait one more day. Besides, after last night, he couldn't leave her the next day again, like he'd done after the Derby. It had weighed on him, that, these long weeks since. He wouldn't be making the same mistake again.

So, he stood here, with the filly Peony and his gelding Homer with what was surely a ridiculous grin on his face because it appeared his ploy might've worked and he would get to spend time with the woman he was hopelessly mad for.

However, after a full ten minutes had passed and still she hadn't reemerged from Sirens, doubt began to prey upon him. Had she reconsidered? For every time the front door opened, it was a gent who stepped through and gave Liam a questioning lift of an eyebrow before going on his way and Liam's heart had to settle down all over again.

Four times, this happened, but with the fifth opening of the door, a miracle occurred and Saskia stepped through, looking smart and lovely in her crimson wool riding habit, the unfussy style and rich color suiting her. As she descended the steps, slipping black kid gloves onto her hands, a shallow line formed between her eyebrows. "We're not having our lesson here on the street, are we?"

He shook his head. "It's just a short walk to Rotten Row. We'll have the lesson there."

The vertical line didn't release. "*Rotten Row?* I don't fancy entertaining all of society with my first riding lesson."

He had a ready answer for this. "Do you believe any member of the *haut ton* is yet out of bed after having danced their feet off at Rake and Gemma's ball last night?"

There. The vertical line disappeared—*almost.* "You and I are out of bed."

"Well, Lady Saskia"—he knew the power of his best charming smile, and he employed it now—"you and I are the special two, aren't we?"

You and I...the special two.

He hadn't planned those words, but how he liked them when applied to him and this serious woman who was, increasingly, the only thing he considered worth thinking about.

Her silvery-blue eyes searched his, something in the air between them releasing.

He dug into his pocket and held out a chunk of carrot. "Offer this to Peony on the flat of your palm and watch her become your best friend."

Saskia did as instructed, a delighted laugh escaping her as Peony's lips gently took the treat.

"Now," he instructed, "give her nose a scratch."

Homer, clearly feeling left out, nosed Liam's shoulder, demanding his treat, too. Treats properly dispensed, Liam handed Peony's reins to Saskia and they set off up Sloane Street toward Hyde Park.

"Sirens is the best circulating library I've ever set foot in." He didn't say the words just to fill the air; he meant them.

She shot him a penetrating glance. "Have you set foot in many circulating libraries?"

"I have. My mam was a devoted reader, in fact. And your library, Lady Saskia, is the best." Before she could wave the compliment aside, he added, "*And* you publish books."

"It isn't all me." What might've been a pleased smile tickled about her mouth. "Sirens is a partnership with my sister Viveca. We each bring our talents to the enterprise. Once Viveca is on a mission, nothing will stop her. It's useful to have someone like that in a business."

Liam chuckled. "Oh, yes, I've been one of Lady Viveca's missions." He gave a bemused shake of his head. "I'm still not sure that I explicitly agreed to the memoir."

"Viveca's rhetorical skills are paralleled by none," returned Saskia, shaking her head with a laugh. "If she'd been born a man, she would've gone down in history as England's greatest barrister."

There was yet a point Liam wanted to make. "But Harriet LaPlume, is all you, isn't she?"

"Aye, she is."

"So, you operate not just one, but two businesses *and* you write novels. Every hour of your day must be spoken for before you even rise from bed."

"Most of them." She shrugged. "But that's how I like my life."

"And on top of all that, you're a lady."

"I don't see how that impacts matters."

"Only because you haven't allowed it to."

She angled her head and met his gaze. "I'm a lady. Not much is expected from me. But *you*," she continued, "are an earl. I suppose an earldom comes with a different set of expectations."

Liam blew out a frustrated breath. Leave it to this woman to strike directly at the heart of the matter. "Bloody time-consuming, it's been, and I don't understand why. Have you seen the betting post at any racecourse in England? Abundant with not just earls, but dukes, marquesses, viscounts, and barons, too. Then there are the balls, musicales, country house parties, and daily appearances at one's club. Insubstantial obligations that can fill every hour of a man's day."

Saskia nodded in agreement. "You should try endless rounds of afternoon teas and shopping for insubstantial obligations. In their world, there is no care whether one is a good person or an educated person. They place a high value on the ideal of the *accomplished person*, but what does that truly mean? That a lady can do perfect needlework? Or a lord can haul himself to his club once a day?" She shook her head. "I have to be more than that."

"Saskia, you *are* more than that."

She didn't hesitate. "And so are you, Liam. That's why you're having difficulty reconciling yourself to the role of earl. You're a man of industry, so you're approaching the earldom from that perspective. Not because society requires as much of you—they don't give a fig if you squander it all at the betting post or on a toss of the dice—but you require it of yourself."

Warmth spread through him. This woman more than liked him; she admired him. And within her admiration existed a kinship, for he admired her, too. Further, they shared the improbable luck that this life—the life of an aristocrat—had been thrust upon them both, hadn't it? They were different people, to be sure, with different goals and aspirations that were personal to them each, but at a profound level, they shared a core sameness that felt fundamental and important.

"I've had a little more time than you to consider this," she continued, "and I've calculated but one substantial, immutable obligation of an aristocrat."

"Even one?"

"Precisely one." She cleared her throat for dramatic effect. "To beget more members of the *haut ton*, so it doesn't cease to exist."

"If that's the case," he scoffed, "then I fear the *haut ton* is going to be sorely disappointed with the new Earl of Bolton."

"I cannot imagine that will be the case."

"Well, to beget a legitimate heir, one needs a wife. A fact I've become all too aware of this last month."

"Fortunately for you, my lord," she said on a laugh, "yours is a condition you shouldn't find too difficult to remedy. I'm not sure there is an unmarried woman in England who would refuse your proposal of marriage."

He lifted an eyebrow. "Not a single one?"

A breathless moment ticked past. It was a cheeky question, and he shouldn't have asked it, but he hadn't been able to help himself.

She cleared her throat. "So, there is your problem solved."

"With respect, I beg to differ." He was under no obligation to speak further on the subject, yet he continued. "It has never been an intention of mine to beget children, heirs or otherwise."

Was that a gasp he heard? Were his words so shocking?

Surprise flashed within Saskia's silvery-blue eyes. "I can't imagine not having children."

Now it was him suppressing shock. But he understood he needed to go carefully... "I would've thought you're so busy with your various enterprises that children might not be for you."

"Oh, they're definitely for me." Within her gaze shone certainty, which only underscored her words. "After Gabriel and Tessa started their families, I knew that was what I wanted." She gave a little shrug. "I suppose I'm greedy and want the world with business, writing, and family. I might not succeed, but I shall try."

If he were being dead honest, Liam didn't like what he was hearing. Except, it wasn't his place to like or dislike Saskia's goals for herself. Her wants and desires were hers, and she was allowed them.

What he didn't like—again, if he were being honest—was that until this moment, he'd thought his goals and her goals might just align.

And they didn't.

"But, Liam?" she asked, angling so she could get a clear look at him.

They'd stopped at Piccadilly, waiting for traffic to clear so they could cross with Peony and Homer. Liam gave them each a treat before turning his attention to Saskia. Really, he'd been buying time, for he knew that look. She was about to ask him a question he might not like.

"Yes?"

"Why don't you want children?"

And there it was—the question she had no right to ask and the question he was under no obligation to answer.

There were details of his life he hadn't yet shared with her, repugnant details. He hadn't been keeping them a secret by not telling her, but, now, he felt if he didn't, he would be. And while he was shaky on what was transpiring between him and this woman, he didn't want secrets threatening their connection. "You know that until a month ago," he began, "I was the bastard of an aristocrat."

A sympathetic smile shone in her eyes. "I and all of London."

He nodded. "But what you might not know is that I was raised in his household."

Her brow furrowed. "Oh?"

"My mam was his cook. The countess was his wife. And Gemma and I were his bastard children. Bolton's life was ordered just as he wanted it."

"I don't understand how that…*worked*."

An abbreviated version of events was all that would be necessary. "Bolton married my mam in Ireland, promptly thought better of it, returned to England, married the countess, then tried to beget heirs and couldn't. So, he fetched his first wife from Ireland, immediately got her with child, and she bore him twins."

"And the countess?"

"She accepted the arrangement."

"Did she know about the first marriage?"

"Not until after his death."

"That must've been devastating."

"Oh, she's devastated."

"What a strange upbringing that must've been."

"I can see it now." He shook his head. "But at the time, it just felt like life, if you take my meaning."

She gave a slow nod, her mind clearly working. "Children don't have any other point of reference."

He'd known she would understand. "Aye. Bolton brought in tutors and had Gemma and me educated, I'll give him that. But I won't give him much more. He controlled us all. Made us feel our lives weren't our own, but only extensions of his. Gemma would call us the shadow children. The children who weren't supposed to be. The countess acted like we didn't exist."

"That's abhorrent." Outrage and revulsion flashed within Saskia's eyes. "You were blameless children."

"After Mam passed, Gemma and I escaped."

"Escaped?"

"Bolton never got out of the habit of viewing us as his. Such is the corrupting nature of total power. No living being should exercise complete domination over another living being." There was the entirety of Liam's beliefs about life in short and plain. "What's clear now is that Bolton was hedging his bets. His marriage to Mam was legitimate, and so were Gemma and I, but if the countess had borne a son, he would've taken the Irish marriage certificate out of his private safe and burned it, destroying my legitimacy along with it."

"But the countess didn't provide an heir."

"And now I'm Bolton."

Would the wonder he felt at that strange outcome never cease to sound in his voice when he spoke it?

"And the countess?" Saskia's eyes made it clear she wasn't nearly finished asking questions. "How does she fit into every-thing now?"

"I asked her where she wanted to live out the rest of her days. She said she'd always preferred Bolton's house near Dover."

That got a lift of Saskia's eyebrows. "After the way she treated you all your life?"

"She thought I would turf her out on her arse. That's how highly she thought of me."

"So, you proved her wrong."

"Aye."

"Good."

"The Dover house was unentailed, so I was free to give it to her, along with the dowry she brought into the marriage. I don't like the countess, and I never will, but she, too, suffered in that household. And she continues to suffer. I won't add to it."

"No living being under your care will ever suffer, will they?"

"Not if I can help it."

"See?"

"See what?"

"That's why you can't be that other sort of earl."

"What other sort?"

"The insubstantial sort. Yes, you're charming and handsome, so society enjoys having you within its ranks." Fervor shimmered about her. "But, Liam, all beneath your care will be looked after. You've done it for your horses all these years, and now you will be that sort of earl. You're a man of substance."

Again, that feeling of closeness...of intimacy...washed through him.

It wasn't because Saskia was writing his memoir that she knew him.

Or that they'd tupped—*twice*.

This kinship linked them at the place of the soul.

A complex thought for ten in the morning.

His mouth quirked into a smile, the one that made his eyes sparkle. "Charming and handsome, you say?"

If he wasn't mistaken, that was a blush pinking her cheeks. She exhaled and shot him an exasperated scowl. "You know this about yourself."

"One never tires of hearing it, nonetheless."

A wry shake of the head was her answer.

He could accept a compliment. His charm, looks, affability, and skill with horses had won him plenty over the years. But it was the deeper compliment she'd paid him that struck home now.

It wasn't merely that this woman saw him.

She saw qualities in him he'd never seen himself.

When the traffic cleared enough for them to cross Piccadilly with the horses, he led them to a cut-through that opened directly onto Rotten Row.

"Here we are," he said. "Ready for your first riding lesson?"

CHAPTER TWENTY-THREE

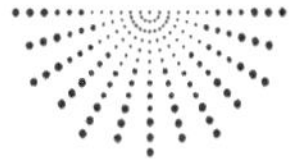

Saskia might've gasped, Liam couldn't be sure.

What he was sure of, however, was that over the course of their walk and conversation the dreaded riding lesson had completely slipped her mind.

Well, it hadn't slipped his.

"I think so." Her words emerged more question than enthusiastic *yes*.

Which wasn't the most auspicious start.

"What we're doing now—simply walking the horses—can be your first riding lesson, if you like."

She turned his offer over in her mind for a moment. "No, you're right. I should learn to ride." Her intention audibly firmed by the word. "And if I'm going to learn to ride, then I want my teacher to be you."

Liam liked those last words. They were words a man could bask in. And perhaps he would, later. Now, he had a riding lesson to teach.

"And see? Your secret will be safe." He gestured toward the surrounding park and specifically Rotten Row with its long, dual rows of plane trees. "Not a single aristocrat in sight."

Still, nerves skittered about Saskia. As she was the most logical person Liam had ever met, he intuited the best approach —to talk her through it. "First, you'll give Peony another treat." He slipped Saskia a chunk of apple to offer the filly. "Now, we'll check that the straps are secure." He led her to Peony's flank and confirmed all was right and tight.

Saskia soaked in his every word and instruction, showing herself to be responsive and teachable.

Like a good filly.

He would keep that observation to himself.

"Now"—he was unable to put off the inevitable any longer— "it's time you put your newfound knowledge into practice."

"Into practice?"

She was buying time. He could only imagine her mouth had gone dry.

"It's time to mount."

He took a step toward her, and she froze. "What are you doing?"

"You'll need my assistance."

"Oh…ah…hmm."

"Saskia." He held her gaze steady. "There's an attuning that happens between horse and rider when you allow it to happen, all right?"

She nodded, though her eyes gave her away. She didn't believe him.

He handed her Peony's reins. "You'll hold these with one hand, and the pommel with the other."

She did as instructed.

He squatted and laced his fingers together. "As we don't have a mounting block, I'll give you a leg up. You'll place your left foot in my hands." When she hesitated, he said with a note of command in his voice, "Go on." Tentatively, she followed his instruction. "Now, on three, I'll lift and you'll push off, then you'll hook your right leg over the pommel. Simple as that."

Her brow lifted with disbelief. "*Simple?*"

"*Simple.*" He gave that a moment to settle, then got straight to it. "*One...two...three.*"

And like that, she was up in the saddle, her right leg hooked on the pommel, her left foot secure in the footrest, an anxious laugh breathing past parted lips, an expression of plain amazement on her face. "I...I did it."

As she stared down at him from her perch, a light flickered in her eyes—*trust.* She'd given over and trusted him. Trust went two ways. Horses had taught him that much. There was trust earned and trust given. There couldn't be one without the other. And this woman...she trusted him.

He knew down to the marrow of his bones that he would never betray this woman's trust.

That was what the light in her eyes said—she knew as much down to the marrow of *her* bones.

Liam swung into the saddle of his mount. "I'm going to give one click, and Homer and Peony will start walking. All right?"

Though trepidation skittered in her eyes, she nodded. He could only imagine her palms had gone sweaty. He clicked his tongue, and the horses eased into motion as they'd been trained to do. After a few steps, he asked, "How does it feel?"

"It feels..."

Liam found himself holding his breath.

She shook her head with a stunned laugh. "Wonderful."

Relief spread through him. "We'll make a horsewoman of you yet."

More laughter sprang from her, and with that laughter, he sensed all her remaining tension release. "Will we go any faster today?" she asked.

"Do you want to?"

"I think I might."

He could see she'd gotten the feel of Peony's motion, her body moving with rather than against it. The attuning he'd spoken of, she'd found it. She was ready to take the pace into a trot.

They reached an offshoot bridleway that veered left. "Let's take this path."

Soon, they found themselves in a more overgrown part of Hyde Park. None of the park was actually wild, but here it was less tamed and less open to public speculation. Here, it was possible to pretend they weren't in the center of a teeming metropolis.

Here, it could be just him and Saskia.

"So, Lady Saskia," he said, playful, "you would like to go faster?"

"Oh, yes."

He reined in Homer and allowed Saskia and Peony to take the lead. "Now," he called out, "give two clicks of your tongue to signal to Peony that you would like her to increase her gait to a trot."

A moment passed while Saskia considered his words and decided if *faster* was what she truly wanted. Then she clicked her tongue and Peony increased her pace. Behind, he waited. He would know fairly quickly if Saskia had taken it too far, too fast —and he would be there if she needed him.

Then he heard it—laughter trailing in her wake. A wild note trilled through that laughter, which shouldn't have surprised him. Here was the part of herself that Saskia accessed when she wrote —the very same place from which Arabella sprang.

The truth was he'd now read two of her books. He'd just been having a bit of fun with her earlier in the library. Her writing was beautiful and insightful—*observed*. This woman had observed life and those flowing through it alongside her. But, also, her writing possessed *this*—daring...wildness...that which ventured beyond restraint.

And that was her now—a daring woman—discovering her love of riding.

It had been important to him that she feel thus, but he hadn't comprehended how important until this exact moment.

For in loving *this*—in loving riding—she loved a part of him, didn't she?

FREEDOM.

The wind in her hair…crisp morning air in her lungs…Peony striding beneath her—*striding* might've been a stretch—Saskia felt free in a way she never had in her entire life.

It wasn't only the ease of movement one experienced with a horse at one's command, but, for example, she'd never once entered this untamed part of Hyde Park, a prospect that would've taken too long on foot. She was a busy person. But on the back of a horse, one could see the world. Alexander the Great might've been on to something with his equally great warhorse, Bucephalus.

Yet it wasn't only about ease of movement and distances covered. Communion existed between horse and rider. *An attuning* was what Liam called it, and he was right. Through some strange alchemy, she and Peony had become attuned to one another, and from there flowed a feeling of joy Saskia had never expected. She'd always kept her distance from horses. Simply, they were too big and humans were too small. She'd never understood how humans came out with all their limbs intact in that equation.

But, now, she understood it.

A trill of laughter—a giggle, really—erupted from her and floated in her wake.

"Enjoying yourself, are you?" came from behind her.

"Oh, aye."

Abandoned to joy, that was her in this moment.

Liam caught up to her, so they now rode side by side. "You're a natural horsewoman, Lady Saskia."

Yet another giggle released from her. How free she felt. "When you invaded my library this morning—"

"*Invaded?* A rather combative way of putting it. Is this how you speak to all new members of Sirens?"

She cut him a saucy glance. *Her...saucy.* "I wasn't sure what to expect," she continued. "Then you said there was to be a riding lesson." She shook her head. "The thing is when I became a lady, I suffered through all manner of lessons." She held up one finger at a time as she counted them off. "Dancing...comportment...tea serving...needlework...oh, you wouldn't believe all the lessons young ladies must suffer."

"But never riding lessons."

"I put my foot down there."

"And now have you experienced a change of heart?"

She twisted to meet his amused gaze. "Liam, I love it. I love... *this.*"

What word other than *this* would've followed had she not hesitated in the split of a second before it passed her lips?

For a word other than *this* seemed to want to follow the two words preceding it.

She swallowed that word down. "And"—she gathered her wits before she became entirely carried away and made a complete fool of herself—"you've been riding since you were a child?"

"Oh, aye, Gemma and I were practically barn cats we spent so much time in the stables."

"Who is the older twin—you or Gemma?" She was making light conversation—the sort of conversation she never made—and found herself enjoying it.

"Gemma is the elder." He snorted. "And believe me when I say she doesn't let me forget it."

"Aren't sisters wonderful?" She gave a teasing roll of the eyes, even as she felt the sentiment in all seriousness.

"Aye, that they are." He felt the same in both regards, that was what his eyes told her.

Really, they felt the same in a great number of ways, didn't they?

"So, Saskia…"

"Yes?"

"What time would you like your daily riding lesson?"

She felt her brow lift. "My daily riding lesson?"

Her question went ignored. "Since you write and tend Sirens in the mornings, I'm thinking afternoons are your best time. Let's say three o'clock?"

"But aren't you leaving London? So, how…" she stammered, "who…?"

He nodded as if she'd just agreed. "Tomorrow afternoon at three o'clock, a groom from Rake and Gemma's stable will arrive with Peony and give you a riding lesson. I know just the lad for the job."

His high-handedness and, frankly, arrogance should've had her shimmering with outrage and giving him a proper dressing down that he would presume to order her days. An invasion, indeed!

But that was her old self.

The self she'd been before this riding lesson…before last night…before the night of the Derby…before Arabella had introduced herself to him all those months ago.

A change had occurred within her.

A change that had sneaked in when she hadn't been paying attention.

Again, the question came to her: was there any risk she wouldn't take if it was Liam doing the asking?

"Saskia," he said. His charm fallen away, in its place, fervency.

While charm might attract, it was fervency that dug in beneath the surface and grabbed hold of one's soul.

"You love riding," he continued, "so why shouldn't you do what you love?"

Words like that held the power to take a lady's breath away.

She dragged her gaze from his—she had to—but the sight before her had her stomach falling to her feet. He must've guided them around—she'd been too heady with the ecstasies of riding to notice—so they'd circled back to the head of the bridleway and were now returning to Rotten Row.

"Oh." No hiding her disappointment in that *oh*.

He shot her a smile. "You'll be too sore to ride tomorrow, if you don't stop soon. It's been nearly an hour."

"That long?"

A dry laugh sounded through his nose. "Oh, you've got the horse madness. Gets in your blood, it does."

"Oh, dear."

"No cure for it, I'm afraid."

Ahead, she couldn't help noticing the park was more populated than it had been earlier. And those who now populated Rotten Row were turning their heads in the direction of Lady Saskia Calthorp and the new Earl of Bolton. Widened eyes and titillated gossip would follow, Saskia had no doubt.

Past them, she and Liam rode. Then it was across Piccadilly and into the quieter environs of Sloane Street. Sure, they'd been noted by a few fashionable people, but those curious gazes held not an iota of sway with her. Tongues might wag, but what were those tongues to her?

Once they reached Sirens, Liam expertly dismounted before coming to stand beside Peony, his head angled back to meet Saskia's gaze. "My lady."

Sudden tension twisted through her. Of course, she was to allow him to help her dismount. *Of course.* She was a lady, and he a gentleman. It was nothing scandalous. What was scandalous, however, was the way her body was reacting to the very thought as she unhooked her right leg and reached out, tipping forward until her hands found purchase on broad shoulders, her fingers digging into corded muscle as her body followed. If it wasn't precisely a graceless tumble as her feet hit the sidewalk, it was a near thing.

But she hardly noticed.

Her feet on the ground and likely steady enough to support her—likely, *not* certainly—her hands remained on his shoulders and his hands on her waist. His mouth was but inches from hers.

A kiss longed to be.

The sort of sweet kiss where their lips would press together for an instant, maybe two, then part wanting more.

The sort of kiss that should've been their first, though she couldn't quite bring herself to regret the first kiss that had been.

In the air between their mouths was the kiss that could've been, but, of course, couldn't be.

Her hands slid off his shoulders, and she took a step back, leaving his hands no choice but to release her. Her eyes held his steadily. "Thank you for introducing me to riding."

His eyes held hers as steadily. "My pleasure."

She could continue with the *thank yous* and the inevitable *farewells*, but she had something more substantial yet to say to this man. "It might not be my place to say this, but I feel I must."

"Saskia, you're allowed to say anything you like to me."

He might reconsider his permission once she said… "You must have children."

The words hit the air like cannon shot, leaden, but not without momentum as he subtly recoiled from their impact.

"But not because of the earldom." If she was to have but one chance at this conversation, then she would give it her all. "You're a good teacher, Liam. You're patient and kind. When you spoke of your father, you mentioned the corrupting nature of total power. But don't you see that's not you? That's not how you would handle your children." When he looked as if he might protest, she continued, "The way you manage your horses

without whip or spur, but rather with guidance and encouragement, that's the sort of father you shall be."

He didn't look as if he fully believed her words, but as if he
were, at least, considering them…considering *her*. "So," he said, at
last, "all roads lead back to the topic of wife."

She blinked. Her eyebrows crinkled together. "I suppose one
would need one."

"A wife who would like loads and loads of children."

Somehow, her fervent, heartfelt argument had veered off
course. The conversation they were now having wasn't the one
she'd begun. "I suppose that won't be too difficult for you."

"Won't it?"

She swallowed against a throat gone parched. "You must
know half the women in the *ton* are madly in love with you."

He snorted. "They're not in love with *me*. They're in love with
an image of me."

Though the words hadn't been directed at her, they stung.
She'd numbered amongst the ranks of those women until
recently—until she'd gotten to know him. "I have another confession," she somehow said.

"Should I become a priest?"

"Definitely not."

Wickedness glinted in his eyes. "What's your confession, Lady
Saskia?"

"That was me."

"Pardon?"

"I was one of those women." Oh, how could she possibly bring
herself to say what she must say… "That first night, at the
Drunken Piebald—"

"I have a vague memory of that night…"

She steeled herself, unwilling to let humor distract her. "It was
why I avoided meeting you for years—you were correct on that
point when you asked why we'd never met. It's why I assumed
the identity of Arabella. Because, you see, I was one of those

women who saw Liam Cassidy and…and…" She inhaled. "And liked what she saw." She exhaled. "And, yes, it was the image of you that formed the basis of my, *erm*, liking, which doesn't make me much different from all those other women who swoon at the sight of you."

"Have you ever swooned, Saskia?"

"Metaphorically."

His eyes narrowed. "And now that you know me?"

"I like you differently."

"*Differently?*"

"More."

She'd never known the effect truth could have on time—that it could make it stop. Or, at least, that was how it felt as she stood on this stretch of sidewalk, her breath caught in her lungs between an inhalation and an exhalation, facing Liam with the truth between them.

At last, he said, "On the subject of wives. Any wife of mine would know me for who I truly am. It's only then that one can give love and feel it in return."

She nodded. "An attuning."

"Aye, Saskia, an attuning."

Though she'd written many such moments of a hero staring intently into the eyes of a heroine, she'd secretly thought such moments might share more in common with fantasy than reality. But, now, she saw how wrong she'd been.

To a point.

In her books, her hero and heroine always found the exact right words to say to one another. But out here, in reality, she struggled and asked questions like, "Weren't you supposed to have left London today?"

A tick of time beat past as he found his footing around this conversational pivot. "Aye, but…"

"But you couldn't leave knowing that I couldn't ride a horse?"

He smiled, as if caught out. "There's a village fête I'm expected to attend," he explained. "Then I'm off to Somerton to see Morningstar prepared for the journey north to Doncaster."

Ah. "So, you're definitely seeing the season through."

"My last." One couldn't mistake the note of loss in his voice. The career that would've been cut short. "I had a good run on the turf."

She nodded. "Better than most."

"And you will be there?" His gaze had lost none of its fervency. "You'll be in Doncaster for the St. Leger?"

"I wouldn't miss it."

He searched her eyes, and must've found what he was looking for. "Until the St. Leger, milady," he said, properly, and even bowed. Then he grabbed Peony's reins before mounting Homer with a smooth, fluid motion. He gave Saskia a final tip of the hat, then clicked his tongue, easing Homer into a walk with Peony trailing half a length behind.

It was with a flutter in her stomach and a lightness in her step that Saskia walked into Sirens. Mrs. Dunlevy's lifted eyebrows greeted her, but she simply nodded at the woman and kept walking and didn't stop until she was in her private rooms upstairs.

No promises had been spoken between her and Liam.

Yet something bound them.

Something more than the physical.

Something more than liking.

It was that sameness.

It was that understanding.

It was that attuning.

CHAPTER TWENTY-FOUR

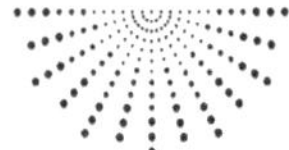

DONCASTER RACECOURSE,
TWO WEEKS LATER

The St. Leger horse race had a fearsome reputation for being cold and rainy and utterly miserable, and Saskia had traveled north prepared for such an eventuality. But morning had blossomed into an absolute beauty of an autumn afternoon—crystalline blue skies…air just crisp enough to put a spring into the step of human and horse alike…not even the whisper of a breeze.

"Perfect race conditions," stated the Duke of Rakesley from his seat down the row.

"Aye," returned Lord Branwell, the war-hero husband of Rakesley's sister, Lady Artemis. "A mudder won't take it today."

Variations on this exact conversation had been swirling around Saskia all day. Of course, as she was seated in the top section of the grandstand where owners and various interested, aristocratic parties of the horse racing world had their boxes, the weather would've been a popular topic.

Twelve days ago, Saskia hadn't yet broached the topic of the St. Leger with Viveca when a letter had arrived in the post—an invitation. Actually, two invitations. The first invited her and her family to stay at Endcliffe Grange as the guests of Lord and Lady

Branwell Mallory. A quick think caught the connection to Liam. Lady Branwell was also known as Lady Artemis, who was the sister of the Duke of Rakesley, who was the husband of the Duchess, Gemma, who was the twin sister of Liam. After a wretched two hours of deliberation, Saskia had accepted the invitation.

The second invitation had arrived a day later. She and her party were cordially invited to attend Sir Abstrupus Bottomley's 1st Annual St. Leger Soirée. A consultation with *Debrett's* had led her to the, *ahem*, bottom of that invitation. As it happened, Sir Abstrupus Bottomley was the neighbor of Lord and Lady Branwell.

Thus, Saskia found herself at Doncaster Racecourse on the day of the St. Leger, sitting with her family to her left—Gabriel and Celia; Tessa and Julian, who also happened to be bosom friends with the Duke of Rakesley; and Viveca and Blaze—and Liam's family and friends to her right. The Duke and Duchess of Rakesley—the duchess bore such a similarity of appearance to Liam that Saskia couldn't look at her without thinking of him… which led her down entire rabbit warrens of contemplation— Lady Artemis and Lord Branwell; Lady Artemis's bosom friend, Lady Beatrix, and her husband Mr. Blake Deverill, known to the *ton* as Lord Devil for obvious reasons related to his dashing dark handsomeness and incredible wealth, and for less obvious reasons that an outside observer could only guess at, but that Lady Beatrix would certainly know very intimately.

The two contingents talked amongst themselves and over Saskia, who felt like the only still point in all Doncaster.

"This will be a two-horse race, mark my words," stated Lady Beatrix. "Morningstar and Lady Midnight."

"Odds are favoring Morningstar, I reckon," chimed Blaze.

"And why do you reckon that?" asked Celia with a bit more fire than was strictly necessary. She could get fiery about her horses.

Blaze didn't rise to the flash of temper. "He took the Derby, didn't he?"

"And the Two Thousand Guineas," said Rakesley over Saskia's head.

"And you got Liam Cassidy—oh, right, the Earl of Bolton—riding him." Blaze shrugged. "He won the Race of the Century five years back. He'll be the favorite."

"On race day, however, anything can happen," observed Julian. Saskia's brother by law was ever the diplomat. "And Lady Midnight thrives on the longer courses."

"Aye," said Lady Artemis, "my money's on the lady." She turned to her brother. "Sorry, Rake."

The duke grunted. "Your disloyalty has been duly noted, sister."

"Lady Artemis," said Saskia, catching the lady's attention, "I must thank you for so generously having us stay at Endcliffe Grange."

Lady Artemis and Lord Branwell had already left for Doncaster by the time Saskia had arrived with Viveca and Blaze. Tessa and Julian had arrived a few days before them.

"And you received the invitation to Sir Abstrupus's soirée?" asked Lady Artemis.

"I did."

"Sir Abstrupus doesn't leave the Roost, so we must go to him." She shook her head as if helpless against facts beyond her control. "And the man loves to host a grand gala. Still, you'll find Sir Abstrupus's hospitality to be slightly unusual."

Saskia's brow lifted. "Oh?"

"The old rascal's hospitality is guided by his whims, which are myriad and unpredictable," groused Lord Branwell. With the scar that bisected his right cheekbone, he was as ruggedly handsome as any war hero in a novel ever was. Saskia wondered if it would be rude to pull her journal and pencil from her reticule so she could jot down a few notes.

"You'll do well to heed Bran's advice regarding Sir Abstrupus," chimed Lady Artemis. "The old troublemaker is his godparent."

Truly, England was a small island.

Lord Branwell held up a finger. "Just don't drink any of the teas he offers you."

Saskia felt her brow gather. "All right," she said, slowly.

"You'll have to trust us on this."

The conversation continued around them as Lady Beatrix caught Blaze's attention. "You don't know something the rest of us don't, do you, Blaze?"

Cheating. She was asking if Blaze had caught wind of any turf skullduggery.

And, of course, Lady Beatrix had every right to ask Blaze such a question for, though it wasn't widely known in society, everyone in this group knew that she and Blaze shared a father and were half-siblings from opposite sides of the blanket.

A small island, indeed.

Suddenly, Saskia began paying closer attention to the conversation. Any underhandedness would impact Liam, grievously, for those were the stakes of horse racing. She could hardly stand it. While she could sympathize with Liam's love of the sport, she couldn't help feeling relieved this was his final race.

Still, he had to make it through the race.

While Saskia still knew little about horse racing, she understood this: before this perfect day had dawned, Morningstar hadn't been favored to win—and now the elements appeared to be conspiring in his favor. She wasn't sure which was better— near-certain loss or an in-the-thick-of-it win. Each outcome carried its own dangers and uncertainties.

To separate herself from the anxiety gnawing at her, she attempted to view the day through the lens of Harriet LaPlume, which served both to store vital details that would go into Liam's memoir and to keep her at an emotional remove.

"Ah, now, I've been clear of the turf rumormongering

business these last few years, Lady Bea." The mischievous glint in Blaze's eye suggested otherwise. "I'm a respectable gent these days, didn't you hear?" Amused silence met his question. "Or as respectable as the majority owner of a gaming hell can be."

This got an equal amount of laughs and snorts. *Incorrigible.* That was the word for Blaze.

"Well, a duke and a marchioness *are* your business partners," allowed Lady Beatrix.

Saskia rather liked Lady Beatrix, as she always seemed to know just a little more than anyone else on any topic of conversation.

"See?" Blaze spread his hands wide and grinned. "Proper respectable."

Through this conversation and others happening all around—everyone seemed to be engaged in two or three discussions at once—people came and went, and it was only now that Saskia realized that to her right sat a new neighbor.

The Duchess of Rakesley regarded Saskia with what could only be characterized as interest in gold-flecked green eyes that precisely matched her brother's. "Do you enjoy the sport of horse racing, Lady Saskia?"

Saskia exhaled a nervous laugh. "Until this year, I didn't know the first thing about it—or even horses, for that matter."

The duchess's gaze remained unflinching and direct. "And how are you enjoying your riding lessons?"

The breath caught in Saskia's throat. *Of course.* Of course, the duchess knew about the riding lessons. The lad, Joe, who was instructing her came from the duke and duchess's stables.

My sister trained her herself.

Those had been Liam's exact words regarding Peony, and the duchess was Liam's only sister.

And all these weeks, she'd thought she and Liam were a secret.

The duchess's eyes suggested it was the worst kept secret in the history of secrets.

"I'm so grateful for the use of Peony, Your Grace." Good manners never went amiss. "She is a wonderful horse."

This pulled a genuine smile from the duchess. Her smile lacked the raw charm of Liam's, but held all its sincerity. "Please call me Gemma." Her smile brightened, as Saskia suspected it always did when she spoke of her horses. "Peony is a gentle soul, isn't she? Please keep her as yours."

A shocked laugh startled from Saskia. "Oh, I couldn't accept such a gift. Where would I stable her?"

"You can, and you shall," said Gemma. "The excellent Cross Street Mews is located a block behind Sloane Street. You shall stable her there."

Gemma had been a duchess for five or so years, but it appeared she'd rather taken to the having-her-way part. That would've been the duke rubbing off on his wife. "Liam was most adamant that you should learn to ride. And the thing about my brother is he doesn't typically become adamant about anything not related to horse racing. Yet..." Her eyes narrowed, a subtle question therein. "He's adamant about *you*."

Only on the rare occasion did Saskia go speechless—and now was one such rare occasion.

"I thought you might want to know."

"Oh, well, thank you."

The thing was Saskia did want to know—and didn't.

What was she supposed to do with such knowledge? Knowledge that warmed her... Knowledge that quaked, shook, and rattled her to her boots.

Rakesley's hand slipped into his wife's, claiming her attention. "They're assembled at the starting line."

Saskia reached for her field-glass. She'd heard Doncaster described as a broad, galloping flat track similar to Newmarket, and she saw that was true, even though Doncaster was pear-shaped rather than straight. At one mile and six furlongs, Doncaster was also the longest track of the racing season. A horse had to have both speed and stamina to win it.

Below, the array of horses held themselves impressively with their rainbow of shiny silks. But unlike the races she'd attended earlier in the season, she now had a true sense of those horses since she'd started riding Peony. Each would have differing personalities, but each would also be possessed of explosive power and speed. Of course, she'd never experienced explosive power and speed during her tame riding lessons, but she now knew the feel of a horse in movement.

At last, she located Liam and Morningstar, as they shouldered their way through the tetchy scrum, angling for the railing. And just as she had at the One Thousand Guineas and the Derby, Lady Midnight was staking her starting position to the outside of the field. The starter hadn't even yet lifted the gun into the air, and already every muscle in Saskia's body had gone rigid with tension. She could only breathe in small sips of air.

Then—*too soon...at last*—the starter lifted the gun, and the familiar anticipatory hush fell over the crowd.

Saskia's field-glass was all but glued to her face with one hand, her other clenched in her lap, her nails digging half-moons into her palms. Though he was hundreds of yards away and nearly a speck through the lens of her field-glass, this was the first time she'd seen Liam in two weeks. As she'd expected, he was intense and focused, clear of intent. Now, thanks to Gemma, Saskia had another word for him—*adamant*. Liam was an adamant creature on the turf—ferocious in his adamancy, but not cruel.

Never far from her thoughts, their last minutes together pushed to the front of her mind. It hadn't been her place to say to him what she had. Yet she couldn't bring herself to regret it. He needed to understand that his ferocity without cruelty was his strength—and what separated him from his father.

Liam was his own man.

She'd needed to say that to him.

She could only hope he'd heard it.

Now, as anticipation threatened to snap the air in two, the gun fired and the horses were off. The crowd roared to life, and Saskia was on her feet right alongside everyone. She couldn't sit primly and properly in her seat while Liam was out there on the turf waging battle, for no mistake that was what he was doing.

Only now that she'd learned to ride did she fully appreciate what Liam could do on a horse at a flat-out gallop. The way he went buoyant in his seat...his hands holding the reins steadily, but somehow also lightly...his *attuning* with Morningstar, who muscled through the initial pack and carved out space for himself as he hit his stride.

Watching this, Saskia experienced a wild whirl of emotions as she willed them to the lead—amazement, hope, anxiety, pride, and something else, too... An unexpected feeling that sparked through her—*desire*. A near overwhelming desire for Liam—a desire that he win...a desire that he remain safe...and, too, desire for *him*, the all-too-attractive man that he was in his talent and his ferocity and his adamancy. That talented, ferocious man who was adamant for *her*.

Her loins, they burned—

No.

That sounded like a syphilitic affliction.

They ached—

Better...but not quite.

They craved.

Yes.

They craved...*him*.

A craving of the loins.

How very sensual was the heat of competition.

She'd never noticed until now.

As Morningstar entered the final stretch, neck and neck with

Lady Midnight, each horse making a strong case for the win, Saskia saw it—Morningstar was slowing. She blinked, at first believing her eyes were deceiving her, but, no, Morningstar was definitely slowing down.

Something was wrong.

Morningstar had been level with Lady Midnight for much of the race, but now, stride by stride, he was steadily dropping back, no longer competing for the lead, or even second or third. From the periphery of her vision, she noticed Rakesley and Gemma rush away along with Lord Branwell and Lady Artemis, and Gabriel and Celia, too. Saskia couldn't move, a fear taken root inside her that if she took her eyes off Liam for even an instant, something dreadful would occur.

"Morningstar appears to be limping," observed Lady Beatrix.

Saskia hadn't wanted to say it—or even believe it—but she saw it, too.

As if it were occurring from a great distance, rather than all around her, the crowd erupted into a celebratory roar.

"Lady Midnight just won."

That was Viveca's voice, but Saskia had no care. The entirety of her being was concentrated on Liam as he, at last, dismounted and led Morningstar to the outside of the course and away from the fray of the surging crowd. As if in silent pantomime, Rakesley, Gemma, Lady Artemis, and Lord Branwell joined him along with Rakesley's head groom, Wilson, and a few lads who stood guard and provided ample space for Morningstar to be examined before he took another step.

"Is Morningstar all right?" Viveca again.

"He's in the best possible hands," said Lady Beatrix, even as worry threaded through her voice.

"What's the time?" asked Viveca of a sudden.

"Half three," came a reply.

"Right on schedule."

Saskia tore her gaze from the track. She could no longer see

Liam for all the bodies now crowding the racecourse. "Is it your afternoon sickness, sister?"

"What afternoon sickness?" asked Lady Beatrix.

Blaze answered his sister. "Every day from four to six in the evening, my wife's stomach gives its contents the old heave-ho."

It couldn't be denied that Viveca had gone a pale shade of green. "And then I'm right as rain until four o'clock the next day."

"Oh, you poor thing," exclaimed Lady Beatrix. "You'll be returning to the Grange now, I suppose?"

"Aye."

"You'll be in good hands there, as taking in sickly animals is their specialty," said Mr. Deverill with a charming wink.

"You say you'll feel better by six o'clock?" asked Lady Beatrix.

"As regular as clockwork."

"Then you'll be able to attend Sir Abstrupus's soirée."

"I've been wondering," said Viveca. "What's a *Sir Abstrupus*, anyway?"

That got a dry laugh from Lady Beatrix. "A rascally baronet who passed his ninetieth year sometime between ten and twenty years ago."

"Sounds like a gent after me own heart," said Blaze.

Soon, Saskia found herself following the flow and leaving Doncaster with Viveca and Blaze. She was under no further obligations as went this day. She'd kept her word to Liam by watching his final race. She hadn't seen him win, but the loss wasn't down to him. Further, he'd come through all right with no injuries.

That was what she'd actually come to see.

As for Sir Abstrupus's soirée later, she was bound by no promises there. The late-night celebratory carousing was a part of the racing world that held no interest for her. She was the owner of a circulating library, which recently released a guide to fly fishing in Scotland. She was no carouser.

No, she was a writer, a solitary pursuit if there ever was one.

What business had she attending raucous revels that only ended with the rising of the next day's sun?

So, now, she would offer her support to Viveca, as a loving sister should do, then, when it was time to depart for Sir Abstrupus's soirée, she would make her excuses and take a light evening meal in her room and write and read as she pleased.

That was the life of Lady Saskia Calthorp.

No all-night bacchanals for her.

Even if Liam was there.

Perhaps, even, especially then.

CHAPTER TWENTY-FIVE

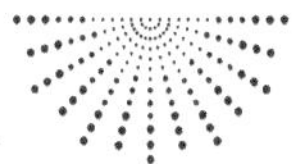

Though rumors of Sir Abstrupus Bottomley's eccentricities abounded, the pipe organ music had been unexpected.

Yet as Liam took in the ballroom so dimly lit that one would call it *atmospheric*, no one else in attendance appeared to feel so—not even the couples whirling across the dancing floor to music that could only be described as dirge-like.

Of course, everyone else in attendance—the whole of the English racing world as far as he could tell—likely hadn't noticed the unusual music, for they would've been bewildered by all the other eccentricities on display: footmen dressed in proper serving attire but wearing *papier-mâché* horse masks…servers circulating through the crowd atop ponies, as they held reins in one hand and silver trays bearing drinks in the other…the fact that the dancing floor wasn't gleaming mahogany but dense, close-cropped racing turf.

In the context of those curiosities, what was a little pipe organ music?

Liam could only admire Sir Abstrupus's commitment to the theme.

His gaze wandered across the ballroom—*again*. This would've been the tenth or hundredth time. He'd lost count.

And, still, he hadn't found her.

Simply, Saskia wasn't here.

As the hour hand was swiftly approaching midnight, he might have to accept she might not come at all.

He hadn't won today.

She would've seen that.

And though he'd wanted to win his last race, badly, Morningstar's safety took precedence over glory.

Saskia would understand.

Still, he'd been disappointed not to have seen her at Doncaster. But apparently her sister had taken ill, so they'd returned to Endcliffe Grange.

Yet he'd held out the hope he would see her here. He had something he wished to say to her—many somethings, in fact, but one something, in particular—and her presence was a necessary element to that discourse.

On the opposite end of the dancing floor, a flash of strawberry-blonde caught his eye. His feet were on the move with a permission of their own, his heart picking up speed against his ribs, a feeling closely resembling joy taking wing inside his chest.

However, as he drew near, he found that strawberry-blonde head of hair belonged not to Saskia, but to her sister, Tessa, the Marchioness of Ormonde. A quizzical smile curving her lips, she said, "Have I surprised you in some way, Lord Bolton?"

Reflex had his jaw tensing—*Bolton*—but his reliable charming smile came to his rescue. "I mistook you for someone else, my lady. My apologies."

Her brow lifted. "Did you now?" she asked. "I wonder who that could be?"

Though he didn't know the marchioness beyond the odd casual social conversation—after all, her husband was Rake's best bosom friend, so naturally they'd occupied the same rooms on several occasions—he thought he might've detected knowing in her direct silvery-blue gaze that bore no insignificant similarity to her sister's. Though a sister, this woman had raised Saskia—and had imprinted no few characteristics onto her, too.

Before he could summon a suitable response for Lady Ormonde, a thin, reedy voice that could've hailed all the way back to the crack of civilization sounded at Liam's back. "Here we have the young Earl of Bolton, formerly of Liam Cassidy fame."

He turned to find a slender rail of a man staring up at him, his pale blue eyes sharp as a wren's, his frizz of white hair appearing to vibrate with barely contained energy incongruent with a man of his years, which had to number near the century mark. This man could be none other than his host. "Sir Abstrupus," said Liam with a bow.

Strictly speaking, an earl didn't bow to a baronet, but even a king would find himself bowing to Sir Abstrupus.

Like a king, Sir Abstrupus wasn't one to suffer mundane niceties. "You didn't win out there today."

Liam had heard a version of those exact words practically from the moment he'd decided to retire Morningstar from the race. "The safety of the horse always comes first."

One bird-like eye narrowed. "I knew your great-grandfather."

"Oh?"

"Ghastly man."

Liam blinked. "I'll have to take your word for it, I'm afraid."

"You prefer it thus, God's truth." Sir Abstrupus's head tipped left, then right. "You're nothing like him. It's in the eyes."

"Thank you…" Liam wasn't sure if he was stating or asking.

Another glimmer of strawberry-blonde appeared at the edge of Liam's eye, and his heart gave a hard thump, then quickly settled. The beholder of this head of strawberry-blonde hair wasn't Saskia, either, but rather her other sister, Lady Viveca.

Sir Abstrupus couldn't help but notice, too. "Now who might that be, perchance?"

"Lady Viveca," replied Liam. "The Duke of Acaster's youngest sister."

"The one who up and married an East-End chancer?"

Before Liam could answer, Blake Jagger stepped into the breach. "Aye, that she did, and the lady hasn't regretted it for even a minute since."

Sir Abstrupus eyed Jagger from gleaming boot to saffron silk top hat with appreciation in his magpie eye. "You and I are going to be friends, aren't we?" Of course, Sir Abstrupus would see a kindred soul in Jagger, as both men were no strangers to flamboyant sartorial choices. The lavender paisley of his waistcoat rivaled Jagger's for ostentation. "Tell me, Mr. Jagger," continued Sir Abstrupus, "have you ever tried naked lady lily tea?"

"Can't say I have."

"But haven't you wished to?"

"Can't say that either."

"Well, you're in for a rare treat."

While Sir Abstrupus signaled the nearest pony-riding server in his bid to introduce Jagger to the gustatory delights of naked lady lily tea, Liam turned to Lady Viveca, who had joined them. "Are you feeling recovered from your earlier indisposition?"

He supposed that was the way a lord would ask a lady about such things.

"Oh, indeed," she said in that breezy way of hers. If one didn't know better, one wouldn't think she'd suffered even the faintest hint of indisposition.

"Have you just arrived?"

He was asking none of the questions he wanted to ask, but was damned if he knew of a discreet way of getting to them.

"A little while ago," she replied. "Blaze and I were, *erm*, exploring Sir Abstrupus's conservatory, which took us quite some time."

Liam's eyes narrowed, noting a telling flush of the décolletage and brightness of the eye about Lady Viveca.

Well.

He wouldn't be pursuing that line of conversation. "And Lady Saskia…" he said, leadingly. "Did she arrive with you?"

"No."

"Will she be arriving later?"

"Saskia won't be arriving at all." Lady Viveca's gaze narrowed on him. "You know how she is."

What struck Liam only that instant was he *did* know how Saskia was.

And he knew she wouldn't want to be here.

One second hardly ticked into the next before his mind was made up. His feet already on the move, he tossed a hasty, "Good evening," toward Lady Viveca. Then he was out the door and off to the stables to saddle Homer. Only a few miles separated Château Bottom's Roost from Endcliffe Grange, so even after riding down unfamiliar Yorkshire roads in midnight dark, he was handing Homer off to a lad at the Grange within the half hour.

He almost made straight for the front door.

But if he knocked on that door, his request to see Saskia would go through one servant, then another and another, until it reached her, then her reply would follow the same path back to him and it would be half an hour gone and he would be none the closer to seeing her.

Another way suggested itself as more like to produce quicker results.

He began circumnavigating the perimeter of the house, his eye on the lookout for a promising lit window on the first floor.

What he hadn't been prepared for was the rooster.

While not aggressive, the fellow clearly considered himself the master of these grounds and all interlopers subject to careful supervision.

In other words, Liam had a rangy, old rooster determinedly dogging his every step.

Oh, and the rooster liked to crow.

The inhabitants of the Grange must've been long accustomed to the bird's sporadic outbursts, for no one had emerged from the house to determine if an intruder stalked the premises.

A small mercy, that.

At last, on the backside of the manor house, Liam found the window he sought—one aglow with mellow candlelight through gauzy curtains.

Saskia would be in that room.

He picked up a pebble and tossed it—*tap*.

He waited.

The curtains didn't twitch.

Another pebble…another *tap*…again, no movement.

The rooster crowed, as if giving voice to Liam's frustration. He picked up a pebble that might've been more accurately characterized as a stone, wound his arm back, and let fly—*thunk*.

A second later, the curtains fluttered, a shadowy form having materialized behind them. Diaphanous fabric swished aside and, hands cupped to the windowpane, Saskia peered through.

Again, the rooster crowed, this time in celebration—or was that Liam's wishful imagining?

He brought his hands to his mouth and called out on a hushed shout, "*Saskia.*"

She remained still.

"*Saskia,*" he called, louder. "Open the window."

A fraught moment later, she lifted the window and poked her head through the opening, her hair falling in a curtain around her. "*Liam?*"

"Aye."

"What are you doing here?"

"You didn't come to Sir Abstrupus's soirée."

"I came to the race." She sounded a mite defensive.

"Saskia?"

"Yes?"

"Aren't you going to invite me up?"

A beat of silence that stretched too long met his question.

Unable to take the suspense an instant longer, the rooster crowed.

"All right," she said, finally.

"*All right?*"

"All right." Hesitation wavered about her. "But, Liam?"

"Aye?"

"Don't let Rodney in with you."

"Rodney?"

"The rooster." A beat. "You can find your way?"

"Oh, aye." Liam's best charming smile found its way to his mouth. "I never met a kitchen door that didn't open for me."

As he pointed his feet in the direction of said kitchen door, Rodney fast on his heels, he might've heard a snort at his back.

Delicate and feminine, but decidedly a snort.

But it was permission granted, and that was all he needed.

SASKIA SHUT THE WINDOW.

Then she returned to her seat at the desk.

But the chair was much less comfortable than it had been mere minutes ago.

So, she crossed the room and perched her bottom on the edge of the bed.

But it wasn't only her body perched on edge.

Her mind was, too.

Liam was on his way…*here*.

Unable to simply sit with that knowledge, she jumped to her

feet and dashed to the door. She pressed her ear to oak, alert to the sound of footsteps.

She should've said *no*, of course.

She should've said she was enjoying a lovely, restful night in and he should try it himself sometime.

But her night in had been neither lovely nor restful.

All that reading and writing she'd planned on? She hadn't been able to string five words together. Instead, her mind had been determined to wander beyond the four walls of this room...across acres of land to the neighboring estate...to Sir Abstrupus Bottomley's soirée...where Liam was. Was he dancing with a marriageable heiress? Was he bringing her punch at this very moment?

Cowardice.

That was what had her in this room.

She'd been a coward all day—leaving Doncaster without speaking to Liam...not attending Sir Abstrupus's soirée.

What was she cowering from, anyway?

For someone who made her living using and selling words, she couldn't seem to find any.

At last, down the corridor sounded the rhythmic thud of confident male footsteps, and her heart performed a neat little flip in her chest. She inhaled deeply to brace herself, but on the exhale, she made the mistake of looking down.

A distressed squeak escaped her.

Upon her return from Doncaster, she'd flung off every last bit of fashionable, uncomfortable clothing and clad herself in her coziest chemise, robe, and slippers—all worn, shapeless wool.

A firm *tap-tap* sounded at the door, and she jumped. Her heart a hammer in her chest, her skin entirely too hot beneath layers of wool that had been pleasantly warm only moments ago, she counted out a slow, steadying five seconds, which she reckoned was the amount of time it would take her to reach the door if she weren't already standing beside it—*five...four...three...two...one.*

She twisted the lock and pulled the handle.

Before her stood Liam, dressed every inch the aristocrat in crisp evening blacks, easy smile curving his mouth, lighting his gold-flecked green eyes, hip subtly cocked in that loose manner of his. His gaze swept down the length of her, then up again. "You're looking...*comfortable.*"

He wasn't being rude, precisely.

He was being diplomatic.

Which was worse.

She crossed her arms over her chest, loose folds of wool bulky beneath, and assumed a defensive, nettled stance. "Women can't spend all the hours of the day dressed as confections for the gazes of men. My sincerest apologies for causing you any disappointment."

There.

Let him suck on that lemon.

His smile only increased in amplitude. "I'm not disappointed in the least. A man craves variety. After all, a man can't live on confections alone. His teeth would rot out of his head. No, sometimes what a man needs is solid, hearty sustenance."

Outrage flashed through her. "Are you comparing me to mutton stew?"

His head canted, mouth turned down at the corners, as if he were seriously contemplating her question. "I wouldn't go as far as mutton. Tender spring lamb and potato pie?"

Her mouth twitched. It didn't want to, but it couldn't help itself. Then it was a giggly chirrup passing her lips...then another...until, against her will, she was laughing.

With an undiminished pleased-with-himself smile, he said, "Come on, Saskia, won't you let me in?"

Of course, she shouldn't.

Experience had taught her what happened when they were alone in rooms together.

But then, in those rooms she hadn't been wearing her most shapeless, most comfortable woolen best.

She stood aside and allowed him entry. He crossed the room and stopped beside the dressing table. She returned to her perch on the edge of the bed. Several feet separated them; it should be a safe enough perch.

"About the race…" The rest of the sentence refused to form. What could she possibly say to the man who had held that race in his palm and then lost it?

But he seemed to want to hear the rest of that sentence. "What about the race?"

"You lost." Inelegant statement of obvious fact.

"Aye."

"Are you…all right?"

"Aye, I'm all right."

And the thing was, he did appear to be all right.

How was that possible? It had been his final race—the final race of the winningest jockey of the last decade—and he was all right after a loss like that?

"I know you wanted to leave the sport with a win."

He shrugged, intriguingly unbothered. "The important thing is Morningstar will be all right."

"What happened?"

"A few furlongs from the finish, I felt him pull up subtly. I suspect it was an overreach injury."

"*Overreach?*"

"When a back hoof strikes the heel of a front hoof. It can happen at high speeds toward the end of a race when fatigue begins to set in."

"Can it cause lasting damage?"

"Oh, aye. It can lacerate tendons and cause infections."

"Could he have finished?"

"Likely."

"Could he have won?"

"Possibly," Liam allowed. "It turned out to be a mild injury. No skin broken or damage to the hoof capsule."

"But you didn't know that, so you took him out of the running."

Liam held her gaze. "Any laurels I receive are down to the horse who allows me to ride him. That horse trusts me to see him through the race. If he comes up injured, I have to honor that trust and put safety before glory."

"You're an honorable man, Liam."

His quick smile flashed. "That going into the memoir?"

She snorted. "And cheeky."

"Enough about me," he said. "Tell me, how are your riding lessons progressing?"

"I love riding." She was grinning. She couldn't help herself. "Well, once my bottom got accustomed to it. Peony is such a dear."

"I thought you would get along."

"Your sister gave her to me."

Liam's brow lifted. "Did she now?"

Saskia's head tipped to the side. "Why do you ask like that?"

"Gemma wouldn't give a horse to just anyone. She must like you."

"Well, I'm honored to have been deemed worthy." The words fell from Saskia's mouth in her usual way—laced with irony—and she immediately regretted her tone, for it was at odds with how she felt, which was truly honored.

She changed the subject. "Watching you today was a completely different experience from all the other races I've attended."

"Oh?"

"Now that I can ride, I'm able to more fully appreciate what you do out on the turf. You're magnificent, Liam."

The lighting in the room was dim—only two candles burning, one on her desk and the other on the nightstand—but she thought a flush might've reddened the tips of his ears. "You'll turn me into an insufferable braggart."

She wasn't finished. "But even though you're masterful and magnificent"—she had no right to say these next words—"I can't like how you've put yourself at risk with every race and get bruised and injured and…and…suffer."

He considered her for a long moment. "But, Saskia, everything in life comes with risk. Even your library."

Her brow creased. "I suppose a bookcase could fall on me."

"You're the writer, Saskia," he chided. "You should know a metaphor when you hear one."

The thing was, she *had* caught the metaphor, but she hadn't wanted to address it, for she sensed its potential to lead to tricky places more comfortably left unexplored.

Liam, however, clearly did not feel the same, for he said, "Sometimes, you must put yourself at risk for what you love. For example, a dog—"

"First mutton stew, now you're comparing me to a dog?"

He continued, undeterred. "A dog loves to have its belly scratched, but that is the most vulnerable place on its body. Still, a dog will roll onto its back and expose itself to get its heart's desire."

"Hmm, you might work on your metaphors."

"Out there on the turf"—fervency shone in his eyes—"I might've gotten battered and bruised and suffered the occasional whip lashing to the face—"

"There's still a silver stripe on your cheekbone."

"But it was all part of being able to do what I loved. But, Saskia," he continued, "those are mere injuries. Riding never caused me a moment's suffering. But you?"

"What about me?"

"Does writing cause you to suffer?"

She snorted. "Bad writing certainly does."

"But you're a good writer."

Oh, the naïveté of the non-writer… "*Good* is subjective."

"Hardly."

"I'll tell you a dirty secret."

"Is this another confession, Lady Saskia?"

CHAPTER TWENTY-SIX

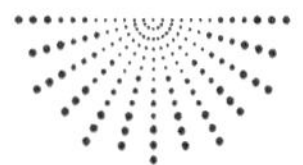

"*Is this another confession, Lady Saskia?*"

It wasn't the question itself that drove a sudden spike of desire straight through Saskia.

It was the suggestive spark in Liam's eyes and the way his voice deepened as he spoke it.

"Sometimes," she began, "I write a perfect sentence. An objectively perfect string of one word following another that comes together with beauty and purpose. But such a sentence is rare. What usually flows from my pen is an imperfect arrangement of words that must be nurtured and pored over and rearranged, then rearranged again. Oh, I suffer."

"Weren't you writing tonight?"

"I…was." If what she'd been doing could've been called *writing*.

His gaze cast about the room, then landed—on the desk in the corner, papers strewn haphazardly across its surface. In the same instant, his intent revealed itself. With graceless abandon, Saskia shoved off the bed at the same moment he lunged toward the desk. It was a short-lived race, however, when her, *"No-no-no,"* transformed into, *"Ouch-ouch-ouch!"* her progress halted by the big toe of her right foot meeting the sturdy walnut leg of an end table.

Instantly, Liam pivoted and rushed toward her. "What's happened? Are you injured?"

Saskia hopped on one foot. "I stubbed my toe." She touched her foot to the floor and attempted to apply weight to it. An instantaneous, *"Urgh,"* escaped her and again she was hopping like a hobbled bunny.

"Oh, woman," Liam nearly growled as he erased the remaining distance between them and scooped her up in his arms, provoking a squeak from her before he deposited her on the bed.

She had to tip her head back to say, "Thank you."

He hadn't needed to carry her. She could've limped back herself. But for those few seconds, she'd been in his arms, and perhaps she was thanking him for that.

He gave a nod, but that was his only movement.

"Truly," she said.

Surely, he understood he was free to return to his former place beside the dressing table. But he didn't. Instead, he lowered to his haunches and reached for her foot.

"Liam, you don't have to—"

"Let's take a look at the damage, shall we?"

He removed her slipper. That slipper was more than ten years old and had followed her into this life from her old one. She could only pray there wasn't a smell.

He held her naked foot up to what mellow light there was and examined it from every angle. She would've seen the humor if it weren't for a few pertinent facts.

One, her toe yet throbbed.

Two, it was possible her feet weren't her best feature. They were functional and useful and she'd never once given them a moment's thought.

But it was the third fact that had the blood rushing hot and jangly through her veins: he was touching her. Awareness pulsed through her with each beat of her heart—of his strong, capable hands upon her, their calluses subtly rough against the tender skin of her foot.

"Can you move your toe?"

She gave it a testing wiggle.

"Ah." He nodded, pleased. "Not broken then. It is swelling and will likely bruise, but it'll come out all right."

"As you're someone who has broken a bone—"

"Three bones over the years."

"—I appreciate your professional assessment."

He nodded sagely. "Do you know what makes a stubbed toe feel all better?"

Saskia searched her mind. "Elevation? A cold compress?"

He angled forward and pressed his mouth to her toe, his lips soft and warm against her, shocking her to her…toes. "A wee kiss," he said, shifting back.

"That's your professional opinion?" How breathless she'd gone, her voice barely above a whisper.

He held her gaze, steady. "Was my kiss effective?"

In truth, she couldn't feel her toe, not with all these other feelings whirring through her. "I, *erm*, yes."

"While we're on the subject of suffering…"

"Are we still on that subject?"

"Oh, aye."

A single hair could flutter to the floor and she would hear it.

"I don't want to give you the wrong impression, Saskia. I suffer."

"Oh?" Somehow, she didn't think they were talking about horse racing or stubbed toes anymore. "What makes you suffer, Liam?"

A smile twitched about his mouth, both serious and amused. "You."

"*Me?*"

"I suffer from want of you. Your presence when we are parted. Your conversation…your mind…your seriousness…your laughter…your…"

"My?"

"Self."

She just caught her mouth before it went agape. "My *self*?"

"You know." He swept his gaze up and down the length of her body.

"How…what a…" she sputtered. "What a shallow appraisal," she said of necessity—the necessity of putting distance between his words and their impact on her.

But those necessary, distancing words had no effect on him. "Every inch of you beneath all these woolen layers is beautiful, Saskia, and I'm only a man. Aye, I want your body. But its beauty isn't why I suffer for it."

The world might've stopped spinning around the sun, and she wouldn't know it.

"It's that this body contains *you*." He shook his head. "I'm not versed in words, like you, so I'm probably saying it all wrong."

She shook her head. "I can't think of a more perfect way of arranging those words."

Opaque emotion, dark and sinuous, passed behind his eyes. Actually, that emotion wasn't entirely opaque. More than a glimmer of wickedness flashed, as he asked, "Does your toe need another kiss?"

"I believe it does."

He was asking permission and she was granting it—for him to kiss her toe…and what was destined to follow.

Destiny, a word that carried mystical weight.

It simply encompassed so much—perhaps everything that is and was.

Perhaps a word that encompassed *them*.

She reclined back onto her elbows and watched down the length of her body as Liam again brought her toe to his mouth and kissed it. Except he didn't only kiss it; he took it between his teeth, provoking a shocked gasp from her as his tongue swirled around, warm and velvety. He bit down lightly. She squealed.

That wicked smile in his eyes, he moved on from her toe, his tongue dragging along her instep, tickling her, but also inciting a now-familiar feeling—*desire*. Higher he trailed—over ankle…up her calf, lifting her robe as he went. When he reached her knees, he hesitated.

She hadn't realized she'd been holding her breath, which, possibly, explained her lightheadedness.

But she didn't think so.

It was *him*.

What he was doing to her now…what his eyes promised he would continue doing.

He unfolded his long, muscle-lean body as he rose. At near eye level, there it was—the outline of his cock, long and rigid, straining against his trousers.

Her mouth went dry.

He shrugged off his evening coat, made quick work of his cravat, his waistcoat promptly following. Before her, he stood in shirt and trousers, looking so very male and so very desirable. He tugged his shirt from his waistband and pulled it over his head. How she ached for him. Unable not to, she pushed off her arms, momentum carrying her forward, the few inches separating them a few too many.

She reached out and hooked a finger into the waistband, pulling him forward into the space between her legs. She took in his male beauty—the corded muscles of his shoulders and arms… his ridged stomach…the dusting of golden hair on his chest, narrowing down his stomach, leading the eye toward…

And there it was—his big cock.

Lust, pure and urgent, shimmered through her as her fingers began working the buttons of his trousers. When his manhood fell free, she heard a gasp—her own.

His throat cleared.

When she lifted her gaze, his eyes sparkled with amusement. She'd been caught staring. *Ogling*, more like.

"I seem to remember you mentioning you've liked what you see for some time now."

Even as she groaned, she couldn't regret having told him of her infatuation.

How bold she'd become.

"Last time," he began. It wasn't necessary to clarify which time was last time. "I noticed something you liked."

Anticipation slipped through her, tempting her into further daring. "Oh?"

"I'd rather show than tell."

Pupils flared with desire and purpose—*intention...promise*—he reached down and wrapped his hand around himself. *Oh.* His hand moved, slowly, deliberately, as he began stroking his length.

Lust, hot and urgent, spiked through Saskia. Her lungs forgot how to breathe. It wasn't only desire shimmering through her, but also a slightly transgressive feeling that she might like.

"Take off your robe, Saskia."

She unknotted the sash and let the garment slip off her shoulders.

"Now your chemise."

She brought her legs beneath her and rose so she was kneeling as she lifted the chemise over her head and flung it away.

"Oh, Saskia."

The way he was looking at her as he stroked himself...with lust, yes, but also with longing. It was *her* he desired, but also her body on its own. Herself reduced to parts—her weighty breasts... her curves...her cunny... How he wanted her. Yes, she liked seeing him touch himself. But she liked this, too—being lusted after...being longed for...

By him.

"Now."

"Yes?"

"Touch yourself, Saskia."

Sudden doubt stirred. *Touch* herself?

"Didn't you once tell me turnabout is fair play?" A wicked smile curled at the corner of his mouth. "And, my love, I think you'll enjoy it."

Her fingers, trembly and uncertain, began at the indent of her throat, tracing down to her breast, touching her nipple. He stroked himself harder. She lightly pinched the taut nub between forefinger and thumb as her other hand trailed down her body to her mons pubis. She didn't know exactly what was expected, so she let instinct take her. Shyly, she spread her legs.

Could one spread one's legs shyly?

The answer was *yes*, for she was split into two selves—shy *and* bold. And in this moment, with this man, inhibition would not hold her back, as she touched herself for his pleasure.

His eyes heavy-lidded with desire, his voice frayed, he asked, "Remember what I did with my tongue?"

Did she ever remember…

"Touch yourself there."

The feel of her sex beneath her fingers wasn't novel, but like *this*, it was. So good and so purely lustful, watching him watching her. *Yet*…soon it felt oddly empty and she knew why. "Liam, I need *you* to touch me." Each word scraped across her throat. "I need *you*."

He released himself and tucked his thumb beneath her chin, tipping her head back as he angled down and caught her mouth with his. Urgently, steadily, he moved forward, pushing her until she was on her back and he was between her legs. Above her, he hovered. Instinctively, she reached down and found his ready shaft and guided him to her. She grabbed his back as he thrust and buried himself deep inside her. "Liam," she cried.

No longer did she feel empty. Lust didn't have to be a hollow, depthless pursuit. In this passion, they were unified—a pleasing of the self...a pleasing of the other. How those were one and the same as their bodies took...as their bodies gave. The weight of his larger, heavier body so delicious and right as he kissed her while he moved inside her.

She wasn't only connected to him, but to herself in a way she'd never experienced. Yet that connection to herself only existed because of her connection to him. This had to be a connection of the souls. She, Saskia, who was so pragmatic and who prided herself on her common sense had become a convert to the spiritual—a believer in the connection of souls.

A feeling began to build deep inside her sex. A feeling that hungered and craved and needed and needed...*more*. And, *oh*, how Liam was giving it to her, but not in a punishing way. In a way that gave her what she needed. How deep inside herself she'd gone, as if there were a universe inside her and it was expanding. Teetering on the edge of climax, she moaned and gasped and pleaded, then on his next thrust, the universe inside her burst, shooting light and sensation through her as he drove deeper inside her.

An illuminated being was she in this exquisite moment of release. A wanton, too. How he and she had transcended the body in this place where their souls met—but how *of* the body, too. This act defied all reason and definition. For if one tried to reason with or define it, the essence of it slipped through one's fingers.

She understood that much.

Better to dissolve into sensation and let feeling take over— feeling of the body...feeling of the soul.

"Saskia, my love, I can't...*oh*..." He pulled from her and took himself in hand and spilled his seed onto her stomach on a long animal groan. Enervated, panting, he collapsed onto his side and reached for her chemise before wiping her stomach. He kissed her neck, the day's growth of his beard deliciously scratchy against her. "I just need a few minutes."

"A few minutes? Until what?"

He smiled against her. "Until we do that again."

Oh.

And she realized that was precisely what she wanted—to do *that* again...*now.*

"We have to wait?"

He chuckled against her, then kissed her neck...her clavicle... his mouth covered her breast... His wicked gaze lifted. "No, my love, we don't have to wait."

My love.

Through all the longing and lust and delight struck a flash of feeling—*fear.*

Fear that she was losing her sense of self.

That she was going too far and a person who went too far wasn't who she was.

Yet...when she was with Liam, she tended to forget that.

He pushed her to dare.

And it made her feel wobbly.

Others wobbled, not Saskia.

But here she was...wobbling.

Even as she gave over to the inevitable and surrendered to his kiss.

A RAY of golden sunshine filtered through gauzy curtains and cast Saskia in the role of sleeping goddess as she lay curled into Liam's side, her head snugged into his shoulder, hair tousled about, her breath light and even in the cadence of slumber.

How lovely she was.

All those men of the *haut ton* who viewed her as fearsome hadn't the faintest notion of who this woman truly was.

If only they could see her now.

But none of those men would ever see her like this.

Never.

He was the only man who would see her thus.

The certainty thrummed through Liam with sudden ferocity.

All those lords and gentlemen could just keep thinking of Lady Saskia Calthorp as fearsome.

He cared not.

He knew the true Saskia.

His stomach gave a loud grumble. After the night they'd shared—which, in truth, had only ended a couple of hours ago—he was ravenous with hunger. But his stomach could wait, for he had Saskia in his arms.

He had all he needed to sustain him.

Her lashes fluttered open, and sleepy, silvery-blue eyes met his. A slow, sated smile curled about her pink lips. "Are you hungry?"

"Oh, aye." His best cheeky smile pulled at his mouth. "Last night's mutton stew wasn't nearly enough to satisfy me."

She buried her face in his neck and giggled.

"Now, I need a healthful, sustaining bowl of porridge to start me in my day." He traced the delicate line of her jaw. "Maybe two."

Her smile froze. "Day..." Her brow crinkled, then released. *"Day!"*

Within the split of a second—it was astonishing what a human body could accomplish within the split of a second—she'd bolted upright and swung her legs off the bed. Her feet had hardly hit the floor before she was frantically dashing this way and that, retrieving articles of clothing. He'd only just sat up when his trousers hit him full in the chest, quickly followed by his shirt.

Positioned at the foot of the bed, she held a boot in each hand. "You must go, Liam—*now.*"

"Why?"

He hoped she didn't plan on throwing his boots at him.

She pointed a boot toward the window. "It's dawn."

"'Tis."

"You're naked." She looked down at herself. "And I'm naked."

She was.

Delectably so.

Her nakedness was, in fact, the lone remaining thing he liked about the last thirty or so seconds.

"You and I are naked in my bedroom."

"And?"

"If anyone were to discover us, there would be a scandal."

Ah. He wasn't sure she would appreciate his opinion on the matter of a scandal involving the two of them, but he was going to speak it, anyway. "Would a scandal be so terrible?"

Her eyebrows creased together.

She blinked.

He'd flummoxed her.

No mean feat, that.

"You know," he continued into this rare opportunity that had presented itself, "there is a way two people naked and alone together in a bedroom can avoid a scandal."

Her eyebrows released, and she sprang back into action, tossing his boots onto the foot of the bed. "That's what I've been trying to say." She lifted another garment off the floor—his cravat. "You must leave before you're discovered."

For a woman who worked with words, she was certainly being obtuse to the ones he was speaking.

"Those two people could marry," he said, to be clear.

The cravat she'd just tossed, fluttered silkily to the bed.

Which was the only movement in the room—aside from the thundering of his heart—for she'd frozen, again. *"Marry?"*

A stunned beat of time ticked past, then another, as the word hung in the air between them. Into that silence, he said, "It's the thing your characters do at the end of all your books."

More stunned silence followed.

"*Book*," she said, at last.

Now, it was his brow creasing. *Book*. He wasn't sure what he'd expected her next words to have been, but it wasn't that. He reached for his trousers. Whatever lay in store for the conversation ahead, he might want to be clothed.

Saskia must've had the same sense for she reached for her robe. "The racing season is concluded."

"Aye."

"I have everything I need to complete your memoir."

"Do you now?"

"All I have to do is write the St. Leger portion, and it will be finished."

"Oh?" he asked. "And that's all?"

A whirl of emotion skittered behind her eyes, and Liam felt suspended on the head of a pin.

He'd all but directly asked her to marry him.

And she'd all but directly said…

No.

Still, she hadn't directly refused.

So, he waited.

Within this indirect space yet lay hope.

She nodded, and his heart leapt.

"Yes, that is all."

From the loftiest heights, his heart sank through him and down through the floor below his feet. He could stand here and fight—fight for what he knew she wanted…fight for a *them*—but he'd always had a nose for the winning line and he intuited standing his ground wasn't the way to secure a victory in this instance.

Instead, he would give her what she said she wanted.

He would leave.

Not a minute later, he was dressed well enough not to shock a passing servant. His hand gripping the door handle, he hesitated. Unable not to, he glanced back and caught one last glimpse of Saskia, looking so delectable in her woolen robe, hair tousled about her shoulders, skin yet rosy from their last bout of lovemaking.

How he wanted this woman.

How he loved her.

So…he had to leave her—and in doing so, perhaps, one day, he could have her.

He gave her a parting nod, swung the door wide, and stepped through the opening, shutting the door soundly behind him before he changed his mind.

Gutted, he took one step, then another, away from her.

A familiar voice rang out behind him, stopping him in his tracks. "Liam?"

He turned to find Gemma approaching. "Good morning, sister."

It was possibly the most morose *good morning* ever to pass a pair of lips. A single eyebrow lifted, she pointedly glanced behind her. "Isn't that the door to Lady Saskia's room that I just saw you emerge from?"

"Gemma"—no mistaking the warning in his voice—"leave it be."

She inhaled a lungful of air and exhaled. Her feet began moving. As she rushed past him, she called over her shoulder, "Come with me to the stables. Artemis needs help with a few ponies that arrived in the night."

"I'm hardly dressed for the stables, sister."

She eyed him up and down. "To be fair, you're hardly dressed at all, brother. Just put on your boots and come with me."

And like that, Liam was conscriped into service, which was

the best thing for him. Otherwise, he would do one of two things —go to his room and brood or turn right back around and knock on Saskia's door.

Aye, the stables were the best place for him.

CHAPTER TWENTY-SEVEN

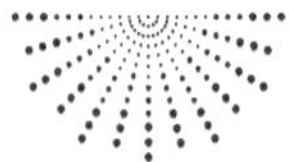

A FEW HOURS LATER

Saskia hadn't been able to return to bed after…

Well, *after*.

She hadn't been able to read.

She hadn't been able to write.

So, she did the one thing she could do: she packed her belongings and sent for a footman to hire a carriage and driver from the nearest coaching inn to carry her back to London.

Now, here she was, in the receiving hall of Endcliffe Grange, surrounded by all the trunks and accoutrements one lady needed to leave her house for even one night, waiting for the hired coach to arrive. It was the correct decision—leaving Yorkshire… returning to London—for the truth was she could be just as miserable and ineffective there as she was here and, at least, in London she could lie sleepless in her own bed.

Had he asked her to marry him?

He might have—or he might not have.

And depending on which, she might have refused him—or she might not have.

It had all happened so fast, and she'd spoken words she might've regretted.

Might presently regret, too.

Might regret for the rest of her life.

The swift *click-clack* of efficient footsteps against marble echoed through the hall, and Saskia had but a moment to brace herself. Not against a polite greeting that would've been necessary if one of the many near-strangers currently housed beneath the Grange's slate roof joined her, but because she knew those footsteps—had known them all her life, in fact. She turned and met her sister's gaze. "Tessa."

"Good morning." Tessa eyed her up and down in frank appraisal, as was her way. "I received your note and thought I would see you off."

"I didn't intend to disturb your sleep." In fact, Saskia had planned on being several miles down the road before any of her family caught wind of her departure.

"I was already up with Ian. He's a ravenous little brute."

Saskia understood she should laugh. Usually, she would have. But all she could summon was a smile that barely lifted the corners of her mouth and surely didn't reach her eyes.

Tessa held out her hand. "Come with me."

"But my carriage will be here soon." Even as the protest left her mouth, Saskia took Tessa's hand.

"Your carriage can wait." She pulled Saskia to her feet. "We're going for a walk."

So it was that Saskia found herself walking the grounds of Endcliffe Grange with Tessa. In the previous century, the estate must have been quite a Palladian gem with formal gardens and mazes and such.

"Do you know much about the Grange?" asked Tessa, conversationally.

"Actually," said Saskia, "the scullery who came to bring fresh water and stoke the fire this morning gave me an abbreviated history."

"Lady Artemis inherited the estate from her grandmother, I know that much."

Saskia nodded. "Over a decade ago. But it wasn't until five years ago—after the death of her beloved racehorse, Dido—that Lady Artemis turned these acres into a horse sanctuary."

"Which turned into a sanctuary for all manner of animals," observed Tessa. "No longer a purposeless aristocratic estate."

One couldn't mistake the current iteration of Endcliffe Grange for anything but a working estate. In the place of those long-ago formal gardens and hedge mazes stood divided pastures and structures for housing the various animals strutting about—horses, yes, but also sheep, goats, pigs, chickens, donkeys, and even a flock of geese and ducks.

"I admire a woman like that," said Tessa. "One who goes after what she wants."

Though Saskia agreed—after all, hadn't she followed her own inclinations all her life?—agreement stuck in her throat. The fact she had to face—that she was waiting to face in the safety of her London flat—was that if she were, indeed, the sort of woman who went after what she wanted, why was she running away?

They stopped at a fence and watched a pair of donkeys graze peacefully in the distance. "So, Saskia," said Tessa, at last.

Saskia tensed. A note sounded in her sister's voice that presaged a *talk*. Whatever Tessa was about to say was what she'd sought out Saskia to say.

She'd turned to face Saskia full-on, leaving Saskia no choice but to meet her sister's too-sharp eye. "How long has Liam Cassidy—" Tessa shook her head. "How long has the *Earl of Bolton* been courting you?"

However much Saskia had been bracing herself, it wasn't nearly enough. "*Courting* me?"

The look Tessa leveled her with would brook no dodging or dithering. "Viveca mentioned he joined Sirens."

Saskia knew.

She absolutely *knew* her sisters had been gossiping about her. Mrs. Dunlevy, too, she reckoned.

"Sirens *is* publishing his memoir." She'd gone slightly breathless—and more than slightly defensive. "It only follows that he would want to join the library to gain a feel for what we're all about."

Tessa's head tipped to the side. "And I suppose that's all he's been gaining a feel for?"

A sudden wash of mortification stripped Saskia's mind clean of any further defense she might attempt, leaving her no choice but to stand beneath Tessa's penetrating gaze, vulnerable and seen down to her very soul.

Her sister nodded slowly. "I suppose you have been spending a bit of time with Bolton, given that you're helping him write his memoir. It's only natural you would become...*close*."

Oh, that the earth beneath Saskia's feet would open up and swallow her whole.

Anything to make this conversation end.

Tessa looked as if she'd only gotten started. "The two of you were seen riding in Hyde Park. I believe there's even a wager in the White's betting book about future prospects regarding the Earl of Bolton and Lady Saskia Calthorp."

A groan escaped Saskia.

"I didn't know you could ride, sister."

"Liam—*Lord Bolton*—taught me."

Tessa's brow lifted as if to say, *See?*

No small amount of satisfaction in the lift of that brow or in the cat-who'd-got-the-cream smile that curved Tessa's mouth. "Well, it's clear."

"What is clear?"

Nothing was clear as far as Saskia could see.

"The man is smitten with you."

"I think you have the wrong end of the—"

"*Saskia.*"

"Yes?"

"It's not up for debate. The man is smitten with you."

"He is?"

"The evidence is irrefutable. And further—"

There was more?

"You, my sister, are smitten with him."

Saskia opened her mouth, surely to launch an unassailable defense, but no such protection came to her rescue.

The fact was she *was* smitten with Liam.

And she'd ruined it.

An unanticipated rush of tears pooled in her eyes.

"Oh, my sweet girl." Tessa gathered Saskia in her arms, encouraging the indiscriminate flood of tears to spill over.

"I just don't know," she sobbed wetly into Tessa's shoulder, "how to navigate that distance."

Tessa pulled back enough to catch Saskia's eye. "What distance?"

"From where I am to where I want to be."

"And where is that?"

A long, shaky exhalation shuddered through Saskia. As if this were a breath she'd been holding since that first night—the night she met Liam at the Drunken Piebald. "With Liam."

"Oh, Saskia, you do know how to navigate that distance." Tessa used her thumb to dry Saskia's eyes, just as she'd done when Saskia was a child. "My dear, you've written entire books on that very subject."

"But that's—" She stopped. Her brow creased. "Wait, you know I'm—"

"*Harriet LaPlume?*" Tessa smiled. "Of course, you're Harriet LaPlume. She could be none other than you. I would know your voice anywhere, sister."

It took a moment for those words to sink in. "Then you know," said Saskia, "what I write is romance. It's fiction."

Tessa gave a chiding shake of the head. "You're wrong there.

Love between two people is that romantic." She took Saskia's hand and squeezed. "And it's real."

Viveca's words from a few months ago returned to her: *I want you to have what I have with Blaze... I want you to have your own version of it, sister. The version that makes you happy.*

Saskia hadn't been ready to hear those words then.

But now, she was.

"You have an important question to ask yourself, though," continued Tessa. "And you cannot dodge it. Which is greater? Your need for the certainty of your present life? Or your love for Liam? Is your love for him great enough to risk lowering your defenses?"

More tears pooled in Saskia's eyes; more tears spilled. "I...I want him, Tessa. With all my heart and soul."

"It's actually there in the title of your first book—*When a Lady Dares.*"

"When a lady dares." Saskia repeated each word as if she were speaking them for the first time.

"That impossible distance you speak of?" continued Tessa. "It's daring that sets our feet on the path that bridges it. Daring to fly. Daring to fall. Daring to give your heart. Daring to love. Saskia, you have so much love banked within your heart. Won't you consider opening it?"

The breath caught in Saskia's lungs.

All along, it had been this simple.

"Yes," came, at last, on a trembly exhalation. Then, strongly, joyously, "*Yes.*"

She still wasn't sure how to navigate this feeling.

She couldn't hide herself away.

She couldn't be Harriet LaPlume or Arabella.

She had to be nakedly herself.

But if Liam was besotted with her, then that was who he wanted...*Saskia.*

"I need to find him, Tessa, before it's too late."

"Oh, my sweet girl, it isn't too late." Tessa's eyes went glassy with unshed tears. "The life you want has only begun." She gave Saskia's hand a final, parting squeeze. "Now, where does one find a horse-mad man?"

Saskia's feet were already on the move. "The stables," she tossed over her shoulder. She didn't know where the proper stables were, but she would scour every inch of Endcliffe Grange until she found them.

Until she found Liam.

Until she knew if she would fall—or if she would fly.

"*Shh, old boy*," soothed Liam, as he ran his palm down the velvety nose of the gray ten-hands Welsh pony whose halter he gripped. This fellow had arrived in the night along with two mares in equally poor condition. Skin and bones, the three were, their coats patchy with muck and hair loss. While Gemma and Artemis tended the mares, Liam steadied the gelding as the farrier and animal surgeon saw to his infected back hoof.

It had been three hours since he'd been pressed into service as Gemma and Artemis's stable lad, and he wouldn't have it any other way. He needed to be essential to events. These last few hours, he'd had time to give life and his place in it some consideration, and he thought perhaps he could be that sort of earl.

Nay, not *perhaps*.

He *would* be that sort of earl. Not the incidental sort of earl who just wanted the title and privilege and said sod all to the rest. He didn't need to cease being a necessary man simply because he now had a title affixed to the front of his name. One only had to look at Rake to know that much. He'd been born to the life of an aristocrat, yet no one would ever say he wasn't the master of his own fate.

The pony gave a low whicker, gently pushing his velvety nose into Liam's hand. "That's a patient lad," he encouraged.

Of course, though he'd used these three hours to sort through certain life matters, a bigger matter remained decidedly, obstinately *unsorted*—*Saskia*.

He'd all but asked her to marry him.

How much clearer could he have been?

And she'd all but said *no*.

He'd had three hours to let that sink in, and with every minute, it only felt worse, as he'd gone from gutted to wretched. In fact, as the pony gave another whicker, Liam wasn't sure who was comforting whom.

Only in the last hour had a reason for Saskia's all-but refusal occurred to him.

Children.

She very much wanted them.

He'd said he didn't—and he'd never corrected the record.

"The way you manage your horses without whip or spur, but rather with guidance and encouragement, that's the sort of father you shall be."

The fact was…she was right.

That was the sort of father he would be.

Further, Saskia believed it of him, which helped him believe it of himself.

So, he'd decided. When he was no longer needed here, he would seek her out, and this time, he would be more clear and purposeful. He would get down on one knee, if that was what it took to make his intention to spend the rest of his life with her more clear.

He liked to win—and he was determined to win Saskia.

"Liam?"

His hand froze. His ears must've been deceiving him, for that voice sounded exactly like…

"Liam?"

One hand still wrapped around the pony's halter, he half turned.

Saskia.

At first glance, she was radiant in the morning light, her strawberry-blonde hair shining golden and her emerald-green pelisse setting off her ivory skin. But as one second ticked into the next, he couldn't help but detect the nervy energy radiating off her. Further, there was the fact that she was remarkably well put together… "Are you dressed for travel?"

"I am."

His brow dug a trench into his forehead. "Are you leaving?"

"I was." She eyed him up and down. "Are you wearing the same clothes from last night?"

"Gemma happened across me nearly the instant I left—" *Your room.* That wouldn't do. One never knew when curious ears were listening, particularly when one set of inquisitive, sisterly ears occupied the stall just across the aisle.

"You're filthy."

He shrugged. "The horse business can be a dirty one." He looked down at himself and snorted. "These togs won't be seeing the inside of an aristocrat's soirée again."

A smile trembled about Saskia's mouth, and all he could think about was kissing it.

"Liam?"

He glanced past Saskia to find Gemma approaching, her hand held out, a spark of mischief in her eyes. "I'll take over from here, brother," she said. "You and Lady Saskia can feed the chickens."

"The feed bag is against the wall outside the gate," carried Lady Artemis's voice from across the aisle.

Saskia lifted her eyebrows and smiled. That was their marching orders received.

Liam couldn't help feeling slightly awkward and observed as they made their way to the chicken yard. Also, he couldn't help wondering… "Do I stink?"

"No more than one would expect."

He nodded, deciding to take that as encouragement. "So, you *were* leaving?" He had to ask.

"I was."

"But you didn't."

"I didn't."

"You came to find me instead."

Why? he left unasked.

She would answer that question in her own time.

They reached the chicken yard, and he held the open bag out to her. She scooped a handful of feed and scattered it in a wide arc. The chickens ran and squawked and boisterously flapped their wings in a frenzy to claim their rightful share.

Saskia's face lit with delight. "What a ruckus they create. So dramatic."

A sudden strident crowing pierced the air, startling them around. "Oh, Rodney," laughed Saskia, reaching into the bag for another handful. The rooster clucked indignantly, but he gobbled up his meal all the same.

"Saskia," said Liam, reclaiming her attention. The time had arrived. It was now or never… "I want children."

Whatever it was she'd come to say, he wanted to ensure she factored that in.

Her eyebrows creased together. "Pardon?"

"I want you to know I've reconsidered my stance on future children, in case you're still thinking of leaving."

She nodded, slowly. "Actually," she said, "I've been thinking about your memoir."

"Oh?" Disappointment sheared through him. She'd sought him out because of the bloody memoir?

"It doesn't have to end with the St. Leger."

"It doesn't?"

"Your story can have a different ending." She hesitated. "We can give it a different ending—you and I."

We...you and I.

Was she saying what he thought she was saying?

His heart wanted to believe so.

"You and I can end with a win."

Perhaps his heart was getting what it wanted, but he needed to say something. "Do you know what horse racing taught me about life?"

She shook her head and waited.

"Horse racing taught me how to bide my time," he continued. "It taught me when to be patient and when to hold my ground and when to fight for the win. It taught me to never give up. And, Saskia?"

"Yes?" Her voice had gone breathless, her eyes glassy silver with unshed tears.

"While I like winning, I've never been in the running for as precious a prize as your heart." He reached for her hand and brought it to his lips. He needed to be touching her. He needed to be kissing her. "I love you, Saskia. I want to spend my life with you, loving each other and raising a family and growing old together. So, tell me, Saskia, have I won *you*?"

A tear broke free and streamed down her cheek. "There is a reason I started writing about love." She swallowed and shook her head. "I began writing about love out of fear. In a fictional world, I could safely explore love without ever having to risk myself. As a result, I became convinced that perfect love only exists on the page."

She closed the distance between them and lifted onto the tips of her toes. Now, only a scant inch of air separated her mouth from his. But he couldn't kiss those sweet lips yet. They had more yet to say.

"But that isn't true," she continued. "It isn't possible for perfect love to exist on the page. Love is an alive thing. It grows with every beat of our hearts. I love you, Liam, and I want to spend the rest of my days growing our love together, always."

"Always, Saskia," he promised.

He took her face in his hands and, at last, brought their mouths together.

From the direction of the stables, he caught the clapping of sisterly hands and, not two feet away, came the enthusiastic crowing of Rodney.

Destiny had chosen him and the woman in his arms for a variety of roles—*writer...publisher...jockey...earl*—but those roles paled beside who they were and would be to each other—*lover... friend...wife...husband.*

Those roles, too, had been destined.

He didn't know what destiny held for them beyond this moment.

But he didn't need certainty.

He only needed this woman.

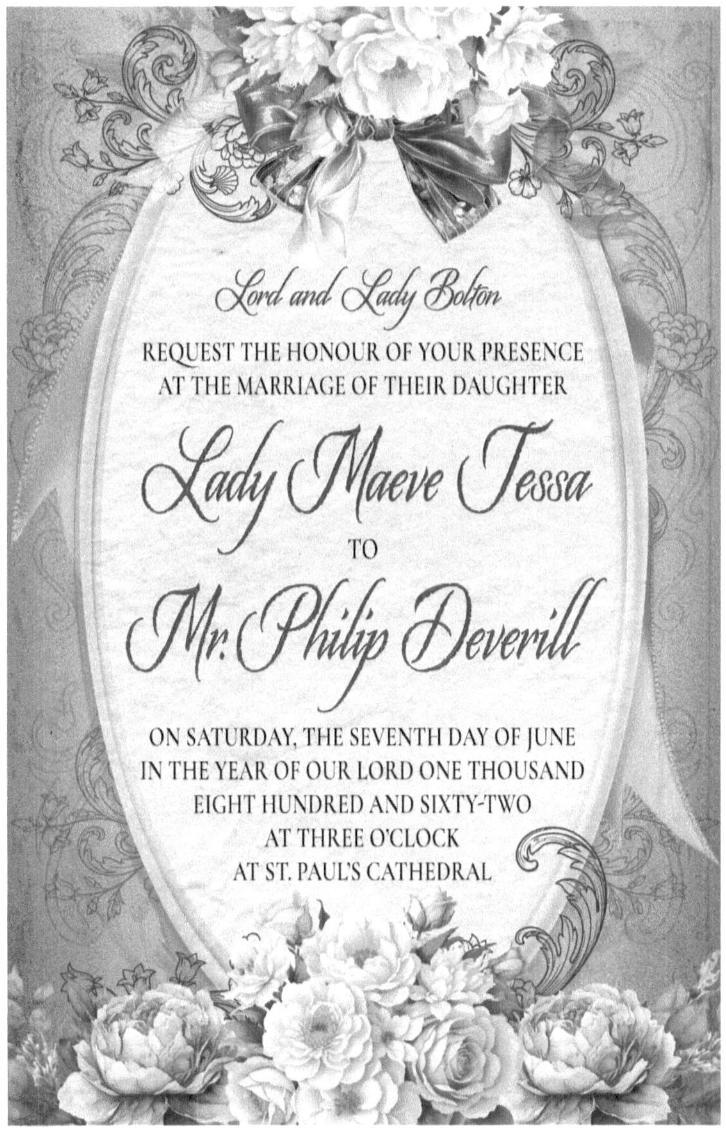

Lord and Lady Bolton
REQUEST THE HONOUR OF YOUR PRESENCE
AT THE MARRIAGE OF THEIR DAUGHTER
Lady Maeve Tessa
TO
Mr. Philip Deverill
ON SATURDAY, THE SEVENTH DAY OF JUNE
IN THE YEAR OF OUR LORD ONE THOUSAND
EIGHT HUNDRED AND SIXTY-TWO
AT THREE O'CLOCK
AT ST. PAUL'S CATHEDRAL

EPILOGUE

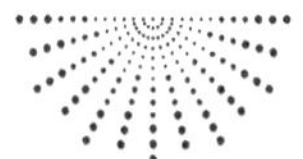

ST. PAUL'S CATHEDRAL,
LONDON, 35 YEARS LATER

"Mama," said Maeve, smiling, laughing. A girl who was always smiling and laughing. "You can stop fussing."

Saskia released the hem of the white lace gown and stepped back. Had she been fussing? She supposed she had.

In truth, she was a fussy sort of mother.

She hadn't seen that coming.

Her throat went tight at the sight of her daughter bedecked in her wedding-day finery—her auburn curly hair a gift from her namesake grandmother...her gold-flecked green eyes from her father...her daring spirit she inherited from Liam, too. Yet Saskia caught something of herself in her beautiful daughter. A willingness to see life unflinchingly and meet it directly.

"You're absolutely radiant, daughter."

Maeve reached for the bouquet of roses that she would carry down the aisle. Roses were her reason for deciding upon a June wedding, so they would be in full bloom.

There was so much a mother wanted to say to her daughter on her wedding day—*too much*. Advice for the marriage...advice for the wedding night. Maeve had put a firm stop to the latter discussion. Her Aunt Viveca had already given her a detailed account of what to expect.

Detailed was the word Maeve had used.

Detailed from Viveca, well, Saskia could only imagine.

So, here Saskia found herself alone with her daughter in the narthex of St. Paul's Cathedral just before Maeve was to walk down the aisle and pledge her troth to her beloved Philip.

"Mama?"

A note sounded in Maeve's voice. A note both familiar and welcome, for Saskia knew what her daughter was about to ask. "Yes?"

"What was the best birthday you ever had?"

Maeve had been four years old the first time she'd asked this question, making it the first occasion of many that Saskia told the story over the years. Through her childhood, it had been Maeve's favorite story about her mother.

Today, on Maeve's wedding day, however, Saskia would tell the story a bit differently, for she had too much to say and only a moment to say it. She reached out and took her daughter's hand. "Thirty-five years ago, your father and I fell in love and decided to spend the rest of our lives together. We had so many dreams and plans for that future, and many of them came true. I wrote more books. Your father involved himself in the reform of horse racing, not to mention the running of the earldom. We were fulfilled by those vocations through the years. But some of our dreams didn't go to plan exactly as we'd hoped."

Maeve stepped closer in that sweet way she always did when she sensed suffering in another.

"I'd always dreamed," Saskia continued, "of having a large family with somewhere between four and ten children."

Maeve's eyebrows winged toward the ceiling. "*Ten?*"

Saskia chuckled. "I hadn't really thought it through. But I'd fully expected to find myself with child within months of the wedding." She swallowed past disappointment down. "Months turned into years, and still, I had no children. I passed my thirtieth year, then my thirty-fifth, and I wasn't a mother. I confess that by then I'd accepted I never would be."

"Then on your thirty-sixth birthday…" Maeve's eyes sparkled.

"Then on my thirty-sixth birthday, I felt nauseous. Nausea unlike any I'd ever experienced in my life and I knew—I just *knew* —I was with child. *You.* And not just you, but you *and* Jacob." The wonder she experienced then, all these twenty-three years later, still resonated through her. "That will always be my favorite birthday. But today, on your wedding day, I would like to tell you what I learned in those years before you and your brother entered my life." She squeezed her daughter's white-gloved hand. "I learned that if you're waiting for life to give you perfection, you'll always be unhappy. There is no perfect life waiting ahead, just around the bend. Find happiness in the life you have, my sweet. All those years we were childless, your father and I were happy, for, you see, happily ever after isn't a state of being. Happily ever after is a state of mind. It's a state of the heart. As long as you carry that belief within you, you will lead a fulfilled life, daughter."

Saskia felt the swift, unrelenting *tick-tock* of time, and yet she had more to say… "And here's another thing I learned: some things matter in life."

An amused line formed between Maeve's eyebrows. "Were you a secret anarchist, Mama?"

Saskia smiled. "It wasn't that I felt nothing mattered, but I'd never actively considered that some things *did.*"

"Oh, you're such a philosopher."

Together, they shared a laugh. The children were always teasing her thus. But she'd never learned the knack for small talk, and now that she was approaching her sixtieth year, it was too late to learn.

"I would like to tell you some of the things that matter." She cleared her throat. "Hope matters. As does faith. Never forget to be kind. And daring, Maeve. Daring matters, but you've known that from the moment your tiny lungs first filled with air and released an indignant yowl informing the heavens of your displeasure at having been born. But, Maeve," she continued, "it's love that matters most. It's from love that every other feeling that matters flows—love for oneself and love for others."

Unshed tears pooled in her eyes, Maeve nodded. "You're the best mother anyone could wish for."

"Second best," said Saskia, reflexively. All these years later, it was still a firm fact in her mind that Tessa was *the* best.

Maeve shook her head. "*First* best."

Saskia swiped away a tear that had broken free. "We still have some work to do on your grammar."

Maeve shook her head with a laugh. As Saskia wiped a few renegade tears from her daughter's cheeks, Jacob strode into the narthex. Sometimes, just for the split of a second, Saskia took him for his father. Well, his father from thirty-five years ago. "What did I miss?" he asked, his eyes bright with the excitement of the day.

Maeve accepted a brotherly kiss on the cheek. "Mama was just imparting her wisdom to me," she informed him.

"That so?"

"But *you* will just have to wait until *your* wedding day."

He flashed the charming smile he'd inherited from his father. The cheekiness was all Jacob. "Then I suppose I'll be waiting quite some time to be blessed with motherly wisdom."

Indeed, it had been a surprise when Saskia had become with child in her thirty-sixth year, but having twins had been a marvel. *Twins.* Of course, Liam was a twin. But she hadn't allowed herself to hope for as much until she'd held one babe in each arm.

And, truly, what a wonder it had been watching them grow and flourish into the people they were today. Maeve with her daring and beauty; Jacob, a future earl, yes, but also involved in the running of Sirens.

"Are you sure you want to go through with this marriage business, my girl?" he asked his sister. "It's not too late if you want to leg it."

Maeve was playfully swatting her brother when Liam entered the room. His hair, once deep auburn, was now salted with gray. Which did nothing to diminish his handsomeness. If anything, he'd only grown more handsome with age. To this day, every hero she'd ever written paled in comparison to the flesh-and-blood reality of this man—*her* man.

Before he took Maeve's arm in preparation to walk her down the aisle, he reached for Saskia. "Can you believe it?" he asked, low, for her ears only.

It—all that had come after they'd spoken their first *I love you*.

She couldn't believe it—and she could.

"Yes, my love, I believe it."

He angled and kissed her within one blink of the eye and the next, over in an instant. But it lingered inside her, as Liam's kisses tended to do. "Now," he said, "go and take your seat. I have our lass from here."

Jacob extended his arm. "Mama?"

Saskia placed her hand on her handsome son's arm and allowed him to escort her into the sanctuary and up the aisle to the front pew. So many familiar and loved faces pointed their way. All their friends and family. All smiling with love and affection.

Her life after *I love you*… She hadn't been able to predict it thirty-five years ago.

After all, she'd never written that part of a love story.

But then, how could she have? She'd only known romantic love as a concept, not as a reality. So, how could she have conceived of the life that followed that first *I love you*.

The years that deepened that love.

Some of the years delivering sorrows unforeseen.

Other years delivering joys unsurpassed.

But all those years delivering on her and Liam's promise to each other—*always*.

The End

ABOUT THE AUTHOR

Bestselling and award-winning author Sofie Darling's passion for historical romance began in middle school the moment she cracked open *Wuthering Heights* by Emily Bronte. An instant and enduring love affair was born.

Sofie spent much of her twenties raising two boys and reading every romance she could get her hands on. Once she realized she simply must write the books she loved, she finished her English degree and set pencil to paper. (Ticonderoga #2 is her quill of choice.)

When she's not writing heroes who make her swoon, Sofie enjoys a nice weekend hike, a visit to a crumbling medieval castle whenever she gets the chance, and a slightly codependent relationship with her beagle, Bosco. Visit her website.

A small press bound by the belief that every voice matters.

Sign up for our newsletter to learn about new releases and more.

Buy directly from us to save on ebooks, book bundles, and special editions.

Follow us on social media:

facebook.com/oliverheberbooks
instagram.com/oliverheberbooks
tiktok.com/@oliverheberbooks
bsky.app/profile/oliverheberbooks.bsky.social
youtube.com/@OliverHeberBooksPublisher
oliverheberbooks.substack.com
amazon.com/oliverheberbooks